# THE Hollow PACK

# KELSEY KARSON

Published by Dobson Ink
Printed in the United States of America
ISBN-13: 978-1-946474-43-8

*To my husband for always supporting me.*

# Contents

## Part Three
## Hollow Threshold

# Introduction

After her aunt's death, Lena Barkstone retreats to the quiet town of Hollow Creek, hoping grief will fade among towering pines and slow, sleepy nights. Instead, she finds herself watched by wolves, warned away from the woods after dark, and haunted by a moon-shaped necklace her aunt left behind.

Hollow Creek is hiding something, and so was her aunt.

Drawn into a world of shifting loyalties and ancient magic, Lena discovers she stands at the center of a growing war between the mortal world and the Otherwood. Three men are bound to her fate: Atlas, the brooding alpha sworn to protect his pack at any cost; Rowan, the tattooed bartender whose steady presence grounds her when magic spirals out of control; and Silas, quiet, watchful, and dangerously attuned to secrets no one else can hear.

As the boundary between worlds begins to fracture, Lena learns her power isn't something she can walk away from, and neither is the bond forming between her and the wolves who guard her. The Otherwood is waiting. Watching. And it wants her.

The men sworn to protect her may be her greatest strength or the very thing the darkness uses to claim her.

*The veil isn't breaking, it's dissolving.*
*And Lena might be the key to saving their world...*
*or the spark that ends it.*

# Part One

---

## *Hollow Inheritance*

Escaping the city life, Lena Barkstone hopes that Hollow Creek will offer her a quiet space to figure out her next steps. Instead, she finds territorial wolves in her backyard, a tangle of secrets, and a magical battle that all hinges on her.

In the middle of all of it are three magnetic men. Broody Atlas, her best friend's older brother, despises outsiders and wants her out of town. Rowan, the tattooed bartender with a gentle heart he tries to keep hidden. Then there is sweet, quiet Silas, who offers help when she needs it the most.

The unexpected suitors aren't just dangerous for her heart, they're shifters bound by ancient magic. With Samhain looming, the veil between the worlds thins, allowing rogues to enter the human world. Lena is left trusting the wolves she knows, against the ones lurking in the dark forest.

# Chapter 1

## *Wolf at the Door*

"Lena!"

Lena opened her eyes, and the bright early morning sunlight that was streaming through the window made her flinch. The plush mattress and warm blankets beckoned her to stay. But the voice calling through her mail slot shouted again, this time louder.

"Lena Barkstone! If you're dead in there, I swear I'll haunt you myself!"

She groaned and rolled out of bed, barely catching herself before her feet touched the cold hardwood floor. The October chill had crept in overnight, and it seemed the heater was about as reliable as her cell signal. Another thing for her endless to-do list.

Grabbing socks from the bottom of the bed, she slipped them on and stumbled to the door. As she passed her suitcase, she snatched the oversized hoodie from the top.

"Len—"

She yanked open the door, stopping her friend mid-word.

Callie stood on the porch, coffee in one hand, bakery box in the other, and with an expression that was both cheerful and judgmental. Lena hadn't seen her in a year, but her old college roommate hadn't changed a bit. Her long, auburn hair, tied up in a messy bun, was the kind that only looked casual but took longer.

"You look like you lost a fight with a haunted doll," Callie said, sweeping into the house like she owned it. "Which in this place is fully possible."

"Good morning to you, too," Lena grumbled, snatching the coffee from Callie's hand and taking a grateful sip. "You're a monster, but this is excellent."

"I bring sweets, gossip, and a warning." Callie strolled into the kitchen as if she'd been there hundreds of times before, dropped the baked goods on the counter, and spun dramatically toward her.

"What's the warning?"

"In Hollow Creek, you don't go into the woods after dark, especially not alone."

She raised an eyebrow. "Why? Because they're haunted? Or because the town sheriff doubles as a scarecrow?"

"The last person who went into the woods at night, alone, went missing for a week and came back speaking in tongues. Literal tongues, you know, different languages. Creepy." Callie flipped open the bakery box, revealing chocolate chip muffins, grabbed one, and took a bite. "Also, the local wildlife's been acting weird. Bolder and coming closer to the houses. Just listen to me and keep your doors locked."

She stared at her best friend, eyes wide. "This is exactly the thing you should've led with before I moved into a house that's hugging the tree line."

Callie shrugged. "Think of it as an adventure, you always loved a challenge. Plus, I wasn't going to say anything that might stop you from moving here. I've missed you."

The black wolf from the night before filled her thoughts. *He was certainly bolder...and bigger.*

She forced the thought away and reached for a muffin. Mentioning the wolf would make what happened real. Or maybe she kept her mouth shut because she didn't want to be laughed at. Again.

She'd been embarrassed before, and wasn't eager to walk down that road again. Callie might not judge her, but she didn't feel like sharing. Instead, she picked at the muffin and dropped onto the kitchen chair.

"So," Callie said, brushing crumbs off her sweater. "You're coming to the bonfire tonight, right?"

"Pass," she said around a bite of muffin. Callie knew that bonfires, or any big social events, weren't her scene. She was more of a curl up with a book type of girl.

"Too bad. I'm not giving you a choice." Callie stepped closer to the table. "I'm not letting you hole up in this house. There's a whole town you need to explore, and there are a couple of people I want you to meet. It will be fun. You love Halloween, and this is the start of the celebration here in Hollow Creek."

*Fun. Not likely.*

The bonfire at the edge of town was already blazing when Lena arrived. Hay bales, pumpkin lanterns, and enough plaid to make a lumberjack weep surrounded the fire. Kids in costumes ran around as music played softly from a speaker perched on a stump, and the smell of woodsmoke and cinnamon cider filled the air.

She spotted Callie in the distance, surrounded by a few others. Too anxious to interrupt, Lena loitered awkwardly by the cider table. *How did I get dragged into this?*

"You look like you want to set the place on fire," said a voice behind her.

She turned to find a man leaning against the table, arms crossed, tattooed fingers tapping the rim of a plastic cup. He was tall, with tousled black hair and a smirk that was either charming or trouble. Probably both.

"I don't like crowds," Lena admitted.

"Then why'd you come?" He tilted his head, clearly interested in her excuse.

"Peer pressure. Threats. Muffins."

"That'll do it." He offered his hand. "Rowan."

"Lena."

"You moved into the old Marlowe house, right?" His gaze met hers, but it felt more intense than it should. "Brave."

"You say that as if the place bites."

He smiled. "Maybe it does."

Before she could respond, he tipped an invisible hat. "Catch you later, city girl." He disappeared into the crowd like fog slipping between trees. Leaving her with a lingering question. What had he meant about the old Marlowe place? Sure, Aunt Mira neglected it some, but his comment hinted at something more sinister.

Pushing the thoughts away, she scanned the crowd. It wasn't like she knew anyone here except Callie. She'd been in town less than twenty-four hours.

*Embrace the night.* She could almost hear Aunt Mira telling her.

The fall celebration was in full swing. Laughter and music filled the air. She was never much for parties or crowds, yet there was something inviting about the event. In the center of the activity, the bonfire crackled, and sparks danced in the air like tiny burning stars. Drawn to the warmth, Lena grabbed a cup of cider from the table and headed into the fray.

"There you are!" Callie waved her over. "I was thinking you would not come."

Tentatively, Lena joined Callie, and the group gathered around her. "I was just...unpacking." She finished quickly. In reality, she was thinking of a way to get out of this bonfire without disappointing Callie.

"That's what tomorrow is for." Callie smiled, guiding her further into the group. "Come on, Lena, you've got to meet the crew. Put a face to the drama I've been unloading on you for years."

"Can't say I haven't been curious." She smirked. "I'm just not sure I remember how to talk to normal people."

Callie grinned and looped an arm through Lena's, dragging her closer to the fire. "These people are hardly normal, but they're mine, and the time is now for you to meet a few."

Butterflies circled in Lena's stomach until her hand shook slightly with nerves. The last party she attended was in college, another one Callie had dragged her to.

Callie stopped in front of a group clustered around logs turned into benches, and Lena forced herself to be present.

"This," Callie paused dramatically, "is Olivia Sandstorm, the only person to be banned from the pie contest. Twice."

"Don't believe her." Olivia glanced up at them, revealing a pale face full of freckles and long red hair twisted back in an artful braid. "Those were technicalities, and the judges were cowards. What can I say?"

"I'm more of a pie eater than a pie marker, so no competition from me," Lena grinned, instantly liking Olivia.

"This is Baxter." Callie gestured to the young man, dressed in faded flannel and worn jeans. "He runs his family's bait shop. Owns too many knives and is the ghost hunter of the town. He knows every ghost story in the country."

"He's the pack's ghost whisperer," Olivia agreed.

"They're exaggerating. The ghosts find me, I don't go looking for them. Well, at least I don't always go looking for them." He shrugged as if it weren't a big deal.

"And the knives?" Olivia questioned.

"I carry only two."

"Sure." The doubt was clear in Callie's tone. "Anyway, this is Lena, my best friend since forever, and the newest resident of Hollow Creek."

"You just moved into the old Marlowe house. Right? Spooky." Oliva looked at her with wide eyes.

"It's a little run do—"

"Any ghosts yet?" Baxter asked, cutting her off.

"Uh..." She glanced at Callie, wondering if Baxter was serious.

"You tell him yes, and you'll never get rid of him," Callie joked.

"Maybe Mira is around. She was flamboyant in life. Can you imagine her as a ghost?" Baxter's eyes lit up.

"Baxter!" Oliva snapped.

"It's okay." Lena let out a light chuckle. "He's right about Aunt Mira. She was always...unique."

"That's one way of putting it." Callie nodded. "Remember the time she showed up at our apartment and decorated for Halloween while we were in class? There were so many orange lights that I'm certain they were visible from space. At Christmas, her house was dark, but on Halloween, she went all out."

"She always embraced the spookiness of the season," Lena agreed.

As a child, that was one thing she loved about Aunt Mira, but when Mira moved back to Hollow Creek, everything changed. Her father no longer allowed her to visit Aunt Mira. The only explanation she received from him was that Mira was crazy. Why? What changed? She couldn't help blaming her father. Even when he was dying, he refused to see his sister. *We both missed so much.*

"So, what's the Marlowe house like inside? As creepy as the outside looks?" Olivia asked before her cheeks heated with embarrassment. "Sorry...I've just always wondered. Mira kind of kept to herself, especially after her husband died."

"It's surprisingly quiet." She glanced at Baxter and added. "No ghosts yet, but I've only been there a night. So..."

"That place backs onto wolf territory," Baxter announced. "Won't be quiet long."

Lena's heart skipped a beat. She watched Baxter, hoping he was joking. Everything about his posture screamed honesty. Was that nervousness in the way he fidgeted?

*Don't tell him about the wolf.*

Her back straightened as she glanced over her shoulder. She

could have sworn it was her aunt's voice, but that's impossible. Callie lifted her cup to her lips, clearly unfazed. Had no one else heard that?

I t was after midnight when Lena pulled into her driveway. She hadn't planned to stay as long as she had at the bonfire, but Callie, Baxter, and Olivia had welcomed her into the group as if they'd known her for years.

Stepping out of the car, she pulled her sweater tighter around her. The cool air seemed colder here. The thick fog coiled around her feet and through the grass as if it had weight. Making the already spooky house feel even creepier.

"Aunt Mira, it seems you had a bit of a following around town. Everyone either thought you were eccentric, crazy, or a bit of both," she whispered as she strolled toward the porch.

"What the..." Unable to believe what she was seeing, she stepped closer.

Except that the proof was right there in muddy brown. A single unmistakable muddy paw print. Big and broad, and definitely not a dog.

"No." Closing her eyes, she shook her head as if suddenly it would disappear. But when she looked again, the paw print was still there. "This isn't happening."

Nearing the door, she fumbled for the right key before quickly unlocking it and stepping inside. It was quiet. Too quiet. It was as if the house was afraid to make a sound. She had tried to brush it off, but there was something unsettling in the air, as if someone or something was watching her.

"Stop it, Lena," she scolded herself. "It was a dog. Nothing more. Just a dog. A very large dog. One with obvious boundary issues. No one is watching you."

But as she turned around to lock the door, something outside caught her attention. Pulling back the curtain for a better view, she scanned the tree line, hoping all she'd see was darkness, fog, and the tangled, unkempt garden. Instead, glowing eyes looked back at her.

Same color. Same stillness. But closer this time, right up against the crumbling stone fence. The animal's nearness made her breath catch. She silently urged the wolf to move. Instead, it stood there, watching, waiting.

"Was it you? I swear you, fuzzy bastard, if you marked my door like a damn chew toy, we're going to have issues." Even as the words left her mouth, she knew it was ironic.

With her heart pounding in her chest, she locked the door and stepped back. The curtain fell back into place, leaving only a sliver of forest visible, yet she could still see the wolf standing there.

The locked door provided her with a sense of security. Relatively safe at least inside, so she forced herself to turn away from the door. As she moved into the house, she flicked on every light she passed.

"Light...wolves don't like light, right?" she asked as if the house was going to answer.

She wanted to believe that if she ignored the wolf, he'd go away, but part of her already knew he wasn't going anywhere.

# Chapter 2

## *Warnings*

As an introvert, Lena hated crowds, yet somehow, she found herself in the middle of the Hollow Creek Harvest Market. Yet another event the small town did to kick off their Fall Festival.

Booths selling everything from homemade apple butter to ghost-themed jewelry had overtaken the town square. Kids darted between scarecrows and hay bales. The jazz band from Hollow Creek High School was butchering "Monster Mash" near the library steps, and someone dressed as a skeleton kept appearing, offering her free samples of witch's brew punch. She was about to make her escape when Callie spotted her.

"Lena!" Callie waved a caramel apple like a wand. "You've got to meet someone!"

She instinctively braced herself. "If it's your cousin again, the one who collects—"

"It's not. And that was a misunderstanding." Callie grabbed hold of her wrist, gently pulling her. "Relax. It's my brother."

Lena froze, unable to take a step forward, but also unwilling to retreat further. "Wait, *Atlas?*"

"Don't make that face." Callie grinned.

"The face I make when you spring things on me without warning? That one?" How was it possible that someone so outgoing and friendly was Lena's best friend? They were complete opposites, yet somehow, they meshed like night and day, or like werewolves and full moons.

Before she could protest further, Callie had already turned and called out, "Atlas!"

Lena glanced around and, for a moment, considered bolting into the corn maze and disappearing forever. But then he walked into view, and it was too late.

Atlas hadn't changed much since the last time she'd seen him. Images of him showing up uninvited at Callie's college party popped into her mind. She could see the way he glared at their friends before leaving without saying a word to either of them.

Now, there he was stalking toward them. The same broad-shouldered man who walked as if he were ready to take on the world. A fight just moments away. The only difference was his dark hair, cropped shorter than before, giving her a better glimpse of the same cold, piercing eyes. Unreadable then and even more so now. He locked his gaze on her.

"Lena," he said, his voice low.

She gave him a tight smile. "Still brooding, I see. Glad to know some things don't change."

Callie shot her a look, warning her to be nice, but Lena ignored it. Something about Atlas had always set her on edge. He walked around as if the world owed him something. That's not how real life worked.

Atlas didn't bother smiling back. "I didn't know you were moving here."

"I didn't either until a dead aunt and a deranged real estate attorney said otherwise." She shrugged. There was a little more to the story, one that ensured she had little choice but to make the move to Hollow Creek, but it was none of Atlas' business.

"You're staying at the Marlowe house?" His lips pressed together in annoyance, though she couldn't determine if it was because of the house, her, or that she was in *his* town.

"I am. Unless you've got a better offer."

Something flickered across his face. Surprise? Frustration? She couldn't tell.

"There have been sightings near that property," he said. "You should be careful."

"Oh, you mean like *wolves*?" She folded her arms across her chest and let out a light chuckle.

Silence descended over them until her shoulders tightened with unease.

Atlas' jaw tensed. "Probably just strays."

"I don't know," she said, feigning casualness. "This one was all black and was big. He was focused and had the *I could ruin your life* energy. Kind of like you, actually."

Callie coughed. "Okay, fun! Anyone want cider?"

Atlas didn't take his eyes off Lena. "You saw it?"

"I did." She nodded.

"Where?"

"In my yard. He was watching me." *Why is he so interested?* But before she could question him, he stepped closer, so close she could feel the heat coming off him. Not just physical warmth, but something alive and just under the surface.

"Did it cross the stone wall?" he asked.

The question was too specific. Too serious.

She shook her head. "No. Just stared."

Atlas exhaled. Not relief. Something more primal.

"You should come by the bar," Callie said quickly, as if trying to cut the tension. "Rowan's working tonight, and he'd love to see you."

Atlas' expression darkened at the mention of Rowan.

Lena caught it. "What's that look for?"

"Nothing." The growl in his voice made her want to step away, as if it held a warning.

"Sure. Real convincing." She held her ground, her gaze locked on his. "You're a terrible liar."

He shook his head, stepped back, and turned to leave. "Just stay out of the woods, Lena."

"And if I don't?" She was never one to take orders, especially not from someone like him, who expected everyone to follow them.

He paused mid-step, then looked back over his shoulder. "Then don't say I didn't warn you."

"He's right, though." Callie watched as her brother disappeared back into the crowd of people. "The woods aren't safe. You shouldn't go near them."

"Why?" Irritation burned within her as she turned toward her friend. "Are you afraid I'll get a little poison ivy and run back to the city? I don't get what the big deal is. What is so dangerous about the woods, and why didn't you bother to mention any of this before I moved into Mira's house?"

"Just stay out of the woods," Callie whispered. "It's no place for you."

Darkness had fallen, but Lena couldn't settle. The anxiety coursing through her was something she couldn't put into words. Unable to sit still, but also unable to focus, she glanced around the living room. Every candle she owned was lit, the flicker of flames casting long shadows along the wall. The aroma of cinnamon and wax drifted toward her as she reminded herself that she lit the candles to be cozy, not to ward off evil lurking in the woods.

There was something off about Atlas. Not just rude and broody, but caged. Like there was too much inside him, and keeping it down took effort. When she mentioned the wolf watching her, he didn't appear to be surprised. Instead, he'd looked *concerned*. The strangest part was that the concern didn't seem to be for her, but for the wolf.

Thinking about the wolf, she wandered to the back door. "Are you out there now?" She stared into the garden. The fog was back. "What is it with this fog?"

As her gaze scanned the area, she half-expected to see the eyes again. Waiting and watching. Yet there was nothing. Only darkness and silence.

As if the thought of silence summoned it, a howl echoed through the night air. Low, long, and very close. A shiver went up her spine as she stepped back from the window. Even in the darkness, she could see shadows moving beyond the crumbling stone wall.

# Chapter 3

## *Scratch the Surface*

After a near sleepless night, Lena stepped out onto the patio into the garden, coffee mug in hand, and breathed in the fresh morning air. The crisp air, the lingering dew on the leaves, and the stillness of the morning were almost peaceful. Unlike the hours before. The howls from somewhere too close to the house and warnings from Callie and Atlas had left her restless.

"Today's a new day." She brought the mug of coffee to her lips, but before she could take a sip, something caught her attention.

Unwilling to believe what she saw, she set her morning cup of coffee on the wooden railing and spun back toward the door. The wood just below the handle had a single, shallow gouge carved into it. Too high for a raccoon but too deep for a stray mutt. Unlike the muddy paw print, she couldn't ignore this. This was deliberate.

"This isn't possible. Some straggly wolf is *not* harassing me."

Picking her coffee up again, she stared at the deep groove, pulse stuttering. It had to be a prank. Someone was trying to chase her out of town. Maybe Atlas. He didn't seem happy she was in Hollow Creek, and come to think of it, he didn't seem thrilled she was staying in the old Marlowe house. Was it just him or a small-town thing where everyone wanted her gone?

She grabbed her phone, snapped a photo, and pulled up Callie's messages, quickly typing up a message.

> Do local wolves know how to knock?

She meant it as a joke, but dread settled in the pit of her stomach like a cannonball. The wolf wasn't just watching from the tree line, it was getting closer. First, a paw print on her porch, and now a scratch in the wooden door. It was no longer just an innocent act, this felt personal. The wolf was getting closer, testing the boundaries, testing her.

There had to be something she could do to keep stray wolves from making themselves at home on her property. Whatever it was, she needed to find it fast before she came out and found one waiting for her. Up close and personal.

Her phone vibrated, and she glanced down to find Callie's name on the screen.

> I know someone who can help. The Hollow Tap, two o'clock. No complaining.

"No complaining, as if I would." A smirk curled up the corner of her lips with the truth of Callie's words.

The Hollow Tap sat just off the main road, tucked into the trees as if it had grown there. All dark wood and warm lighting, it was more of a rustic lodge than a bar. As Lena strolled into the building, she glanced around, hoping to spot Callie, but something told her she wouldn't.

"Hey Lena, welcome to The Hollow Tap. What can I get for you?"

Her gaze drifted to the bar, more importantly, to the bartender, Rowan. The same guy she'd met at the bonfire. His black hair was just as tousled as it was a few nights ago, only now his smirk seemed to be more trouble than charming. The black T-shirt and jeans he wore only accentuated the bad boy persona he was projecting.

"Rowan." Surprise laced her tone as she stepped closer to the bar. "I...you work here? I mean, I didn't realize—"

"It's my place." He cut her off before she could finish. "Not what you expected, huh?"

"Um...I just..." She forced herself to take a deep breath and relax. "No, actually, it's kinda perfect. It suits you."

"What can I get you?" He moved closer to her end of the bar.

His gaze studied her, like a predator eyeing his prey. Swallowing fear, she leaned in against the bar, closer to him. "You wouldn't have any more of that cider, from the bonfire, would you?"

"Good choice." His slow drawl was intoxicating. "It's my special brew."

"Have you seen Callie around?"

"Callie?" Grabbing a mug from the shelf above the cooler, he raised an eyebrow. "Naw, it's too early for her. Why?"

"Then why am I out in the wild?" she muttered to herself.

Rowan grinned from behind the bar and placed the cup in front of her. "Because you secretly like my devastating charm."

"You're lucky the cider's good." She wrapped her fingers around the mug, enjoying the warmth. "I saw you hanging out with Atlas at the bonfire. That knocks your *devastating charm* down a peg or two. What is his problem?"

Rowan's smile faltered. "He's...complicated."

"Are you trying to politely say he's an ass?" She took a sip, letting out a light sigh as the warmth spread through her.

Watching him, she traced her finger along the rim of the glass. The cider was a specialty of The Hollow Tap, sweet and crisp with a hint of spice that reminded her of autumn mornings, cinnamon, and the faint scent of burning wood. It held the perfection of the season in a single taste.

She took a sip, the warm liquid sliding over her tongue. Smooth with a tart sweetness, only to be followed by a lingering mellow aftertaste. There was something familiar and grounding about it. *This alone could keep me in Hollow Creek, at least in the Fall.*

"He's protective." His words pulled her from her thoughts. "It comes with the territory."

"What territory?" She set the mug on the bar and looked at him. "It's weird how you talk around here. Today, *territory*, but at the bonfire, I heard someone say something about a *pack*. What is that all about?"

He didn't answer, and before she could push further, the door opened with a soft chime.

A man stepped in, letting the door swing shut behind him. In the amber glow of the hanging lights, she could see he was tall, lean, dressed in worn denim and a soft flannel that looked as if it had survived at least two decades. His pale gray eyes scanned the room before landing on her.

"You're the one in Marlowe's place. Right?" he asked as he neared the bar.

"Wow." She blinked. "Word sure travels fast around here."

"This is Silas," Rowan explained. "He handles gardens, tree trimming, and scaring off crows with just a look."

"Lena," she said, holding out her hand.

Silas hesitated for a moment before taking it. His hand was rough, warm, and calloused, like someone who worked for a living.

"Callie said you needed some help to get the landscaping under control." He let go of her hand, but his gaze stayed locked on hers. "I drove by on my way here and saw the overgrowth out back. I can clean it up if you want."

"That'd be great." She was surprised by how calm his presence made her feel.

Rowan stepped back from the bar, grabbed a rag, and started wiping down the bar. Even as he did, his gaze flickered to hers frequently.

Silas glanced out the bar's front window as if he could see her property, but she knew he couldn't. "You've got deer trails running too close to the property line. *Things* come through."

"Things?" The way he said it made the hairs on the back of her neck stand on end.

He didn't answer. Just tilted his head, as if listening for something she couldn't hear, before adding. "Don't stay out after sunset."

"Wow." She let out a soft chuckle. "Do you all have a town script you're working from?"

Silas turned to her, a smile barely curling up the corner of his lips. "We don't say it for fun. You'd do well to listen."

He tipped his head to Rowan and slipped out as quietly as he'd arrived.

Rowan watched him go before turning to her and shrugging. "He's not wrong."

"Okay," Lena said, draining her cider. "What exactly is *in* the woods that has half the town acting like I'm living next to a murder forest?"

Rowan gave her a long look, then smiled. "The better question is, what's already *watching* you from it?"

That night, with her boxes unpacked, Lena turned to Aunt Mira's old belongings, things she had no use for. Mostly old clothes and personal keepsakes.

Cleaning out a dresser drawer, she found an old journal stuffed under a sweater. Running a finger over the worn black leather cover, an engraving caught her attention. There in the middle was the head of a wolf, snarling upwards, as if tipped toward the moon. Something about it felt strangely familiar.

This wasn't the first time she had discovered a piece of Aunt Mira's old life hidden in the house. Most of it was old family photos, trinkets from another life, and bits of long-forgotten notes scattered throughout the rooms. As she opened the journal, a piece of paper dated a year before Aunt Mira's passing slipped from between the pages.

Dearest Lena,

If you're reading this, then I must be gone. I'm both heartbroken and relieved at the thought. You've grown so strong, more than I ever could have imagined, but there are things you must understand about your inheritance—about this house and the land that surrounds it. Things I never had the courage to say aloud but must share now.

I know you have questions. This house may seem like nothing more than a crumbling old building right now, but there is more to it. More to you than you have been told. This house and land belong to our bloodline. It belongs to you now.

It's time for you to understand the legacy I never shared, and for you to come into your own. I regret not telling you all of this before, but I thought you would be safer away from it, away from the pull of the woods and the power they hold. Hollow Creek, and this destiny is why your father cut ties with me. But this is our family's burden to bear, and you've always been drawn to the untamed. You've heard whispers in the wind. I can see this power within you, and it runs deeper than you realize.

*This house was never just a home, Lena. It's a place of protection, a sanctuary for our family—even if your father denied it—and for those who walk with us in the shadows. There are things I've kept hidden from you, secrets about your true nature. You are of this land. And the wolves that roam these woods, that watch from the edge of the forest, they are not only beasts, Lena, they're protectors. Our protectors.*

*You've already met Atlas and others, and you've felt the pull, the attraction. That bond is ancient, as old as the land itself. It wasn't just fate that brought you here, it was me, too. I only hope you're ready.*

*You're not an outsider in Hollow Creek. You're part of the bloodline that connects us all—human and wolf. Your future is tied to them, to this land, in ways you cannot yet comprehend. In time, you will.*

*I have faith in you. But remember this: there are ancient forces at work here that would see the balance tipped, that would use the power of the wolves for their own gain. You must stand firm. Stay strong for your own sake and for the sake of those who have kept this town and this land safe.*

*I wish I could be there to guide you through it, but I know you'll be fine. I believe in you. Don't fear the power you possess, embrace it. You're ready.*

*With all my love,*

*Mira.*

She stared down at the letter, unable to believe what she had read. Was this what the whole town was talking about when they mentioned territory, pack, and wolves? What is the reason everyone kept telling her to stay out of the woods?

"No, this is too crazy." She folded the letter and slipped it back into the journal. "Maybe Aunt Mira was as crazy as Dad said."

As if on cue, a wolf howled. Close.

Dropping the journal onto the desk, she grabbed the flashlight and stood. She'd had enough. This was her home, and she wasn't about to let some flea-infested, mangy wolf intimidate her. She stalked to the kitchen, toward the back door, and grabbed a knife from the island as she passed. She knew it was stupid. A little kitchen knife would not be much defense against the full-grown wolf she had seen hanging around, but it was better than nothing.

With her free hand, she pulled open the door. The fog had settled within the overgrown garden. Unnerved, she swept the garden with the flashlight that was next to the door. Looking for the eyes that seemed always to be watching her. But there was nothing. Just silence.

"Where did you go?" she shouted, anger emboldening her as she stepped off the porch.

A twig snapped. She spun to the left, light catching a glimpse of sleek silver fur before it vanished into the trees. Her pulse spiked.

"Okay," she whispered. "You're not crazy. You're just being stalked by an apex predator that may or may not be some sort of town cryptid."

Another rustle of leaves, this time closer. Fear winning out, she backed up toward the door, risking one final glance out into the trees. Her gaze found a figure standing at the edge of the woods. Not a wolf, but a man. She froze, each breath tightening within her chest. In the dark, she couldn't make out his face. He stood there, completely still, watching.

"Hello?" she called, but there was no response.

In the blink of an eye, he was gone.

"I'm seeing things." She tried to convince herself as she stepped inside and slammed the door. As she locked it, her phone buzzed in her pocket. She pulled it out and unlocked it. A text from an unknown number displayed on the screen.

You shouldn't be out there alone.

# Chapter 4

## *Secrets in the Woods*

Lena had planned to spend the day completing chores around the house. Yet the day had slipped away from her without her realizing it. She kept glancing at her phone, at the message she had received the night before.

> You shouldn't be out here alone.

She had tried to ask who they were. No name and no reply. Silence. It felt like she was stuck in a horror movie, waiting for the next shoe to drop.

Too many things had happened for it all to be a coincidence. The wolf, who had been watching her. The paw print and claw marks. The letter from her aunt about a legacy and a bloodline. Now, the man who was standing at the edge of the trees. He wasn't just passing through on an evening walk. There wasn't a house for more than a mile. He was watching her. As she thought back to what had happened, she couldn't help but think it was a different wolf than the first time. Though she hadn't seen the movement in the woods for long, the fur seemed lighter.

As dusk settled and the light turned golden, she stepped out of the house and into the garden. Something within her changed, she was no longer naïve to what seemed to be happening in the woods. She also recognized the change in the air, it was sharper, sinister. The fog hadn't rolled in yet, but the woods beyond the stone wall were already dark with shadows.

*I should have stayed inside.*

Instead, with a small knife tucked into the trim of her boot and a flashlight in hand, she stepped over the crumbling wall. She saw the old dirt path her aunt had likely once used, overgrown but still visible, twisting between the trees as if swallowed by the darkness.

Standing on the other side of the wall, the world shifted. No hooting owl, no wind, just silence. The only sound was the soft crunch of her boots on the damp leaves. Suddenly, something moved ahead of her. Through the trees, she glimpsed him. The wolf. Dark as midnight with silver streaked through the fur and massive. With her chest tight and her heart beating faster, she watched as the wolf moved slowly this time, pausing between the trees like it wanted her to follow.

"Okay," she muttered as she followed. "This is either extremely dumb or fate taking Halloween a bit too seriously."

The wolf led her deeper into the forest, past mossy stones and half-fallen trees, until the path widened into a small clearing, revealing a ring of twisted birch trees with silver bark and dark, reaching limbs. The wolf stopped at the center and turned back to her. Their gazes met.

"Wait..." Her chest tightened, not in fear but recognition. As if she knew him.

Before she could speak, the wolf turned and slipped silently into the shadows, disappearing. As she stepped further into the clearing, something on the ground caught her attention. Something disturbed the dirt, leaving a small mound near the base of one of the trees. As if someone had uncovered something under the dirt, then tried to conceal it again in a hurry.

Curiosity got the best of her, and she knelt, brushing aside the leaves until her fingers hit something solid. A box. She pulled it free and swept away the remaining dirt on the lid, revealing old wood carved with symbols. One of the symbols, a snarling wolf head, just like on the journal, caught her attention.

After a moment of hesitation, she pried open the lid. Inside the plush red velvet was a small silver pendant shaped like a crescent moon on a thin chain, along with a piece of paper. Yellowed and weathered, she could still make out Aunt Mira's loopy handwriting.

*Lena,*

*If you found this, the boundary is weakening. Stay out of the woods on All Hallows' Eve. Don't trust wolves unless they bare their throats. And whatever you do, don't look into the pond when the moon is full.*

*Aunt Mira*

A twig snapped behind her, and fear flooded through her veins. She snatched the knife from her boot, stood, and spun around, the box nearly falling from her grasp. However, behind her was no wolf, instead, a man stood. One she recognized. Rowan. His expression was unreadable. His gray eyes locked on the box in her hands.

"You weren't supposed to find that *yet*," he said quietly.

Her grip tightened. "Why? What is this?"

"You should go home." He tipped his head toward the path that led her here.

"Why do you all keep saying that? What is going on in this town?"

He stepped closer, coming to stand only a few feet from her. "This place is older than it looks. The trees remember and the land keeps secrets."

"Yeah, well, I'm done playing clueless tourist. My aunt left this for me. She knew something was coming. So don't tell me to walk away when I'm already in it."

His gaze softened. "You're not ready to know."

"Try me." It felt like she was the only one in this small town that wasn't aware of whatever was going on, and she was tired of it.

Silence hung between them as Rowan studied her. But she refused to back down. After a moment, he simply held out a hand. The air around him shimmered. It was faint and almost imperceptible, but for a moment she saw a shape flash beneath his skin. A tall, powerful wolf.

*He's one of them...*

The thought was enough to get her moving toward the path. "Fine."

Without a word, he fell into step behind her. It was darker now, and she was thankful for the flashlight, allowing her to see where she was walking. But behind her, Rowan didn't seem to have an issue. He moved through the woods silently. Without the warmth of his body behind her, she might have forgotten he was there. As the house came into view, he slowed.

"Goodnight, Lena."

She stepped over the wall, crossing back into the garden, and immediately, the air became lighter, easier to breathe. She glanced over her shoulder as she neared the porch, and he stood there at the tree line, watching.

No, guarding. Like something worse was just waiting for her to turn her back.

It was past midnight, but Lena was still awake. Sitting on her sofa in the dark with a butcher knife in her hand as if she were waiting for someone to break in. Three quick raps on the door echoed through the house, followed by silence.

She wanted to ignore it, but something compelled her to move toward the door. The usual creaks of the house echoed, louder than usual. With one hand on the wall, her gaze locked on the door only steps away, she paused to listen. For what she wasn't sure, but she paused, nonetheless.

The knock came again. This time slower, softer.

She forced herself forward, the knife clenched in her hand, ready. She opened the door a crack, the chain still latched, because something was happening in Hollow Creek, she wasn't completely aware of. But it was becoming clear that the strange things didn't just happen in the woods anymore.

Silas leaned heavily against the doorframe, his normally crisp shirt torn and stained dark across the ribs. His face was pale, but his eyes were wild.

"Silas?" She blinked, unable to believe he was standing there. "You...you're bleeding!"

He shot her a half-smile, like it was only a slight inconvenience. "Bit of a disagreement," he said, his voice hoarse. "Can I come in, or should I bleed out dramatically on your porch?"

She unlatched the door before she could second-guess herself, and Silas staggered inside. One arm wrapped tight around his side. The moment he was out of the way, she shut the door and locked it. Her gaze scanned the trees at the edge of the property.

"You look like hell." She tried to keep her tone light as she laid the butcher knife on the counter.

"Thanks." He chuckled under his breath. "You know how to lift a man's spirits."

Wrapping her arm around his waist, she helped him to the kitchen table and into a chair. Each movement caused him to wince. It was clear he was hurt more than he was letting on. She didn't ask what happened, at least not yet. There were more important things. She grabbed the first-aid kit from under the sink.

"Shirt off," she ordered, snapping on gloves. "Otherwise, I'll cut it."

He gave her a faintly amused look but obeyed. The fabric peeled away with an ugly *pop*, revealing torn skin along his ribs and a nasty bruise already blossoming with black and blue.

"Shit, Silas, that's not a 'disagreement,' that's a mauling."

He didn't respond, only watched her as she opened the first-aid kit. He hissed as she dabbed antiseptic across the worst of the gashes, the cotton pad staining deep red almost instantly.

"Hold still," she muttered, leaning closer, her hands steady. The cut was deep, long claw marks arching across his left side just beneath his ribs as if something had tried to rip him open. The sight of it made her stomach twist, but she didn't flinch. She pushed her emotions aside and focused on the task at hand.

"I'm trying," he mumbled through clenched teeth.

His skin was hot beneath her fingers, almost feverish, and she could feel his exhausted muscles tighten with pain. Silas wasn't the type to show weakness, and yet here he was, bleeding in her kitchen, shirtless and silent.

With a clean pad, she wiped closer to the wound, and a low growl escaped his throat, no doubt from the sting of the iodine.

"You growl now?" she asked, eyeing him.

"Consider it an occupational hazard." His lips curled up into a half smile.

"Of moonlight brawling?"

"Something like that." His gaze flicked to her face, the humor disappearing from his features.

She grabbed a pair of tweezers from the kit and leaned in again. "I need to clean the edge of the wound. It's got dirt or something in it."

"Are you expecting me to scream, or something?"

"I say it because if I were you, I'd rather be unconscious for this." With tweezers in hand, she leaned in, carefully removing a shard of bark and something else that shimmered like a sliver of obsidian. "What the hell is this?"

Silence. Why did that seem to be the theme of Hollow Creek?

She glanced up, but Silas was staring up at the ceiling, as if he couldn't bear to look at her.

"You're not going to tell me what did this to you, are you?" she asked, hoping she was wrong.

He let out a breath, his shoulders shifting slightly, but he still wouldn't look at her. "If I did, you wouldn't sleep tonight."

"Too late for that." She dropped the tweezers and some debris on the table, then grabbed a towel. "I wasn't doing much sleeping before you showed up. Or didn't you notice the butcher knife I answered the door with?"

Pressing gauze gently to his ribs, she started wrapping the bandage. He winced but said nothing, letting her work. The silence stretched long, filled only by the sound of tape tearing and their breathing. Finished, she stepped back. "There, you're put back together. For now, at least."

"You're good at this." He grabbed his torn shirt and slid it back on.

"I've had practice. But you're the first injured wolf to show up at my door lately."

His gaze shot to hers, sharp now. "I never said—"

"You didn't have to." She leaned back against the counter and crossed her arms. "I can connect the dots."

For a brief second, his mask slipped. A flicker of vulnerability beneath his usual sarcasm. Then it was gone.

"You're smarter than most." He rose from the chair and turned to the door. "I shouldn't have come. But thanks for not asking too many questions."

"I've asked plenty, you just didn't answer any of them," she said flatly.

"Goodnight, Lena." Gingerly, he stepped toward the door, his fingers on the deadbolt, when she called to him.

"Silas..." Her words trailed off, unsure how to put her concerns into words. "Whatever you're not saying...it's getting closer. Isn't it?"

He didn't turn back or answer. Just opened the door and disappeared into the dark.

Her gaze landed on the blood-streaked towel on the counter. It was all the answer she needed. Whatever lurked within the forest was getting closer, and she needed to be prepared. Silas' wounds weren't from a fight, an animal had clawed him. Something was out there, and it wasn't playing by the same rules anymore.

# Chapter 5

## *The Alpha Problem*

The next day, Lena didn't wait for the wolves to come to her. Instead, she dressed, grabbed her coffee to-go, and headed out, looking for them. Specifically, Atlas. She couldn't explain why, but she knew he was involved. Rowan's earlier words echoed through her thoughts: *He's protective. Comes with the territory.*

She had enough cryptic warnings, enough people telling her she *wasn't ready*, and enough half-truths to drive her up the damn wall. Her aunt had left her something, and now it was clear she wasn't just a clueless outsider stumbling into local lore, she was *in it* up to her neck. Atlas, with a scowl carved from stone, knew more than he was saying.

She was *done* being handled. It was time for answers.

The Hollow Tap was mostly empty when she stormed in. Only a few locals were sipping beer and discussing deer season. Rowan was behind the bar. He tipped his head toward the back.

"Office."

She marched by him without a word or even a sideways glance. She would save her anger for Atlas.

Not bothering to knock, she barged in, her gaze landing on Atlas behind the desk, paperwork scattered across the surface.

"I figured it was a matter of time," he said, leaning back in the office chair.

"You know, most people say hello first." She slammed the carved wooden box onto his desk.

He glanced at the box, but there was no visible reaction. Nothing.

He leaned forward, his finger teasing along the carving before he opened it. The change was immediate. Jaw clenched and muscles tightened. When he glanced up at her, no amusement lingered. Now, only heat, unfiltered and barely controlled. "Where did you find this?" he asked, voice low.

"In the woods. Where your *pet wolf* led me."

He stood slowly, coming around the desk, and for a moment she thought he might growl. "You shouldn't have gone out there."

"You shouldn't be hiding what my aunt was into," she snapped. "That symbol on the necklace? It matches the one on the journal I found. It's the same with the carvings on the box. She left it for me, Atlas, not you. So, stop acting like I'm some clueless city girl who wandered into your territory."

He leaned back against the edge of the desk and focused his gaze on her. "You're not clueless, you're reckless. There's a difference."

Anger fueling her, she took a step toward him. "And what are you? Broody forest boss with a territorial complex?"

"I'm the one keeping this town safe while you play detective in cursed woods."

"Oh, *screw you, Atlas.*" The air between them snapped tight, like a wire stretched to the breaking point. She could feel the tension in her bones, but she wasn't about to back down. She deserved answers.

"You have no idea what that thing means or what it can do." He slammed the box shut, causing her to jump a little. "Your aunt wasn't just some sweet old woman into herbal tea and fairy tales. She was a guardian. That land, your land, Lena, sits on a threshold, one that *should've closed* when she died."

"A threshold to what?" She swallowed the anger that had been burning within her. She was finally getting answers, and she wasn't about to let her temper get the best of her.

He stared at her. "The Otherwood."

The words meant nothing, and yet, they *felt* like something ancient and dangerous.

"Your house..." His words trailed off as if he wasn't sure she was ready.

"My house, what? Damn it, Atlas, tell me! I don't know what's going on or what this Otherwood is, but something about the house has shifted. It feels...different."

"Your house is sitting on a seal, and it's weakening. It's why you're seeing things in the woods, and it's why the wolves are watching. Something is coming through, Lena. And if you don't stop poking at it—"

"You'll what?" she cut in. "Growl at me? Send Silas to shadow me again? Bite me?"

He moved. Fast. Too fast for her to follow.

Before she could blink, he was in front of her. Not touching, but *close*. His presence filled the space between them, all heat and intensity, with the heavy scent of pine.

"You think I haven't wanted to?" he said, voice quiet and dangerous.

Her breath caught in her throat as she stared up at him. Heat bloomed in her chest at his closeness. She hated how much her body reacted. How she wanted to reach out and touch him. "Go ahead, prove me right."

His gaze dropped to her lips, and for one hot, charged second, she thought he was going to kiss her. But then he pulled back. Just enough so that she could breathe more easily.

"I'm not going to give you what you think you want," he said, voice like stone. "Because once I do, there's no going back."

"What does that mean?" Her pulse thundered in her ears.

"It means I'm already breaking the rules just by letting you stay."

Putting distance between them, he walked around the other side of his desk and sat down.

She stared at him, fury and confusion warring within her. "You don't own me." Snatching the box from the desk, she took a step toward the door. He clearly wasn't going to give her the answers she needed.

"No." Atlas paused, leaning forward until his elbows rested on the desk. "But if you keep walking this path, something else might try to."

Images flashed before Lena's eyes too fast to hold on to, as if she were trying to catch lightning in her hands. Trees on fire, flames licking up bark, and ash rising into the sky. As quick as that appeared, it disappeared. Only to be followed by red eyes blinking at her in the darkness. Too low to the ground to be human. Whatever it was, it stood between the trees, watching her from the shadows.

With her feet in the water, she glanced around the pond, looking for something, but only found darkness. *You're not alone.*

She glanced behind her and found she was no longer in the garden. She was now in her bedroom. A wolf, massive and still, crouched at the edge of the bed. Its fur was darker than night, so black that it seemed threaded with shadows. Its glowing molten red eyes, unblinking. The wolf didn't growl or even move. It stood, watching, waiting.

She tried to speak, but her mouth wouldn't open. Unable to move, as if pinned beneath an invisible weight, she was left waiting for whatever was about to happen. The wolf tilted its head, and she could feel herself sinking. The forest, fire, and water were closing in on her.

She bolted upright, completely awake, with her heart hammering against her ribs. Despite the chill in the room, sweat clung to her skin, and her breath came in sharp, uneven gasps.

No fire, forest, or wolf. Only a dark room, with moonlight spilling across the wooden floor.

"Just a drea—" Her attention drifted to the nightstand. Sitting neatly beside her lamp, as if whoever placed it there wanted her to find it immediately, was the pendant from the box she'd found in the woods.

"I left this in the car." She stared at the pendant, unable to believe what she was seeing. "After seeing Atlas...I know I left it in the car." Yet, there it was. The chain was clean, and the pendant was shimmering in the moonlight.

# Chapter 6

## *Teeth Beneath Skin*

Throughout the day, Lena's thoughts circled the pendant and the wolf standing at the bottom of her bed. By evening, she was certain of two things. The pendant was important, though good or evil, she wasn't sure. She hadn't been meant to find it right away. But now that she had, what did it mean?

The other thing she was positive about was that the wolf knew her. Was it Silas? Atlas? Or someone else? More importantly, how did it get into the house? Each night before bed, she made sure to lock every door and window. Did the wolf move the pendant? Why?

She stood by the kitchen window, looking over the overgrown garden. Is this why the wolves keep coming? Because it's overgrown? Or because of the deer trails Silas had mentioned? Even as she considered it, she knew there was more to it than that. Yet, she made a mental note to ask Silas again about his offer to clean up the garden.

The last rays of sunlight were peeking through the trees when Rowan strolled into view. Two beer bottles and a grin when he spotted her in the window.

"Peace offering," he hollered, holding them up.

She stepped away from the window and opened the back door. "Why?"

"Heard you and Atlas nearly burned down my bar." He shook his head. "You were gone when I came back out of the kitchen, but I wanted to make sure you were okay."

"I didn't start the fire," Lena muttered. "I just poured the gasoline."

He let out a deep chuckle as he stepped inside. "You okay?"

"No," she admitted honestly. "But I'm not leaving, if that's what you're about to suggest." She watched him lean against her kitchen counter as if he'd done it a thousand times before. He looked comfortable in her space.

"Wasn't going to." He popped open the beers and handed her one. "I like trouble. You keep things interesting. It's a nice evening. How about we take these out to the porch?"

Taking the offered beer, she nodded. If she were alone, she wouldn't have set foot outside again at night, but with Rowan there, she felt safe. She stepped out, glanced around the perimeter, and plopped down onto the back step. The fog was curling. Low, but thick.

"What is it with all the fog?" she mumbled.

"It's Hollow Creek," he answered, sitting down next to her.

He smelled like wild sage and the first spark of a bonfire. His presence alone eased some of the tension within her. Allowing her to breathe for five minutes without looking over her shoulder. Yet there were still so many unanswered questions.

"Tell me the truth," she said. "You're not normal."

"We've met, so yeah." He smirked.

"No." She turned to face him. "You're not *human*. Are you?"

The smirk faded, and silence stretched for a long moment before he leaned in closer.

"Would it scare you if I said no?" he asked, his voice low.

She held his gaze. "Depends on what you are."

His smile returned, but it didn't quite reach his eyes. "You already know, don't you?"

A howl cut through the air before she could answer. Long, low, and close. *As if that wasn't the story of my life. Why won't they leave me alone?*

Rowan's gaze snapped toward the trees. Tension rippled through him like a pulled thread. His eyes glowed. *Wolf.*

"What was that?" she whispered.

"Trouble, and not the fun kind."

He stood, fast but graceful. "Go back inside, Lena."

"No."

He glanced down at her, expression suddenly serious. "I'm not playing now. Please, just go in and lock the doors."

She took a shaky breath. "Rowan—"

Before she could finish, his body jerked forward. Bones cracked, and his body contorted. She would have expected the transformation to be painful, but Rowan made it look natural. As if his human form was just a mask being peeled away. His hands curled into claws. Fur rippled along his arms and shoulders. His mouth split, stretching back to reveal a snout and fangs.

In seconds, he wasn't a man anymore. Silver-furred, golden-eyed, taller than anything natural, and beautiful in a way that stole the breath from her lungs. He was a wolf. *Her wolf.* The one that came to her before.

She stumbled backward, heart pounding, as her gaze stayed locked on him. The wolf—Rowan—stood utterly still, watching her, waiting to see how she reacted.

But before she could assure him, another wolf, massive, black, and angry, burst from the trees. With a snarl, it lunged at Rowan.

*No!*

Rowan intercepted it mid-air, the two beasts colliding in a blur of teeth and fury.

For a moment, she wasn't sure what to do, but Rowan's earlier words rang through her thoughts. *Please, just go in and lock the doors.* Scurrying backward, she grabbed hold of the door and pushed it open. Her gaze stayed on wolf Rowan as she slammed the door shut and locked it. Safely inside, her heart thundered in her chest. Outside, the sounds of the fight: growls, snaps, and finally a yelp echoed through the air.

*Please don't let that be Rowan.*

Silence. Eerie silence fell over the house, and her chest tightened. She wanted to push the curtain aside, but fear of what she might find froze her in place.

A soft knock echoed through the house, louder in the silence.

"Rowan..." she whispered as if praying it was him.

She forced herself forward and opened the door enough to peek through.

Rowan stood there, naked and bleeding from a cut above his brow. Breathing hard, he met her gaze. "Now you know."

With those three little words, his eyes rolled back into his head, and he dropped to the ground, barely missing the door frame as he did.

She reached out, trying to catch him, but he was heavy. Too heavy to keep upright. The best she could hope for was to ease his landing. "Rowan!"

# Chapter 7

## *Lines in the Dirt*

With more effort than Lena wanted to admit, she managed to drag Rowan's body inside. She wasn't sure it was adrenaline or blind panic that kept her upright as she managed to get him onto the sofa. Letting out a deep breath, she grabbed the throw blanket from the back of the sofa and covered his naked body.

Besides the cut above his eye, a few scratches, and some bruising, she couldn't find a reason for him to be unconscious. Even the claw marks along his side were mild, at least compared to what happened to Silas.

Grabbing the first-aid kit from the kitchen, she made a mental note to restock her medical supplies. If this kept up, she'd be out of iodine, ointment, gaze, and bandages before the week was over.

"Rowan..." she called softly to him as she sat down on the coffee table in front of the sofa and began to clean his wounds. Nothing. He lay there, unconscious. "Damn it, do I need to call an ambulance?"

Unsure how to explain his wounds, she waited, carefully cleaning each laceration, while watching him closely. Now and then, he stirred, muttering something incoherent. Under her fingers, he felt feverish. He was too hot, unnaturally so.

"You could've warned me," she whispered, pressing gauze to the worst cut. "A casual 'hey, I turn into a wolf' wouldn't have killed you."

He didn't answer.

"What about the other wolf? Damn it, Rowan, I need you to wake up. I need you to tell me if I should call someone." She tossed the last of the bloody gaze aside and pushed the hair away from his eyes. "What am I supposed to do?"

Outside, the woods had gone still again. Like the forest itself was holding its breath. There was no peace to it. Like a storm waiting for the right moment. Whatever was out there was closer now.

She looked down at him, her voice softer now. "Why me? Why was I led to that box? Why *show* me? What am I supposed to do?"

She didn't expect him to answer. As he lay there unmoving, a knock came from the front door. Loud. Sharp. Angry. There was only one person who it could be, but how? How did he know?

With one last glance at Rowan, she stood and moved toward the door. She opened it just wide enough to see Atlas standing on her porch. The scowl on his face warned her that he wasn't in the mood for questions.

"Where is he?" He glanced over her shoulders.

"Hello to you, too," she snapped, stepping outside and pulling the door shut behind her. "I'm fine, by the way. Thanks for asking."

Atlas' jaw clenched. "Lena. Move."

"Not until you tell me what the hell is going on. And don't give me more cryptic one-liners. I've seen what he is. I know *you're* the same. Silas, too."

Atlas stepped closer, his voice low and furious. "Did he shift in front of you?"

"Yes."

"Did he touch you?"

"What the hell kind of question is that?"

Atlas didn't answer. But the silence, full of possessive, vibrating jealousy, told her more than words ever could. Her heart beat faster, but now for entirely different reasons.

"Oh my…" She let out a soft, disbelieving laugh. "You're jealous."

He doesn't deny it, just looks at her like she is losing her mind.

"You don't get to feel possessive." She stepped closer. "You've been nothing but cold since I got here. You warn me off, push me away, and then get mad when someone else doesn't treat me like I'm made of glass?"

"He's not safe," Atlas said tightly.

"Neither are you."

From the way his eyes burned, full of pure fury, her comment had landed, and for a heartbeat, she thought he might say something reckless. Instead, he let out a deep breath.

"Let me see him."

She hesitated for a moment, then opened the door.

Atlas stepped in, his entire body stiffening when he saw Rowan on the sofa. He crossed the room in two strides and crouched beside him, checking the wound with practiced ease. There was something fierce and protective in the way he moved, but also regret. Like Rowan bleeding out in her living room was the last thing he'd ever wanted to see.

"Who attacked him?" she asked quietly.

Atlas stood. "A rogue."

"A rogue…like another human that turns into a wolf?"

"Shifter." He nodded once. "Something's stirring them up and bringing them out of hiding. We've kept them out of Hollow Creek for years. Now they're coming through the boundary like it's nothing."

"Because of me?" *Wasn't that the only logical reason? The only change in Hollow Creek. Aunt Mira died, and I moved to town.*

Atlas didn't answer.

She stepped in front of him. She needed answers, and now that he was on her turf, it was time to get them. "Tell me the truth."

"You really want it?"

"I'm not a child, Atlas." She crossed her arms over her chest and waited.

"No," he said, voice rough. "You're worse. You're a damn lightning rod. The land answers to you now, even if you don't understand it. Your blood called the wolves, and your presence *woke* something. You want to know why I'm angry? Why I'm scared?" He took another step, crowding her against the wall. "Because I can smell you on the wind every time you step outside. Because every part of me wants to follow it."

"You don't get to say that," she whispered. "Not after all this time pretending I don't exist."

"I didn't say I didn't *feel* it," he said. "I said I couldn't act on it."

The air between them turned molten. His chest rose and fell like he was barely holding something back.

"Th...then stop holding back." Her voice shook, but she refused to look away.

Atlas reached toward her. His fingers hovered near her face. "I can't, because if I start, I won't stop. And that would make me just as dangerous as everything else you're afraid of."

She didn't know whether to slap him or kiss him, but before she could decide, he stepped away.

*Coward.*

"She's fiery," Rowan said behind them, voice hoarse but amused.

They both turned.

Rowan sat up slowly, bloodied and grinning. "This is going to be fun."

# Chapter 8

## *Awakening the Bloodline*

Morning light spilled through the kitchen window as Lena sipped coffee and tried to make sense of the past month. A few weeks ago, everything was calm, or rather, normal. Now she found herself neck deep in something otherworldly. The truth wasn't clear yet, but it was becoming less blurry. She wasn't just some city girl with a penchant for folklore, she was part of something older, something alive.

"No wonder Dad never wanted me to come to Hollow Creek. He knew what I'd find here, what I'd become part of."

She set the coffee aside and opened Aunt Mira's journal again. This had to have the answers she was seeking.

*October 15th*

*The woods whisper tonight with a voice both old and hungry. I can feel the pulse beneath my feet and almost see the blood of those who came before me. The seal holds, but only just, and I write this not knowing if I will live to see another autumn.*

*The wolves are restless, and the pack grows uneasy. Shadows beckon where light once lived. It can only mean one thing: the boundary is thinning.*

*The Otherwood waits beyond the trees, beyond the pond's glassy surface, waiting for the moment the seal cracks. My blood is the anchor, and I fear what will happen if that bond breaks. I have no choice. To protect this town and the pack, I have bound myself to the land in body, spirit, and soul. The pendant holds the key, a lock on the darkness beneath.*

*I wonder if my niece will understand what she's inherited and have the courage to carry the weight.*

*Will she listen when the wolves call her home?*

*May the moon guide her.*

*— Mira*

Lena closed the journal and rose from the table. As she moved toward the counter to get more coffee, her gaze focused on the pendant lying on the table. It was the key, but the key to what?

Movement from outside caught her attention. Silas strolled through the back gate, and she let out a sigh. Dressed in faded blue jeans and a white T-shirt, she hoped this was a social visit, not some mission from Atlas.

She set her mug aside and opened the door as he stepped onto the porch.

"You're awake early," he said, voice low, gaze flickering with something she couldn't determine.

"I don't sleep well anymore," she admitted. "I keep thinking... about Rowan, Atlas, and whatever is happening in these woods."

"You're caught between two worlds." He nodded, folding his arms.

She met his gaze, curiosity battling frustration. "And you? Which world do you belong to?"

"Both. Neither," he said cryptically. "But today, you'll start learning to belong to your own."

He tipped his head toward the kitchen table. "That pendant..."

She let her gaze fixate on the pendant lying on the kitchen table. She wasn't sure why she'd brought it downstairs, but something made her want to have it close. The question that kept coming to her mind was, why did Aunt Mira have this in the box, buried in the woods?

"Mira's pendant isn't just a charm, it's a key. Now close your eyes," he instructed.

Listening, she let her eyelids drift shut. Instantly, the world shifted. Around her, the garden disappeared, and the air thickened until every breath held the scent of pine and wet ground. The pulse of the land beat under her feet, synced with her heartbeat.

"Feel the energy. That's the blood of your ancestors flowing through this soil. Through you."

Images flashed within her mind. Moonlight forest, wolves, a woman standing before a glowing circle carved in stone. No...it wasn't any woman, it was Aunt Mira.

"Lena, you're the last guardian." His voice was low, and she could feel the heat coming from his body as he stepped closer. "The seal your aunt protected is weakening because of *you*. Because you have not accepted what you carry in your blood."

"Why me?" she asked breathlessly.

"Because you *choose* to be here. To fight." He dragged his finger along her arm. "Open your eyes."

"Sil—"

"Not now," he cut her off. "Atlas is by the pond. You need to go to him."

"That's the last thing I need."

"Trust me." There was an urgency in his voice.

"Fine." Even as she said it, she could hear the annoyance in her tone. Yet she stepped away from him and strolled toward the stone fence, toward the pond just on the other side of the trees.

Stepping through the tree line, she spotted Atlas near the edge of the water. Unlike the night before, anger and annoyance no longer poured off him. Instead, his lip curls up into a half-smile.

"You need to see this." As she neared, he knelt beside the pond and traced the edge with a finger. "The pond is the other side of the seal. The line between our world and the Otherwood."

"I thought the boundary was the forest."

"It's more than that. It's a force that runs through everything here. Mira kept it anchored, but without her, it's fraying."

"If it breaks?" She glanced down at him.

"Then the wolves won't be the only things crossing over. There are things worse than any rogue shifter waiting in the Otherwood." His eyes darkened, and she could almost feel the fear coming from him.

"What happ..." She swallowed hard and pulled the courage from deep within her. "What happened the last time the seal broke?"

Atlas looked away, jaw tight. "Blood spilled, and families torn apart. A war no one here talks about anymore."

She reached out, placing her hand on his shoulder. "Then *we* make sure it doesn't happen again."

He looked back at her, the walls around him cracking just a little. "That can only happen if...if you're with us."

# Chapter 9

## *Blood and Bone*

The sun dipped low in the sky, casting long shadows through the trees and onto the clearing where Silas waited. He stood there calmly, but his gaze held the same sharp intensity Lena had seen when she first met him at The Hollow Tap. His easy nature clashed with the intensity in his eyes, making him seem like a man bearing the weight of centuries.

Atlas stood beside him, arms crossed, watching her as if she were a spark that would ignite the forest. As the mood struck, he seemed hot or cold. "Are you wearing the pendant?"

She reached up, pulling the necklace from beneath her shirt to show him the small, silver crescent moon. When Atlas called to inform her that Silas would meet her for her first training session, he advised her to wear the pendant only if she was truly with them. Embracing it meant she couldn't go back. "I'm with you, Atlas."

"Ready?" Silas asked.

"I guess." Her heart pounded against her ribcage with anxiety.

"First," Silas stepped closer, closing the distance between them. "You need to learn control. The magic of this land flows through you, but it's wild like a wolf pup. If you don't tame it, it will tear you apart."

He stepped forward, extending a hand. The pendant around her neck thrummed against her chest. It was so strong she wanted to step back, away from him. *Is he causing this?*

"Focus on the energy. Don't fight it."

She closed her eyes and concentrated on the pulse of the earth beneath her, a slow, steady heartbeat. The scent of pine and rain drifted toward her on the thickened air. Then, warmth spread from the pendant, flowing through her veins like fire and ice at once. A flicker of silver light shimmered behind her eyelids.

"Good," Silas said. "Now, open your eyes."

She did. The clearing was the same, but her vision sharpened. The colors vibrant and the shadows deeper. Faint traces of energy flowed between the trees, like veins of magic beneath the bark.

Atlas stepped forward, breaking the quiet. "Now comes the hard part." He handed her a dagger, worn but well-balanced. "Defense. If you're going to protect yourself and this town, you need to be prepared."

She wrapped her fingers around the dagger's handle, feeling the weight, and tried not to think of what *protection* might mean. The first strike came fast, before she was ready, and stole her thoughts away.

Atlas moved with the grace of a predator. He was holding back. It was clear in the way he moved. Slow, giving her a chance to predict his next move. Still, she dodged clumsily, adrenaline flaring.

"Focus!" Atlas barked. "Don't let your fear decide your moves."

She bit back a retort and steadied herself. What she wouldn't give to knock him on his ass.

Each time he charged at her, the pendant pulsed faster, the magic within her stirring. He circled her, coming left when she faked right, but this time she expected it. She arched the dagger through the air and barely made contact, cutting his shirt and staining it with blood.

"Oh, Atlas!"

With a nod, he lowered his dagger. "Not bad," he admitted, a ghost of a smile tugging at his lips.

"Not bad...you're bleeding because of me." She stared at him wide-eyed.

"It's just a scrap. Don't worry, we heal quicker than humans."

"Do you not see what this means?" Silas asked, pulling her attention to him. "Atlas moves faster, even when he's trying not to, and yet you still got him. Your skills are improving in just that quick session." He nodded in approval.

"I don't want to hurt someone on our side. I—" A howl cut off her words. Harsh and unfamiliar.

"That's not one of ours." Silas' expression darkened as he stepped closer to her.

"Rogues," Atlas agreed.

"More are coming, and they won't stop until the seal breaks," Silas said grimly. "That's enough training for tonight."

She swallowed hard and glanced around the woods, almost expecting something to move. The weight of the necklace seemed heavier now, as if it were an anchor pulling her toward an unknown destiny.

But there was one thing for certain. She wouldn't run. She would face whatever was coming head-on.

# Chapter 10

## *Shadows at the Edge*

Standing in the clearing beside Atlas and Silas, Lena's gaze strained against the darkness, searching for movement. Something was out there, watching, waiting. She couldn't see it, but she could feel it.

"Rogues don't follow the old rules," Atlas said quietly, voice tight. "Boundaries and treaties go out the window. All they care about is breaking the seal. They'll burn this town down if that's what it takes."

Silas shifted beside her, muscles tense, and she could see his eyes flickering gold in the moonlight. "They'll come in force. We don't have much time."

Lena's breath caught in her lungs as figures emerged between the trees. Wolves, twisted and wild, their eyes glowing red, and their snarling teeth bared like weapons. She started to take a step back, then stopped herself.

"Get ready," Atlas growled low in his throat.

Silas shifted. Right in front of her, his human form blurred. Fur replaced skin, bones reshaping until he stood as a massive wolf, powerful and fierce. It all happened in one clean motion.

Atlas didn't hesitate either. He moved with wolf-like grace, ready for the fight that was coming.

Then there was Lena. She stood there, heart pounding, dagger in hand, doubting she was ready for this. But she didn't run.

An ebony beast stepped forward, the clear alpha. He wasn't just taller, he seemed to drip menace, enough to make the others stay back a step. "You don't belong here," he snarled.

"This is our land," Atlas growled.

With that, the conversation ended, and the air exploded with movement. Snarls, growls, and the pounding of paws on the ground. Atlas and Silas fought with savage precision, but the rogue pack was bigger than she expected. She gripped the pendant, feeling the magic thrumming as her mind raced, searching for a way to help.

A sudden lunge from a rogue wolf caught her off guard, but before it could strike, Silas was there. A blur of fur and claws, pushing the attacker away. She stumbled back, breathless, but thankful.

"Lena, focus on the pendant!" Atlas' voice cut through the chaos. "Feel the land...use it!"

She closed her eyes, reaching deep for the power. Energy coursed through her veins, cold and sharp as moonlight. She grabbed hold of it, trying to push it out toward the fight. A wave of shimmering light burst from her hands, washing over the rogue wolves.

The rogue wolves yelped and quickly retreated, leaving only snarls of frustration in their wake. The rogue alpha gave one last furious growl before melting back into the shadows.

Silas shifted back to human form, breathing hard as he stood there naked.

"Not bad for a rookie." Atlas clapped a hand on her shoulder.

"You guys must go through a lot of clothes." She smiled, shaky but proud.

"We fight because we have to, not because we want to," Silas said, as if to explain the loss of wardrobe. "Don't worry, we keep clothes at work, in our trucks, and well...pretty much everywhere."

"We fight because we have to." She nodded, understanding exactly what he meant. "And, I'm not going anywhere."

"No," Silas said, his gaze drifting to Atlas. "You're ours now."

# Chapter 11

## *After the Storm*

The forest's stillness made Lena uneasy. Not a single sound, not even the wind, and all the energy that had coursed through her moments ago had vanished. With trembling fingers, she reached up and traced the edges of her pendant. The magic inside still hummed faintly, pulsing like a second heartbeat.

*It's not the pendant, it's within you.* She glanced over her shoulder, almost expecting to see Aunt Mira, but only darkness and trees were there.

Silas leaned against a nearby tree, clearly exhausted. His breathing was slow but labored. Atlas had disappeared. Mumbling something about chasing away any strays. Leaving her alone with Silas, both needed a moment before they could make the trek back to her house.

"Is it always like this? The fighting, the hiding, and the endless danger?" she asked, breaking the silence.

Silas glanced at her, eyes tired but steady. "No, it wasn't always war, but the rogues don't care about peace. They'd rather have chaos, and that means we always have to be ready."

"I'm not just some outsider anymore, am I?"

"No." He gave a small, bitter laugh. "You're a part of the pack. Whether or not you like it."

"I know it was you." She glanced at him. "Why did you show yourself to me? You brought me to the box. You could have scared me away."

"Because you needed to know." His gaze softened. "And because I trust you more than I should. Maybe also because...I wanted you to see me, all of me."

"I see you, all of you, Silas." She lifted her gaze from him and looked up toward the sky, unable to meet his eyes. "I'm scared," she admitted quietly.

"Good." He stepped closer, closing the distance between them. "Fear keeps up sharp. But Lena, you're stronger than you think."

The moonlight danced across his face, revealing a vulnerability she hadn't expected. She reached out and brushed her fingers along his hand. "Teach me, Silas. Help me belong."

His fingers curled gently around hers. "You already do."

For a moment, the chaos faded, and they were just two people.

"I come bearing gifts," Rowan hollered, stepping into the clearing. "Clothes."

"About time." Atlas stepped out of the trees, strolling toward Rowan.

"Good, everyone's here." She didn't pull her hand away from Silas, but looked at each of them. "I deserve some answers, and for once, you're going to give them to me. Now."

Lena hadn't exactly invited them into her home, but after the incident in the woods, it was clear the conversation couldn't wait any longer.

"Rowan, how did you know to come out into the woods?" She glanced at Atlas and added. "Did you call him?"

"Not in the way you're meaning." Atlas stood with arms crossed near the door. She wasn't sure if he was ready to leave or if he was going to barricade it shut.

"What does that mean?"

"As alpha, he can communicate with us," Rowan explained, taking a seat in the corner chair.

"Oh..." She stood, arms folded, trying to ignore the intensity of three supernaturally handsome, deep, dangerous men watching her. "Let's start with what I'm actually dealing with."

As the silence stretched on, she glanced at each of them until her gaze landed on Silas, who was slouched on the sofa, eyes still shadowed from his healing wounds. "Seriously? I've had wolves watching me in my backyard, someone marked my door like it was a chew toy, and last night I had a dream so vivid I could smell smoke when I woke up. Oh, and let's not forget this pendant that I left in my car was suddenly back on my nightstand like that's normal bedtime behavior. So, someone talk to me."

The tension between them was sharp like broken glass. Until Rowan spoke. "You're not wrong to be scared, but it's time for you to know the truth." He glanced at Atlas, who gave a reluctant but resigned nod.

"I'm not a fighter." Silas rubbed the back of his neck. "Not like the others. I'll fight when I have to, like tonight. I heal, but I...if I'm being honest, I feel too much. Fear, pain, guilt, it all bleed off people, especially when they try to conceal it.

"You're an empath?" She'd heard of it but had never known anyone with the ability before.

"Something like that. My talent relies on emotion and touch, which I suppose makes me good at mending bones and keeping secrets, but it's..." He gave her a tight smile. "Draining."

Her gaze drifted to Rowan, waiting for his story. He leaned forward, elbows on his knees, as his gaze found hers. "I wasn't born to this pack. I was a lone wolf for most of my life. Keeping my head down, I moved through towns, searching for something. Atlas offered me a place here. He didn't ask for loyalty, just honesty, and that was enough. Eventually, I became his beta."

"What made you stay?"

Rowan glanced toward Atlas before looking back at her. "Sometimes you don't realize you need a home until someone offers it."

She nodded because she knew what he meant. She hadn't known she needed something more in her life until she ended up in Hollow Creek. Though she wasn't sure she was up for the challenge it presented. "And you, Atlas? You're the alpha?"

"I am," Atlas said, tone clipped.

"How?"

The simple question seemed to bring a tension she hadn't expected. She didn't understand it, but based on Silas' downcast gaze and Rowan's twitching jaw, she knew she had asked a loaded question. But Atlas didn't seem to flinch as if he knew the moment was coming.

"My father died in a rogue attack, and I inherited the position. We weren't ready. I wasn't ready...I was only twenty, the youngest alpha in my pack's history." His voice was steady, but the bitter undertone betrayed his true feelings. "My father wasn't only the alpha, he was the spine of this town's protection. When he fell, the mantle passed to me. It didn't matter if I wanted it or not, I had to step up and do what was right by the residents."

The anger she'd been holding slipped away. She wasn't the only one thrust into this role. "Atlas, I'm sorry."

He didn't say anything, he didn't have to. The look in his eyes was enough.

"I didn't want you here, Lena. I didn't want you to get involved in this. But I think your aunt knew what she was doing when she left you the house. In Hollow Creek, we don't believe in accidents."

Her gaze traveled over each of them. Silas sat open and aching in a way she wasn't sure he even meant to be, while Rowan sat unreadable and grounded. Then there was Atlas, who pulled her in like gravity. Dangerous, certain, and impossible to ignore.

The tension between them was almost unbearable. Not from the mystery or the answers still waiting. The undeniable force between them hummed in her blood like a forgotten chord being struck.

"So, what happens now?" she asked.

"Now we keep you alive, and we figure out what is waking up in these words. And we decide if the bond forming between you and this pack is a gift..." Atlas' voice dropped low, and his gaze heated in warning. "Or a threat."

Even with every muscle in her body screaming caution, she didn't want to run. She would stand her ground even if it broke her.

# Chapter 12

## *The Otherwood Curse*

After the conversation with the pack, everything seemed too quiet, like a hush before the storm. Uneasy, Lena stood near the window, staring out at the forest.

"Tell me what's really going on," she demanded without turning. "No more half-truths. I want it all."

She glanced back to find Rowan standing near the fire, now only embers. His eyes were shadowed and heavy. Silas sat on the edge of the armchair, hands clasped. While his expression had softened, his eyes told a different story. Finally, she turned to Atlas, whose presence seemed to charge the room. Still, no one answered.

"Every Samhain, the veil thins between this world and the Otherwood." Rowan ran a hand over his face before looking at her.

"You guys keep mentioning the Otherwood, but what is it exactly?"

"Another realm." Silas' voice was low. "A kind of in-between place where old things sleep and stranger things wait."

"On Samhain, the barrier between the two weakens," Rowan stated again.

"And every year, something tries to come through." Atlas met her gaze. "This year it's starting earlier. The veil is too thin already."

"That doesn't explain me or this house," she snapped.

"They built this house as a ward anchor point. It's one of the few places strong enough to hold the boundary, and your family were guardians. You're a guardian now, Lena." Atlas' voice was steady, but his words hit her like a hammer.

"Aunt Mira knew about this?" Even as she said it, she knew the answer. It was written in her journal. Scraps of truth hidden within the words, but Lena had thought they were just stories. No, she had wanted to believe they were just fantasies.

"She did more than know. Her blood, magic, and presence here were the only things that kept the veil intact," Silas explained.

"Why didn't she tell me? Why leave me in the dark until it was too late?" Frustration rose within her like high tide pounding the shore. "She's dead, and what if I hadn't come? What if I just sold the house?"

"She thought she had time," Rowan said quietly.

"We talked about it," Atlas admitted. "She wanted you to live your life. Have the freedom she never had. Then, when she had no choice, she'd have told you."

"What matters now is that the veil is growing weaker. The things on the other side are becoming bolder." Rowan steered the conversation back to the issue at hand.

"You've seen them, haven't you?" Silas asked, and the way he looked at her, it was like he already knew the answer.

Her thoughts flashed to the red-eyed wolf at the edge of her bed. The pendant being moved to her nightstand. The dreams that plagued her every time she closed her eyes.

Rowan nodded, clearly knowing the answer without her voicing it. "They recognize the bloodline and have been trying to reach you."

"We don't think it's a coincidence that Mira died just after the last thinning." Atlas stepped closer, his voice rough around the edges. "Or that you came back, right before this one."

"What happens if something gets through?" she asked, her voice barely a whisper.

"Then Hollow Creek burns and everything beyond it," Rowan answered without hesitation.

The weight of everything crashed over her all at once as she sank down onto the window seat. Everything was connected, and she sat at its center.

# Chapter 13

## *Marked*

Lena ran through the trees, barefoot, breath steaming in the night air. Branches clawed at her skin as something *followed*. She couldn't see it, but she could feel it.

She knew she was dreaming. She wasn't actually running through the forest, but unable to wake up, she couldn't help but feel true terror. This dream was not surreal like the others. It was sharp, cold, and felt real.

Within the darkness, a voice echoes. *Claimed...taken...*

"What?" She turned in the direction of the voice, but nothing was there. Just pitch black, the darkest she'd ever seen.

Distracted by her search for the voice, she didn't notice the hands reaching toward her until it was too late. Long fingers wrapped around her arms. She tried to scream, to wake up from the nightmare, but her body wouldn't move.

Suddenly, in front of her, a figure appeared. Shrouded in darkness except for his eyes that blazed like fire. The figure reached forward, touching the edge of her collarbone, where it met her shoulder.

Pain erupted from his touch, bringing tears to her eyes. She struggled, trying to escape his grasp, but they held tight, pinning her in place.

Shooting upright in bed, Lena let out a strangled cry. Sweat slick across her skin, her breath ragged. She reached up, touched her neck, and pulled her nightshirt to the side.

There on her shoulder was a strange sigil, fresh and red, pulsing beneath her skin. It wasn't a scar or a tattoo, it was a mark.

"What? How?" She shot out of bed and dashed across the room to the mirror above the dresser. She stared at it in the mirror, unable to believe what she was seeing. "What does this mean?"

Three quick knocks echoed through the house. Any other time, she'd be terrified, but in that moment, she knew it was Silas. Letting go of the shirt, she stepped out of her room and headed toward the front door. Opening it, she found Silas standing there in only black shorts and sneakers, his hair tousled from sleep.

"I felt it," he breathed, gaze sweeping over her. "What happened?"

Without comment, she pulled her pajama shirt to one side, revealing the mark. As she did, Rowan and Atlas stepped onto the porch.

"Inside," Atlas ordered, ushering everyone inside before he turned and locked the door behind them.

"She's been claimed," Silas said quietly, hovering his hand over the mark.

"It's Otherwood magic," Rowan added.

"I don't understand. I didn't even leave the house. It happened while I was dreaming." She stared at them, hoping for answers.

"That shouldn't be possible, not with the protections on this house." Silas turned toward Atlas.

"They're not holding anymore." Atlas glanced at each of them before his gaze settled on Lena. "Whatever's behind that veil, it's not just testing boundaries, it's reaching through."

"I want it off!" she snapped, her voice shaking. "I want it gone, now."

"We can't." Silas put his hand on her arm.

"Not yet, at least. It's like a tether. If we don't sever it correctly, it could hurt you or pull you under," Rowan explained.

"So, I'm just stuck with this mark? Alone, with this thing…"

"You're not alone," Silas assured her as his attention turned to Atlas, who was silently standing there, fist clenched at his sides. "There's no denying she's part of this now."

"She's tied to the veil." Rowan looked at Atlas, as if waiting for something.

"To the house and her bloodline." Atlas nodded.

"We'll keep you safe." Silas looked down at her.

The softness in his voice made her want to believe it, but this was dangerous. Could the three of them really keep her safe? "Now what? You guys just babysit me until Samhain and hope I don't get eaten by the creatures in my dreams."

"We protect you," Atlas announced as if that answered all her questions.

"Literally, magically, and emotionally, if you'll let us." Silas ran his hand along her arm, offering a small comfort she desperately needed.

She wanted to believe them and embrace the safety they were offering. But the dream left her feeling raw, exposed. How could they protect her from something she couldn't see, something that only attacked at her weakest moments, when she was asleep?

As the night wore on, Silas and Atlas left to check the perimeter, leaving only Rowan by her side. Exhausted Lena leaned back against the sofa. She desperately wanted to sleep, but the very thought terrified her.

"Come here." Rowan lifted his arm, welcoming her into his embrace.

She debated it for a moment, but she scooted closer, and he gently cuddled her into his body and draped a warm blanket over them. The draw to him was powerful and undeniable. He didn't say anything, he didn't need to. His presence was enough. As she lay her head against his chest, Rowan let out a soft breath, like something uncoiled inside of him. His heartbeat steadily thumped against her ear, easing the stress within her.

"Sleep, I'll keep you safe." His fingers teased along her forearm, caressing.

In his arms, she found warmth and safety. Something she hadn't felt for longer than she could remember, and especially since arriving in Hollow Creek. She let her eyes close, embracing the moment. She wasn't sure when it would happen again.

The soft creak of the front door opening woke Lena. With a soft moan, she pulled the blanket up, using it to block the morning light peaking in around the edges of the curtain and snuggled closer to Rowan's side. With him, there she felt safe. She didn't need to worry about the door opening, because if it were anyone other than Atlas or Silas, he'd have reacted.

As Atlas stepped into the room, she forced herself to open her eyes to look at him. His gaze settled on her curled against Rowan's side, the blanket tangled between them. From the way his brows knitted together, she was certain his thoughts were going much further than the truth. Not that she hadn't wanted to explore more with Rowan, but exhaustion had won out.

Atlas' jaw flexed, pulling the lines around his eyes tighter. "Looks like I missed the sleepover."

"She needed someone here." Rowan straightened but didn't move away. Rather, his arm tightened slightly around her.

"I'm sure she did." Atlas' voice was level, but the tension in the air was like static under her skin.

"It wasn't like that." She glanced up at him from the comfort of Rowan's embrace.

"Didn't say it was. But maybe next time you let me know when there's a change in the rotation."

"So, what is this guard duty?" Rowan lifted a brow in question.

Atlas didn't answer. He looked at her again for a moment before he turned and walked out, shutting the door behind him.

"Well, that went well," she mumbled.

# Chapter 14

## *Pack Rules*

Twenty minutes after he stormed out, Lena found Atlas on the front porch. Arms crossed, he leaned against the deck support post and stared out at the forest as if daring something to come out. Morning sunlight filtered through the tree branches, casting a welcoming golden glow across the garden, beautiful even in its overgrown state.

"Are you going to sulk out here all day? Or are you going to come inside and talk to me like an adult?" she asked, coming up behind him.

"I'm not sulking." He didn't glance back at her, but his shoulders tightened, warning her he wasn't in the mood.

"My mistake." She shook her head. "You're just brooding so hard the temperature dropped."

He spun around to face her. His eyes were dark and unreadable.

"You walked out like I wounded you. So, let's not act like you don't care." She was on unsteady ground, but she couldn't stand the tension that was lingering since he stormed off.

"That's the problem, Lena. I do care."

His words were sharp, cutting deeper than she expected. Not

sure what to say, she stared at him for a moment, the air heavy with silence. "You saw Rowan on the sofa with me, and you made assumptions."

"No, I witnessed Rowan holding you like you're already his," he corrected.

"Word games." She stepped closer. "I was scared, Atlas. Something marked me in my sleep. Something from another world. Something I couldn't fight against. I needed comfort, and Rowan was there. You weren't."

Atlas opened and closed his mouth to say something, but instead looked away.

"Say it, Atlas. Say whatever is on your mind."

"I don't like him touching you." His voice was low, but he turned back to look at her.

"Why?"

"Every time I get too close, you push me away. But with Rowan, you looked like you belonged there."

"Be honest, Atlas, you never tried to be anything. You've always acted aloof, as if I weren't worth your time. You want to set boundaries with your pack? Then do it. But don't act as if you wanted something from me before Rowan made his move." Anger flared within her, and she backed away from him.

His gaze shot to hers. "Then let me."

"Huh?" She blinked, confused.

"I want rules, but not for the reason you think." He stepped toward her, closing the distance she had just put between them. "I want them because this is spiraling, and if I don't do something now, I'm going to lose you before I've had the chance to reach you."

"I want you safe, but I also want you close." He reached out, and she braced for his touch, but it never came. Instead, his hand hovered near her wrist, as if waiting for permission. "I hate that I'm bad at this, this being soft...I wasn't built for it. I'm an alpha."

"You were built for control," she murmured.

"You tear that control apart every time you look at me like this."

No longer waiting for permission, he wrapped his fingers around her wrist, pulling her closer, as his gaze dropped toward her lips.

"Tell me your rules." Her words came out breathier than she intended.

"One, no more secrets. This isn't a game, and you're part of this now. Part of this pack and this land."

"I haven't had any secrets." She raised an eyebrow at him. "Unless you mean my cuddle session with Rowan. Atlas—"

"You need to be ready for what's coming." He cut her off.

"You're jealous." She raised an eyebrow at him, daring him to admit it.

"Two, if you need someone at night, physically or emotionally, you call me first."

"Pushy." But that was enough to prove her point. He was jealous. He was alpha, and his pack was moving into places he wanted to be.

"Three, no more distance. I'll stop pretending I don't care that you're tangled up in this mess. I'm in it...with you, Lena. We all are."

"Why do I feel there's another one coming?" she asked.

A small smile curled up the corner of his lips, cracking the tension in the air. "Four, you stop pretending you don't feel this too."

# Chapter 15

## *Legacy Unearthed*

A crate of leather-bound journals now sat on the desk in Lena's bedroom. These were all that remained of Aunt Mira's life and now held the secrets and truths Lena needed to survive. Each entry seemed to unravel part of the mystery while also raising new questions.

*The seal is not just a boundary. It's a promise. A pact made centuries ago between the wolves and the land itself. My ancestors were chosen to guard it, to keep the balance safe.*

As she read the words, her pulse quickened. Until the journals, she hadn't realized the depth of Aunt Mira's sacrifices. Now, as she stared at the faded photograph that had been stuck between the yellowed pages. She finally understood what was expected of her. In the picture, Mira stood beneath the full moon. She wore the pendant that was now around Lena's neck, even in the photograph, Lena could see a soft glow. In the background, Atlas, Rowan, and Silas flanked her. Not in human form but as wolves.

"This is my future. My destiny."
She turned the page to the next entry.

*If the seal falls, the Otherwood will spill into our world. Not all who cross will be wolves. Darker things lurk, hungry for freedom and blood.*

She slammed the book closed and leaned back against the hard wooden chair, trying to ground herself despite the fear.

Her phone buzzed across the surface of the desk. A message from Rowan lit up the screen.

> Meet me at the pond. We need to talk. It's about the rogues.

*Standing, she reached up and brushed her fingers across the pendant. In that moment, she embraced the future she was a part of and the one she was trying to build. She was no longer a visitor to Hollow Creek. She was a guardian, and the fight was only beginning.*

"I'll keep this town safe," she vowed as she caught a glimpse of Aunt Mira's picture. "*We'll* keep everyone safe," she corrected as her gaze drifted to the wolves behind her aunt.

Mist curled along the surface of the forest as Lena made her way toward Rowan. The closer she got to the pond, the heavier the air. As if an invisible force was pressing down from above. The smell of moss and distant smoke hung in the air, but what caught her attention was the water. The surface of the pond, usually still and glassy, rippled without wind.

Rowan was crouched near the water's edge, focused.

"What's going on?" she questioned as she came up beside him.

"Look closely." He nodded toward the pond.

She stared down at the water, squinting. At first, she didn't see anything. Then, glancing up at the trees, she understood. The reflection was wrong. In the watery reflection, the forest was nowhere to be found. Now, the pond shimmered with something else. She could see twisted shadows and a flicker of movement that didn't match the sky above.

"The veil is thinning here, faster than it should." His tone held urgency and a hint of fear.

"Because of the mark?" A chill ran up her spine as she scanned the water, searching for a clue. Something to tell her what was coming and how to stop it.

"Partially, but *they're* adapting."

"They?" She glanced down at him.

"Creatures from the Otherwood." He stood, still not meeting her gaze. "Skinwalkers, Hollow-Wights, and things without names. Most of them are mindless, but some appear to be working together."

"And you know this how?"

"Last night they took someone."

The words shot through her chest like a knife. "Someone... someone from Hollow Creek? Who?"

"Cliff." He reached out and put his hand on her back, caressing her softly. "Retired mechanic. He lived on the edge of town, near the highway. He has coffee in town at the diner every morning. When he didn't show up, Atlas got a call. On the surface, it didn't mean much, maybe he overslept, maybe he tied one too many on last night, but when we saw his front yard..."

"What?" She spun toward him. "What did you find?"

"It was...wrong." He hesitated. "There were paw prints circling his porch, but they weren't from pack members. Then there were the mirrors. Every single one shattered, but..."

"But what, Rowan?" she demanded.

"Not from the outside." He looked at her. "The mirrors were shattered from within."

Her stomach churned. It was her responsibility to keep this town safe, and she was already failing. "So, we're losing people now?"

He nodded. "The things that are coming...they know about you."

"Because of the mark." As if on cue, the wind picked up, sending leaves tumbling. The ripples on the water deepened, spreading outward in waves. "Well, that's new."

He grabbed hold of her arm, gently pulling her behind him, protectively standing between her and whatever might emerge from the water. "They're testing this spot. Trying to see how far they can reach, finding the weak points."

"We can't stop this alone." She kept her voice low, afraid that whatever was on the other side would hear her uncertainty.

"We're not alone," he reminded her as he glanced over his shoulder at her. "We need to bring the pack together. All of us and soon."

"Let's go." She stepped back from the pond. Even as she did, she kept it in sight until the trees blocked the view. "I started reading my aunt's journals. The seal is a pact...a promise. If it breaks, everything changes."

"We'll stop it," he assured her as he took her hand. "We fight this together. You, me, and the pack."

She squeezed his hand and nodded. "I'm ready."

This was her town, and she wasn't going to give it over without a fight. It was a silent vow against the oncoming storm. One she wasn't sure she was ready to face.

# Chapter 16

## *Lines in the Dark*

The night seemed heavier than it was when Lena made her way from the pond, as if the upcoming battle was already pressing on her. Every step seemed to make more effort, and the shadows seemed to hold more fear.

"Go on in," Rowan encouraged as they stepped over the stone wall. "I promised Silas I'd help him load some stuff."

Every ounce of her being told her to hold on, but she let go of his hand and stepped onto the porch. *You promised Atlas you'd call him if you wanted comfort.* The thought popped into her mind, but she didn't pull out her cell phone. Instead, she opened the door and stepped inside.

"We need to talk."

Her pulse quickened as she turned back to find Atlas standing in the doorway to the kitchen. His eyes burned with emotion.

"You're getting too close to him." Atlas' voice was low, but sharp.

She let out a soft chuckle and met his gaze. "Rowan? We're allies. We need to trust each other."

"Trust?" He scoffed. "You think this is just about the pack? About fighting rogues? It's more than that."

The weight of his words hit home, a warning, yet also something more. "Atlas, I don't know where you get off thinking you can decide who I can trust or who I spend my time with, but—"

"Rowan's...complicated." He stepped closer, his voice dropping to a harsh whisper. "Dangerous. If you're not careful, you'll get hurt. He's the pack's enforcer for a reason."

"I'm not afraid of him." Her heart pounded not from fear, but from something she wasn't willing to put into words.

"You should be afraid of what you're stirring up." He stared down at her, as if waiting for her to argue.

For a moment, everything else faded away. It was just them. Two people with too many unsaid words and emotions tangled like the vines in her garden. But in a split second, it ended as he stepped back.

"Watch yourself, Lena."

She couldn't determine if Atlas' comments were out of concern, jealousy, or maybe both. But she wasn't naïve. She was aware that the pack was complicated. Her bond with Rowan wasn't about rivalry or power, it was about trust and survival.

Tired of the cryptic messages and the power struggle, she headed to her bedroom, to Aunt Mira's journals. The veil was weakening, and somewhere within those pages had to be a way to stop it.

*I just have to find it. For my sake, the town and the pack.*

"You warned her?" Rowan's voice drifted down the hall, pulling Lena out of the latest journal entry.

"Had to." Atlas' voice was rough. "She's walking a line none of us want her near."

Those words got her up and moving toward the door. What line? What didn't they want her near? She needed to know as much as she needed to find a way to stop the veil from opening.

"She's not some outsider to keep at arm's length," Silas said.

Her eyebrow rose at the sound of his voice. She hadn't heard him come in. Where had he been all day?

"She's not pack." The anger in Atlas' voice made her step closer. "Not *yet*, at least. That changes everything."

"Maybe that's what this pack needs...change." Rowan's voice dropped. From where she stood, she could see him pacing near the fireplace.

"Or maybe you both need a good kick in the butt." She stepped out of her room and strolled toward them. "Did I miss the part where the veil is no longer thinning? Because otherwise I think we have more important issues than fighting among ourselves."

"Lena, they don't m—"

"Don't." She cut Silas off before he could make excuses for the others. "They're both adults, they can make their own excuses, they don't need you doing it for them. But honestly, I'm not interested in it. We have enough to deal with. Where were you today?"

"I—"

"He had work for the pack." Atlas cut him off.

"I took Callie to visit her cousin," Silas explained. "With Cliff going missing, Atlas wanted her somewhere safe."

"No wonder she didn't answer my calls or texts." Lena's shoulders relaxed as she stepped further into the room.

"Cell service is spotty at Jim's place." Atlas leaned against the side of the fireplace, but he wouldn't meet her gaze. "She's safe with Jim's pack. They'll protect her while we deal with things here."

"Guys..." She looked at Rowan for a moment, then Silas. "Would you mind giving us a few minutes? I need to talk to Atlas *alone*."

"Come on, Rowan." Silas tipped his head toward the back door. "I need to check some things in the garden, anyway. Need to order more stones for the wall to make sure we keep this boundary solid."

"I..." Rowan hesitated for a moment before nodding. "We're going to need more than stones."

As they made their way out the back door, leaving her alone with

Atlas, she dropped onto the sofa. "Atlas, I understand you're worried about me and Rowan..." Her words were quiet, but she took a deep breath and continued. "I'm not just some girl who stumbled into your world. I want to be part of this...part of your pack."

"You're playing a dangerous game here, Lena." His usual stony facade flickered with something that seemed almost like reluctance. "Maybe you don't realize how much this means to me."

"I'm not your enemy, Atlas." Her voice softened. "I can be a friend, or I can be so much more, if you open yourself up to it."

"Prove it."

The words were soft, daring, and full of desire. But she was ready to prove to him that she was a value to the pack. The path ahead wouldn't be easy, but maybe they could walk it together.

# Chapter 17

## *Moonlight and Bonds*

The forest bathed in moonlight cast soft shadows along the path. Crickets hummed, and the wind whistled through the trees. In comfortable silence, Lena walked beside Silas. She hadn't been sure what to expect when he asked her to take a walk with him, but still she accompanied him.

As they walked in companionable silence, a heaviness hung in the air. The deadline of Samhain was close, and if she failed, the veil would open, and Hollow Creek would burn. That alone was enough to terrify her. But with Silas by her side, the world felt lighter.

"I figured a walk might help. You've been...tense." His posture was relaxed but watchful.

"I wonder why," she said, drying, though her lips curled almost in a smile. "The wood—"

"We can go back." He cut her off before she could finish. "If you're uneasy about being in here after dark, we can..."

"No, Silas. I feel safe with you." She reached out but stopped herself before she could make contact. "It's just...whatever is out here they...." She stumbled over her words, uncertain how to say what she was feeling. Instead, she reached up to where the sigil marked her skin, hoping he understood.

They stepped into a small break in the trees where the moonlight filtered through. Silas stopped and turned to her. "You're marked, but it doesn't change who you are."

She let out a soft laugh. "I don't know who I am anymore. All of this...it changes everything about me."

"The fact you're still here, fighting this with us, says everything."

With her gaze focused on him, she stepped forward, closer to him. Without thinking, her fingers brushed along his side, the place where, only days ago, he'd been torn open and bleeding. He didn't flinch. "Healed?"

"Completely." His voice was soft as he stared down at her. "You don't have to worry about me."

"But I do." The air around them buzzed with electricity and magic.

He stepped closer, closing the last bit of distance between them. Their breath mingled in the cool air as his hand hovered at her waist for a moment before daring to touch her.

A howl echoed through the air, distant, but a reminder of everything at stake.

With her mouth inches from him, her heart thundering, the last thing she wanted was to be practical, but she whispered, "We should go."

"I know."

With the moment gone, she stepped back and dropped her hand from his side. She didn't want it to be over. She wanted to forget about everything else and explore the heat that inexplicably pulled her toward these men. But losing control meant more missing town residents or worse.

As they neared the stone wall, Silas paused. "Go on, I need to check something."

He stood there, waiting as she stepped over to the safety of her garden. "Be safe."

He gave her a subtle nod and disappeared into the trees. As she turned around, she found Atlas stepping out of her house. "You guys just come and go as you please. Making yourself at home in *my* home."

"Mira's house was always our second home." He stepped to the edge of the porch and leaned against the railing. "You need us now more than ever. After Samhain, if you want us to stay away, just say so, but for now, get used to it."

Although she wouldn't admit it, the last thing she wanted was for any of them to stay away. Each of them brought a smile to her face, but Atlas tended to be the most annoying of the pack. Assertive, grouchy, and used to getting things his way.

"Well, why are you out here? Seems like something is on your mind." She stepped up onto the porch, her gaze on his.

"Out of respect, I'm telling you this first, but I'll be speaking with Rowan and Silas soon. I don't want anyone to go near you alone anymore. It's not safe."

"What you're saying is, you don't trust me," she snapped.

"Lena..." he let out her name on a breath, annoyance lacing his tone. "The Otherwood marked you, and with each night that passes, we're one step closer to the veil cracking open."

"You don't get to tell me who I spend time with or what I do."

"No, but I do get to tell *my pack* w—"

Her hand was on his chest before she realized. Anger burned hot within her as she pushed him back.

Catching her wrist, he didn't move away, instead, he pulled her tight against his body.

The moment they touched, everything snapped. He leaned down, pressing his mouth to hers. The kiss was furious and breathless. He pushed her up against the house, one hand tangled in her hair, the other gripping her hip to hold her close.

A moan escaped her lips as she clawed at the hem of his shirt, dragging it upward, desperate to feel his skin against hers.

He pulled back from her, breaking the kiss. "Tell me to stop." His eyes were wild, and his voice ragged.

She didn't want him to stop, she wanted more. Rising onto her toes, she pressed her lips to his.

He reached under her butt and lifted her. She wrapped her legs around his waist as he stepped away from the wall. Without breaking the kiss, he carried her into the house and kicked the door shut behind them, as he sat her on the kitchen counter. Running his hands up her back, he pressed her close before working his way lower. His mouth found her neck, kissing along the curve as he worked toward her collarbone, his teeth grazing her skin.

"You drive me insane," he growled.

"Good, I'd hate to be forgettable," she whispered, dragging her fingers through his short brown hair. "I need this...I need you. Take me to the bedroom."

He glanced up, watching her for a moment with hungry eyes before lifting her off the counter and strolling toward her bedroom. The world may be going to Hell outside, but this moment was something they both deserved.

Before Lena even opened her eyes, she reached across the bed, searching for Atlas, only to find the space empty. The covers were crumpled and thrown to the side, a clear indication that last night wasn't a dream, but what she had really wanted was to wake up beside him.

Slipping out of bed, she quickly pulled on jeans and a T-shirt before heading to the kitchen. Even before she opened her bedroom door, she knew she'd find all three of them there. Embracing the connection with Atlas had changed something. She couldn't describe it, but she could feel that last night had changed everything. The connection between her and her three wolves was stronger now, undeniable.

As she stepped into the kitchen, she found Silas cooking. He smiled at her, but it didn't quite reach his eyes. Rowan and Atlas sat at the table. Atlas glanced up at her but didn't say a word. Rowan didn't bother to look up from his coffee.

The tension in the house wasn't just sexual, it was pack-related, and she was right in the center of it all. An invisible thread tied her to each of them, delicate but undeniable. It wasn't about choosing, but rather bonding through mating. The connection between her and the pack was alive, and they all felt it.

# Chapter 18

## *Full Moon Rising*

Everything about the night felt wrong, and it was like everything around Lena sensed it. The forest was empty, no animal stirred, not even the occasional owl. Even the wind was still as if holding its breath, waiting. The moon hung low, full, and bright, bleeding through the tree limbs around the pond.

As she neared the edge of the pond, the pack followed in silence. Atlas, to her right, was stone-faced and watchful. On her left, Rowan was steady, and Silas was silently behind her, focused energy rolling off him in waves. Her gaze fell onto the pond, and the surface rippled. Once again, the reflection didn't match, but the image was clearer now. Something from the Otherwood was already stirring.

"Positions," Atlas commanded, his voice low but urgent. "Now."

Like clockwork, each took a corner around the pond. The stones they'd prepared, etched in runes and soaked in Lena's blood, saltwater, and ash, were placed at cardinal points.

"Lena, remember," Silas glanced at her from across the pond. "The pendant belonged to Mira, but now it answers to you. Embrace it."

As if to confirm his words, the crescent moon charm around her neck pulsed.

"Once we begin, you can't leave the circle," Atlas warned from his spot to her right. "No matter what happens, stay where you are."

"Promise?" Rowan pushed.

"I promise." She glanced at each of them, assuring them she was in it with them. Without her, the circle wouldn't be complete, and they'd die. "We're in this *together*."

Atlas began chanting, low and in an ancient tongue she wasn't familiar with. He lifted his head toward the moon, and as he did, the clouds shifted, as if moved by his words. Rowan joined in, his voice harmonizing with the same resonance, while Silas murmured. With each word, the binding threads of magic wove through the air, grounding the energy.

Sounds echoed around her as if the forest recognized and answered their pleas. Stones cracked and roots shifted. The hairs on her arms rose, but it wasn't until it felt as if the ground reached up and took hold of her ankles that her heart began to race. She thought it must be vines wrapping around her ankles, but when she looked down, there was nothing there. "What—"

The sigil on her shoulder flared hot, then froze, cutting off her words and sending a shiver down her spine.

Beneath the surface of the water, something slammed into the barrier. Startled, she flinched but didn't move. With every breath she took, the pressure within her seemed to grow. She could feel the hunger of the Otherwood pressing against the veil, howling to be recognized.

Smoke curled from the stones, but it was the wind that held her attention. *Lena.* It seemed to whisper, but she knew it wasn't the wind, it was from the other side. The Otherwood knew her name now, and as the sigil glowed, it called to her, urging her to switch sides.

She froze as the veil opened, just a tear, but enough to split the pond's surface like an open mouth underwater.

Shadows spilled onto the shore. They weren't creatures as she'd been expecting, at least not yet, but it was silhouettes and spirits of beings, not full shapes. Whispers echoed around her.

"Hold the circle!" Atlas barked at the others before looking at her. "Now, Lena, now!"

Dropping to her knees, she clutched the pendant and tugged the necklace free. She pressed it into the dirt around the edge of the pond, with such force that the ground beneath her crumbled.

"By blo...blood, bon..." Her voice shook, and she forced herself to take a deep breath and let it out before starting again. "By blood, bone, and name, I call back the barrier. I offer breath for boundary. Flesh for flame and heart for hollow."

Under her hand, the pendant burned, and smoke curled out from between her fingers. Around the pond, the runes flared, and the screams echoed throughout the forest. Just as quickly as it started, the veil slammed shut.

Exhausted, she collapsed onto the ground and stared down at the pond. The water was still, but something told her it wouldn't last for long. The Otherwood would find a way to push back, and if she wasn't ready, it would break free.

"Not on my watch." She whispered, pulling the pendant free from the dirt.

One by one, each of the men joined her. Breathing heavily, Atlas offered her a hand, and when she took it, he pulled her upward. Silas and Rowan were right there, coming to circle her.

"You did it," Silas said, brushing her hair from her face.

She shook her head, looking at each of them before correcting. "*We* did it."

She might not have fully understood the magic yet, but deep within her, she could feel the tether between all of them. *Pack*. It wasn't because of the magic or the ritual, it was because they'd chosen each other. The Otherwood might have marked her, but she was wanted here, by them. That was what mattered.

# Chapter 19

## *Shifting Ground*

The soft pop of embers in the hearth echoed throughout the silent house. Curled up on the sofa beneath a warm blanket. Lena watched as the men drifted into silence, each absorbed in thought. The ritual had left her body aching and raw. But her heart felt full. They didn't need to say it. She could feel it in her bones. She belonged to them now, the pack, and for the first time since arriving in Hollow Creek, she wasn't worried. No matter what the future held, she was ready as long as they were by her side.

She looked at each of them in turn. Atlas sat near the fire, elbows on his knees, staring at the floor. Always the protector, Rowan stood watchfully near the door with his arms crossed. Then there was Silas, the softest of the guys, settled on the floor, close enough that his shoulder brushed the side of her leg.

"It's over, right?" she questioned.

"For now," Rowan answered.

"The veil is sealed for now." Atlas nodded. "The curse is...quiet, so we've brought ourselves time."

"Time and balance," Silas added.

"I don't even know what that means or who I even am." She looked down at her shaking hands. "I'm not a wolf like you. I'm not Mira, or even a witch. Yet something feels as though it's been rewired within me."

"You're a tether now, an anchor." Rowan stepped closer, coming up next to the sofa, allowing her to truly see him.

"With Mira's death, the veil began to crack, but it didn't tear until you got here. It also didn't close until you stood in the center of all of it," Silas explained.

"So, I'm..." Her throat thick with emotion, she looked at them. "I'm your human paperweight? Boat anchor?"

"No." Atlas let out a soft laugh. "You're the glue that holds this pack together when everything is being pulled apart."

"We're bound to you, Lena," Rowan stated when Atlas failed to.

"Magically?" She raised an eyebrow in question as she looked at him.

"Emotionally too." Silas brushed his fingers against hers.

"In every way." Atlas' gaze locked on hers.

"Wait..." She paused, unsure how to say what was circling through her thoughts. "I should have to choose...shouldn't I?"

"You don't," Silas was the first to answer.

"No," Rowan echoed.

Atlas shook his head. "The bond formed naturally, we all felt it. What we have doesn't follow anyone's rules. It doesn't have to. If it works for us, then that's all that matters."

She glanced around the room, each of them so different. Rowan was the quiet, resolute one. He considered everything before he spoke, and when he did, he meant every word. Silas wore his heart on his sleeve and felt more than he let on. While Atlas was all fire, fury, and control. A true alpha in every way.

"So..." Her lips curled up into a smirk. "I'm magically linked to a bunch of protective wolves."

"Mates...that's what we are." Silas nodded.

"You're *ours* now." Atlas rose from where he was sitting near the fireplace and came to sit beside her on the sofa. "In every way you want to be."

She swallowed hard and took his hand in hers. "I want all of it with each of you."

Rowan came around the sofa and knelt in front of her, gently taking her other hand into his. "You'll have it."

For a moment, they let themselves sink into the warmth and safety of the moment.

"Guess, it's time you meet the rest of the pack." Silas' words were soft, but their weight hung in the air.

"It's time." Atlas wrapped his arm around her shoulders.

"Wait..." She glanced at Atlas. "I thought you three were the pack."

"We're part of it, but not the whole. We're just..." Atlas' words trailed off.

"The protection," Rowan added. "Atlas is the alpha of the pack, and we're...well, I guess you could say we're his right-hand men."

"The pack is family and bond. Now you're part of it." Silas ran his hand over her leg.

"Did it escape those wolf brains of yours? I'm not a shifter. Sorry to disappoint." She stared at them wide-eyed.

"Doesn't matter." Atlas' lips curled up into a smirk.

"You stood in the center and held the line. More importantly, you chose us and we chose you." Rowan squeezed her hand. "Don't look like that, it won't be that bad."

"Really, because this sure feels like meet the parents, shifter edition," she teased.

Silas chuckled. "Sort of, but the worst thing that could happen is something challenges you to a race through the woods."

"Most will just try to feed you." Silas shot her a grin. "We'll be there and so will Callie. You won't be alone."

"They need to see why you're ours, and we're yours." Atlas' finger caressed over her shoulder. "They need to see that we made a strong pick."

She looked at each of them before letting her attention settle on Atlas. "Okay, let's meet this pack of yours."

With each of them beside her, their hands on her body, she felt confident. If they could overcome the Otherwood, she could survive meeting the pack.

# Chapter 20

## *Hollow Ground*

F og crept along the grounds like long fingers as Lena Barkstone stepped out of her car, directly into a puddle. *Of course.* She stared up at the sagging house that was now hers. It loomed before her as if it regretted having survived yet another year. The paint peeled, and the iron fence bordering the property did nothing to keep out the mist coiling through the overgrowth.

"This is fine," she muttered to herself as she opened the back door before she dragged a cardboard box from the backseat of her car. "This is totally fine. This house isn't trying to eat my soul, it's just old and creaky, not haunted."

The tape at the bottom of the box gave way, sending Halloween lights and decorations tumbling onto the cracked driveway.

"Of course," she said flatly.

Weeks had passed since Aunt Mira's death, and still Lena couldn't decide what to do with the house. Keep it or sell the old house and forget about the note that was left that simply read:

*It's yours now. Keep the wards up. Stay away from the woods on All Hallows' Eve.*

Whatever that meant.

She hadn't been close to her aunt, but something about the place called to her. Maybe it was the fog. Perhaps it was the fact that she had nothing left in the city but terrible memories and a lease she could barely afford. Or maybe she just needed a place to disappear. Whatever it was, it felt like the fresh start she needed.

Leaning down, she gathered the scattered contents of the box. Hopefully, her day wouldn't continue the same way it started. With everything in her hands, she stood and took a deep breath, filling her lungs with the scent of wet leaves and something earthier. *Home.*

Heading up the old wooden stairs, the house greeted her with a groan, the type that came from the bones of a building, not its walls. Still, the stained-glass windows glowed in the late afternoon light, and the front door opened without protest. Inside, it was dark and chilly, but the structure seemed solid enough.

She just had to look through the dust and neglect to see that the place had potential. There wasn't any doubt in her mind that the house needed work, but with a bit of elbow grease, she'd restore this place to its former glory. It didn't have to be her forever home, but it could provide a place to sort out her life and decide her next step.

Over the next few hours, she unpacked what little she'd brought and fought her way through cobwebs to find a functioning kitchen. It was a bit of a nightmare, but with some work, she'd get it up to standard. The bathroom, on the other hand, reeked of mildew, and she was pretty sure the attic growled at her.

She stepped out onto the porch and scanned the garden. While it was likely once beautiful, it had now become a tangled web of overgrowth. The rose bushes were overtaking the fence, and the stone path had more broken pieces than solid ones. Everything was covered in silence so thick that it made breathing difficult.

Halloween was her favorite time of year, and with the creepy house vibes, she was going to lean into the spooky nature of the season. She pulled out a couple of ceramic jack-o'-lanterns and placed them near the door before setting her sights on the archway leading to the garden. The string of orange lights would be perfect there. As she pulled them from the box, she froze. Her gaze shot up, glancing around the outdoor space. It almost felt as if she were being watched. She stilled, listening. The wind blew, and leaves rustled, but the hairs on the back of her neck didn't lie. Something was out there.

Slowly, she turned toward the woods. Just beyond the cracked stone fence, trees tall and close together, like they'd grown that way just to keep people out. The fog was thicker there, clinging to trunks, winding between roots. Then she saw them.

Eyes. Glowing faintly gold. Low to the ground. Too steady. Not a flicker of reflected light, but something alive. A wolf.

She froze. It was huge. Bigger than any she'd seen. Dark fur with threads of silver mixed in, head low, watching her with predatory stillness.

Slowly, she reached into the pocket of her jeans, pulling out her cell phone. With a flicker of her gaze, she looked at the screen. *Shit! No bars.*

When she looked up again, the wolf was gone.

Just gone. No sound. No movement. As if it had never been there.

"Cool." She let out a shaky laugh. "A hallucination. Love that for me."

Leaving the lights unplugged, she stepped toward the back door. Her gaze was still searching the wood line, as if expecting the wolf to reappear. She needed to get inside. Inside meant safety. At least from wolves. The house, no doubt, had its own safety issues.

Without turning her back to the darkness, she stepped into the house and shut the door behind her. With a quick flip of the deadbolt, she let out a sigh.

"Just a wild animal passing through." Even as she said the words, she didn't believe it.

# Part Two

## *Hollow Anchor*

Hollow Creek isn't the sleepy town Lena believed it was. Living in the house she inherited from her aunt, she realizes there's more to the town than meets the eye. Shadows move in the woods. Wolves aren't just animals, they're a pack of shifters. Magic exists in ways it never should. At the center of it all is her, the anchor and a target rolled into one.

With three men by her side—Atlas, the brooding alpha, Rowan, her steady protector, and Silas, the empathic healer—Lena discovers some family secrets are darker than the forest. Some desires are impossible to resist.

This Halloween, the veil will break, the wolves will fight, and Lena will learn that magic has a price and love has no rules.

# Chapter 1

## *Embers*

Before coming to Hollow Creek, Lena couldn't recall a single dream she had. Now, every night, her dreams were vivid and filled with things that didn't belong in this world. They haunt her dreams and stay with her when she's awake.

She'd never realized how exhausting dreaming could be. When she awoke from running through the forest, she felt as though she'd actually done it. There were moments she was certain she could smell the ash and smoke from the burning branches. Almost every dream involved a wolf, but tonight this one was different. This wolf had heterochromia, one eye red and the other as dark as the night sky. Whenever she stopped running, he was there, standing among the trees, watching her. He'd tilt his head back to howl, but no sound came.

As she lay there clutching the sheets, she couldn't shake the feeling that something was coming. The veil was shut, but they were still pressed against the other side, trying to break through. The ache in her chest eased with each breath she took, but Aunt Mira's pendant around her neck continued to glow faintly.

*It's not over.* The words hit her like a speeding train. Protecting

Hollow Creek was a lifetime commitment, but after the ritual, she expected things to settle down. At least for a while. Instead, the frequency of her dreams increased to the point she couldn't sleep without seeing the Otherwood. She had survived this world full of curses, wolves, and magic, but this dream was different. Personal and raw. It was as if the Otherwood was no longer coming for Hollow Creek, it was targeting her, too.

With sleep off the agenda, she got out of bed and headed toward the kitchen. The moment her bare feet touched the floor, she felt the boundary anchor vibrating beneath the house. The wards were working, but the Otherwood was becoming more desperate.

As she entered the kitchen, she spotted Atlas at the kitchen counter, shirtless, his hair still damp from a shower. He didn't look surprised as she approached him.

"Another dream?" he asked, reaching for the coffeepot.

"Worse this time." She pulled out a kitchen chair and dropped onto it. "I haven't seen this wolf before. His eyes were different colors."

"That's not one of ours." He poured her a cup, and with it in hand, he turned toward her.

"I figured." She reached up and took the coffee from him, and his fingers brushed her hand for a moment longer. "Why are you up so early?" He was a morning person, but this was extreme even for him, the first rays of light weren't even peeking over the horizon yet.

"Something has been spotted moving near the ley line. Rowan's been out tracking it for about an hour now, and Silas is on his way back now. He said it smells wrong." He pulled out the chair next to her and sat down. "I'm calling the pack together today."

"And me?" she asked.

"You're part of this now." He reached over and let his fingers tease along the back of her hand. "You'll come with us. We talked about it before, but now is the time."

"Couldn't we wait for less...I don't know magical drama?" Even as she said it, she knew it wasn't an option.

"You're part of the pack now, Lena." His gaze met hers, and she could see the truth in his eyes. "We'll be with you, but it's time."

"I just..." Her words trailed off as she took a timid sip. "We've talked about it for a while, but now it feels...undeniable."

"That's because it is. This connection is." He laced his fingers with hers. "You belong with us."

"When?" she asked.

"Rowan and Silas should be back within the hour and then—"

"An hour?" She cut him off. "You expect me to be ready for meet the family, pack edition, in an hour?"

"Better drink up and get ready. I'm calling everyone together." He pulled his cell phone from his pocket.

"Women don't like to feel rushed." She pushed her coffee aside and rose from the table. "I'm going to make you regret this one day."

"Couldn't be helped."

She almost argued, but he was right. The magical chaos happening wasn't something they could put off. If there was something moving out by the ley line, they needed to identify it. Informing the pack would allow more people to patrol and for everyone to be on guard. The Otherwood was still active, and they didn't seem deterred by the new wards.

Sitting on the porch steps, Lena tugged her sweater tighter around her, attempting to keep the chill in the air at bay. Leaves blew across the stone garden path. Over the past few days, working alongside Silas, they managed to whip the garden into shape by clearing the overgrowth. Though with the weather growing colder each day, she wasn't sure how often they'd be able to use the beautiful outdoor space.

Movement in the corner of her gaze caught her attention, and she turned to find Rowan strolling toward her. His jeans rode low on his hips, but his bare chest was what caught her attention. As he spotted her watching, a slow, cocky smile tugged up the corner of his lips.

"See something you like, darling?"

"Oh yeah..." She stood up as he neared.

With his alpha tendencies, Atlas took control of the situation. Rowan was the protector who always made her feel safe. While Silas, her sweet wolf, was the emotional connection within the pack. His presence settled the restlessness within her, especially when it came to the magical aspects of her newfound life.

Rowan pulled her against the front of his body, dragging his hands up her back. "These nightmares are taking a toll on you."

"I'm fine." She glanced up at him, not wanting to admit aloud how draining the dreams really were.

"Here." Atlas stepped out of the house, stealing the moment from them, and tossed a shirt at him. "Find anything?"

Rowan caught the shirt but didn't pull away. "Something has been moving through our woods. It's circling, making the track difficult to pinpoint, but it's been close and is sticking to the area."

"It's a Hollow-Wight," Silas announced as he stepped into the garden.

"A what?" She moved away from Rowan and held out her arm to him, welcoming him back to her. He smiled, soft and genuine. The power coming from him was a now-familiar weight that settled the storm within her.

"A spirit beast from the Otherwood." Silas wrapped his arms around her, pressing her tight against him, and kissed the top of her head as he looked up at Atlas. "They were once guardians of the threshold between realms, but now they're creatures leaking magic."

"They're drifters." Atlas placed his hands on the railing and let his gaze meet hers. "They seep through where ley lines are weak. The boundaries will keep it from the house...for now."

"It's scouting the area," Rowan added.

"As if rogue wolves weren't enough." She leaned into Silas' embrace and reached out to take Rowan's hand in hers.

"We'll keep you safe." Atlas stared beyond her, toward the trees, his mouth set in what lately seemed to be a permanent pout.

"Atlas," Silas whispered.

He looked at them for a moment before stepping off the porch and coming to stand in front of her. "Sorry, Lena."

He took her other hand, and instantly the connection between them flared within her. Surrounding her, their touch on her skin, the pull was the strongest. It wasn't just romantic, it was possessive. She belonged to them. To the pack.

"We said it before, but we need to take her to the pack." Rowan squeezed her hand as if he expected her to argue.

"Already?" Silas' calm energy flared with anger.

"She's part of the bond, and the pack needs to see it." Rowan glanced down at her. "They need to feel it."

"It's already been decided." Atlas let go of her hand and brought his fingers up to the side of her neck, teasing along the bare skin. "It will be fine."

"We'll keep you close, you'll be safe," Rowan assured her.

"But if you're going to *truly* be one of us, you need to know the pack." Atlas' gaze met hers.

"What if they don't like what they see?" she questioned, raising an eyebrow at him.

"They will." Silas wrapped his arm around her waist.

"You give them a reason to trust you, and they'll be eating out of your hand." Rowan's lips curled into a confident smile. "Just like we do."

"Many of them knew Mira. So, being her niece gives you a foothold. And..." He tipped her head up toward him. "I'm alpha, and I trust you by my side, that counts for something."

"Let's do this before I lose my nerve." She licked her lips as she teased her finger along Atlas' hip. *Or drag you all upstairs.*

# Chapter 2

## *The Gathering*

The deeper they walked into the forest, the more charged the air became, until it felt as though Lena was trying to swallow smoke-filled air. Every step felt heavier than it should. Everything within her told her to turn around.

"Look at me, Lena," Atlas ordered.

"You're focusing too much on the wolf energy." Silas slid his hand along her arm as the three of them circled around her.

"You've felt our wolves, you know the power they carry within them." Atlas cupped her cheek, all she could smell was the cedar that always seemed to radiate off him. "You've seen and felt the magic you're capable of. That magic you carry within you, like the breath in your lungs. Close your eyes and embrace it."

"Go on." Rowan nodded when she hesitated.

Closing her eyes, the first thing she noticed was the thumping of the ley line beneath her boots, and the air was sizzling around her. Her skin buzzed, and the pendant around her neck warmed.

"They're going to look at me and decide I don't belong. That I'm a threat." Even with the beat of her own magic coursing through her, she couldn't see why the wolf pack would accept her.

"No," Atlas growled. "They're going to see the truth. "They'll see the woman who stood in the circle against the Otherwood. You held the line, and that is remarkable. There are wolves who wouldn't do that. They'll see the power within you."

"That is what you should be focused on," Rowan agreed.

"That is what you will embrace as we walk into the pack tonight." Atlas' lips were against her ear. His breath teased along her skin. "Just like Silas, you feel too much, and you carry the burden of it. But Lena, that's not a weakness, that's what makes you what you are. You're our veilheart."

"What?" she questioned.

"The veil listens to you, it bends to your power, and you hold its heart and *ours*. Our veilheart." A moment passed between them before he added. "I don't care what anyone says, I'm not walking into fire without you beside me. Beside us."

Opening her eyes, she looked at Rowan and Silas. Though his face was out of view, she could feel Atlas' breath and hear his heartbeat pulsing close. She knew he wouldn't lie to her. Every word he said was honest, and that meant more than anything else.

"Veilheart, huh?" Her voice was soft, and he pulled back enough to look at her. The smile on his face was real and, on him, truly a rare thing.

"You're ours, Lena, no matter what anyone says. Remember that."

Words failed her, but she stepped into him and pressed her body against his. Her forehead rested gently against his chest, and he didn't hesitate. He wrapped his arms around her, cradling her in his embrace. It wasn't until that moment that she realized how much she needed to hear that.

As Rowan and Silas placed their hands on her back, she felt the stress leave her, dropping to the ground like the fall leaves. For a moment, she just let herself enjoy it. A quiet moment with the three of them was everything she needed.

"Okay, let's do this." She tipped her head back to look at Atlas. "Let's go scare the hell out of a bunch of wolves."

"Another reason you're the perfect person to have by my side," Atlas smirked.

Taking her hand in his, Atlas stepped back from the group, signaling it was time to go. As he stepped up next to her, Rowan joined her on the right, while Silas stood at her back. Each of them surrounding her, protecting her.

As the clearing came into view, it was clear most of the pack was already here. Wolves and humans crowded around the fire, while others gathered in smaller groups. The moment they stepped out of the tree line, all the attention turned toward her. There were dozens mingling about, but she felt calm. Without breaking stride, she painted a smile on her face and reminded herself of what she was capable of.

Without turning, Rowan glanced at her as if wanting to make certain she was okay, and the little check was grounding. They had her back, and with them, she could do anything. She'd already overcome everything the Otherwood threw at her, and instead of breaking her, it made her stronger. *No, it made us all stronger.*

The bonfire flames licked higher, revealing their true colors of blue and violet. Tethered magic. She hadn't seen it before, but Aunt Mira's journals had mentioned it.

"Ceremonial fire," Silas whispered from behind her. "Reacts to intent. Legend says it shows your truth, even if you don't want it. A mirror to our soul."

"A magical lie detector, just what everyone needs," she muttered.

"Keep your focus," Rowan whispered. "The fire sees all and will tell the pack everything they need to know about you."

As Atlas stepped into the crowd, others gathered around him. He didn't let go of her hand, but he stepped forward, almost as if shielding her.

"Thank you for gathering tonight on short notice. This is Lena. Some of you've seen her in Hollow Creek, but every one of you has felt her. She stood with this pack at the ritual, keeping everyone safe. She's bound to the ley line, to this land, and to us."

A low murmur ran through the crowd. A few nodded, welcoming and acknowledging her, but there were also numerous side eyes or grunts. She expected them, but she knew she belonged here. Belonged with Atlas, Rowan, and Silas.

"She's not a shifter, but she *is* pack," Atlas announced.

"Isn't that convenient?" A man stepped through the crowd. Board with a scar along his cheek, salt-and-pepper hair, and sharp gray eyes.

"Calder," Rowan whispered as she took in the man.

"She arrives in Hollow Creek, and the veil thins. Yet, no one seems to think she's the reason. The Otherwood is stirring because of her, and yet you want us to accept her as a bondmate? She may carry magic in her veils, but that doesn't mean she's loyal or safe."

"You're out of line." Atlas' jaw flexed.

"I'm saying what others are too afraid to say," Calder glanced around the crowd as if waiting for someone to agree.

"Relax, Calder," Rowan growled. "Be grateful she's on our side. Otherwise, she could probably burn down the forest by accident and not think twice."

"You think I wanted this?" Lena stepped forward before considering the consequences. As she neared the fire, it crackled, growing larger. "That I showed up in Hollow Creek hoping to get cursed, marked, and pulled into your magical war?"

The gathered crowd murmured almost as if agreeing with her, though she couldn't make out for certain what was being said. Instead, she kept her attention on Calder.

"I stood in that circle, facing the veil, when others would have run." She watched Calder pale and drop his gaze, ashamed. "If you want someone to blame for your fear, look at the veil, not me. Neither the veil nor the Otherwood cares that I'm not a wolf. It saw me when I stared into its depth."

As she finished, silence descended over the pack, only the fire crackling in the background could be heard.

Movement from the edge of the pack caught her attention. Callie strolled out of the crowd, her auburn hair pulled up in a messy bun, and a mug in her hands. Her lips curled into a smile as she started across the clearing toward Lena.

"Sarcasm and spine, just what this pack needs," Callie announced.

"What are you doing?" Atlas whispered to her as she neared.

"What I always do, helping you soothe the idiots." She smirked up at her brother before offering Lena the mug. "Spiced cider, sort of a rite of passage to the pack."

"Thanks." She took the offered mug and met Callie's gaze. They'd been friends since college, yet she never would have guessed she was part of a wolf pack. Or that there were such things as wolf packs.

"Don't worry about Calder, he's all growl," Callie whispered.

"He's right about one thing." Silas stepped closer behind her, his voice low.

"What part?" She wasn't sure she wanted to know, but it was better to face whatever it was head-on, not wait for the other shoe to drop.

"There is a shift occurring within the pack. Some wolves don't like change, and you being here...well, it changes everything." As Silas spoke, he ran his hand along her back, as if offering her comfort.

"Stay with her," Atlas ordered, barely looking at Rowan and Silas.

She watched as Atlas headed toward the crowd with purpose. Something had caught his attention, otherwise, he wouldn't have left her. The heat of the flames urged her closer, but as she stepped toward the warmth, the fire brightened, sending the flames higher. As it grew in intensity, wolves shifted uneasily, as if sensing something too.

*A mirror to our soul. Did it like what it saw?*

# Chapter 3

## *Anchors Born*

The tension in the air still pulsed, but the focus was no longer on Lena. Looking out into the crowd, she allowed herself to relax a little. She sat on a log near the fire, watching the flames as if they held some hidden knowledge. Silas was on her right, while Callie sat on her left. Atlas was moving about, talking to pack members. Rowan was nearby, talking to a small group, but his gaze kept drifting back to hers.

"You know, Mira came here a couple of times. She mostly kept to herself, but she was always watching. Like she knew something the rest of us didn't. Guess in a way she did." Callie brought the mug of spiked cider up to her lips and took a sip before glancing over at Lena, who was looking at her. "What?"

"Mira...she knew? I mean, about you and this pack? Is that why yo—"

"Oh, Lena, no. You think Mira encouraged me to befriend you at school?" Callie cut her off and reached over to take her hand, and let out a laugh. "If anything, she warned me to stay away from you."

"Mira and Atlas had numerous conversations about you and

Callie's friendship." Silas leaned in. "She couldn't forbid Callie from friending you, but she could ensure Atlas stayed far away from you."

"That's why he left that Halloween party we threw during college. He stopped by to see me, but when he spotted you, he had to leave," Callie explained.

"Why?" she asked.

"He needed Mira's help to keep Hollow Creek safe. Staying away from you was her one condition," Silas whispered.

"I don't understand."

"Mira wanted you to have a chance at a normal life. She knew it would be limited, but she wanted to give you that freedom, no matter how short-lived it was. The only way to do that was to keep this legacy a secret for as long as possible." Callie put her cider on the ground and turned toward Callie. "College was my chance to forget about the pack drama. When I first met you, I didn't know you were Mira's niece. You were like a magnet that drew me in. I couldn't help it, even though we're opposites in so many ways. Looking back, maybe my wolf recognized something within you. But I wouldn't change it for the world. You're my best friend, Lena, and I hope you'll always be."

She thought about the Halloween party they threw in college and the way Atlas had strolled into the house, but immediately turned the moment he spotted her. He'd always seemed to be a distant jerk whenever he visited Callie at school or picked her up for holiday breaks. Was all of it because of Aunt Mira?

Watching him now, she tried to connect the Atlas from her college days to the man who was quickly stealing her heart. Well, one of the men. She glanced at Rowan for a moment, their gazes locked, and she shot him a smile before turning to look at Silas. With each of them, she had something different, something special. It might be new and difficult to put into words, but it was real.

"I wish she'd have told me." Her fingers reached up to the pendant necklace. "Instead, she left me the house, pendant, and a magical war."

"She wasn't the first." Callie reached into her pocket and pulled out a silver pendant similar to Lena's, only older and more weathered. "She won't be the last."

"That's a..." She stared down at the silver crescent moon pendant in Callie's hand.

"It was my mother's. Though weaker than Mira, my mother was an anchor too." Callie ran her thumb along the edge of the pendant. "You're not just bonded to the guys, Lena. Your bloodline ties you to Hollow Creek and to the veil. You're part of this place in every sense. The mark on your shoulder isn't a curse, the veil recognized you."

"The question is, recognized me as what?" Her voice was soft, her stomach tightening with apprehension.

"You're an anchor, more accurately an anchor born, the last true one left," Callie explained. "An anchor born carries magic in their blood. You physically keep the boundary stable, keeping the mortal world safe from the shadows and twisted magic the Otherwood holds."

"What does that even mean?" she asked, having a hard time wrapping her thoughts about it all.

"There will be times, like on Samhain, when the veil thins, and creatures slip through. Anchors keep it stitched shut magically." Silas caressed a hand along her back. "You're the balance of this pack. Your presence can stabilize the pack, or if you're not careful, tear us apart."

"You've got power that calls to us. It's probably why I was drawn to you in college." Callie glanced toward the fire before looking back at her. "You saw how the fire responded to you when you stood up to the pack. It knows you, and while the pack may not fully accept it, we need you."

Looking into the fire, she realized Callie might be right. She'd survived being touched by the Otherwood, the nightly dreams, and shadows plaguing her every step. Yet tonight, she realized this involvement with the pack was bigger. It was alive, and if she wasn't careful, they had claws and teeth.

# Chapter 4

## *The Flickering Boundary*

Exhaustion clung to every muscle in Lena's body as they made their way back to her house. The pack gathering was full of expected tension as they tried to determine if she was truly one of them, or if she'd been like Mira, a welcomed guest, or worse yet, an outsider.

She wasn't sure she'd won all of them over, but after her conversation with Callie, she had forced herself to get up and mingle. Silas, always there, gently guiding her, but most of the time, Rowan or Atlas were at her side as well. Though whenever it was Atlas, the conversation seemed more hesitant or hostile. It was clear that certain members of the pack—Calder, being one—didn't want her there. Even with her magical abilities, she was still human.

"Something's wrong," Rowan mumbled, reaching out to take hold of her wrist to stop her from moving forward.

Stopping, she glanced around but couldn't see anything. Yet, the air pulsed with expectation. The forest was eerily quiet.

Silas squatted down and placed his hand near the ground. "The ley line is pulsing. Something from the Otherwood is leaking through the seam."

Without thinking, she leaned down and pressed her hand against the mossy ground. As her fingers made contact with the soil, energy spiked, shooting up her arm. It wasn't unpleasant, but unexpected. Her vision shifted, revealing another dimension. That's when she saw them.

People walked into the shadows of the trees, most of them she didn't recognize, but one familiar face caught her attention: Cliff. He had been missing since before Samhain, yet there he was, slowly walking into the woods, as if drawn by some invisible force. One by one, each person vanished into the dark. She pulled her hand back, breaking the connection.

"What is it?" Silas asked, concern lacing his tone.

"I..." Her words trailed off as she tried to get control of her emotions. "I saw them. All of them. Cliff walked into the woods as if someone..." Her voice faltered.

"Someone what?" Atlas questioned.

"As if someone controlled him."

Silas crouched beside her, his hand steady on her back, grounding her. "The magic from the seam is bleeding into our world."

"We need to go," Rowan encouraged. "The forest is too dangerous now."

"But Cliff..." Rowan and Atlas stepped closer, and Silas grabbed her arm, pulling her up to stand. "What's—" A rustle from deep within the trees cut off her words.

"Let's go." Atlas' voice was low as he kept his attention on the trees.

Before they could move, the shadows morphed, twisting unnaturally, and a figure emerged from the darkness. It didn't walk, it was as if it simply slid through the space. Translucent skin and hands that were stretched into jagged claws, but what caught her attention the most were the hollow pits that should have been eyes. It was as if she were staring into a black hole, the pull was so immense.

"Stay behind us," Silas whispered, as the three of them surrounded her.

As the creature moved closer, the symbols on her shoulder pulsed. It was like an itch on the inside of her skin, before it grew hot.

"Lena, where did you go?" Her aunt's voice drifted toward her, and she froze.

"Aunt Mira..." Even as she said it, she knew it wasn't possible. Mira was dead, but that voice was perfect. An exact copy.

She stepped forward, squeezing between the guys, heading directly for the trees. Somewhere in the darkness, the voice was there. Mira was there.

There in the distance, Mira stood. Her long brown hair was tied tightly back in a braid, and that same cardigan she loved so much was draped around her shoulders. "Aunt Mira..."

"I've been wondering when you'd come to see me." Mira held out her hand, inviting her forward.

Her arm brushed against the tree, the coldness of the bark pulling her back from the moment, allowing her thoughts to clear. Her heart hammered in her chest as one of Mira's journal entries floated through her thoughts.

*Hollow-Wights are corrupted spirit beasts. Once guardians of the threshold, but now they leak magic, distorting it all. Those empty sockets where eyes should be stared through me, as if looking into my soul, my memories. They feed on the memories. If you ever encounter a Hollow-Wight, don't listen to its voice.*

"No!" She pressed her hand against the bark, digging it into her skin, trying to ground herself from what was happening. "You're not Mira!"

As if her words were enough to pull the façade away, Mira's projection morphed into the creature. Standing in front of her, Hollow-Wight still held out his hand with the long claws, as if he was waiting for her to take hold. "Your connection with her is strong. So, I took her voice to pull you in."

"You don't belong here." Feeling the pull from the creature, she dug her nails into the bark, reminding herself to focus. She couldn't be pulled into its spell again.

"The door is open, anchor, because you carry the mark of the Otherwood. The blood that sealed us out will open the veil again."

Gripping the tree, she swallowed past the lump in her throat and tried to calm her racing heart. As she did, she realized a fog had surrounded them, making it impossible to see the guys. Where had they gone? They'd been right next to her, but now she couldn't even hear them.

Instead, she saw the forest in a new light. It was no longer dark, instead, she could see pathways left by Otherwood creatures. It was as if the forest around her was now a living, breathing threat. One that wanted to eliminate not only her but also Atlas, Rowan, Silas, and the Hollow Pack. *I won't let that happen.*

"That will never happen!" she shouted, letting all her rage fill her words, as she pushed out with her magic. "They're under my protection."

As the Hollow-Wight disappeared, the fog lifted, revealing Silas and Atlas. "Rowan?" Her voice was soft as she looked at them.

"I'm here." Rowan stepped out of the trees, coming toward her, but his gaze shot to Atlas. "It completely ignored me. It was after her."

"The forest isn't safe. Lena..." Silas stepped forward, coming to her side. "Your magic is spiking, and the forest isn't just reacting, the Otherwood is responding."

"That Hollow-Wight tried to pull you through." Atlas and Rowan joined Silas at her side, but it was Atlas who reached out and touched her.

The warmth of his fingers against her clammy skin calmed the storm within her thoughts. She glanced up at him. "It said the door is open."

"What exactly did it say?" Rowan placed his hand on her shoulder. "We need the exact words if you can remember."

"It's burned into my memory." She tipped her head back to look at him. "The door is open, anchor, because you carry the mark of the Otherwood. The blood that sealed us out will open the veil again."

"They don't want to just escape the Otherwood." Silas' voice was soft as he looked to Atlas. "They're trying to rewrite the anchor. She's a target, she's..."

"The goal," Rowan supplied when Silas trailed off.

Each breath feels as though she's trying to swallow glass. The fate of Hollow Creek depended on her, and if they rewrote what essentially she was, it would mean she couldn't protect them. Not only were the residents of Hollow Creek in danger, but the three men in front of her would be at the center of it because of her connection to them.

"What if she's not just the anchor, but the hinge?" Silas questioned.

"A hinge?" She glanced toward him.

"The thing everything swings on."

As he explained, a shiver crawled along her spine, as if something within her was moving. She dropped to her knees, the forest glowing under her. She wasn't sure how to put the sensation into words, but she was certain something within her had been touched by the Otherwood.

*You're no longer human or just anchor born. You're more. You're a tether hybrid. Part anchor, part Otherwood touched. The sigil changed something within you.*

# Chapter 5

## *Shifting Allegiances*

I n the back room of Rowan's bar, The Hollow Tap, Lena stared at those who were gathered around the table. The pack meeting wasn't just tense, the power within the four walls was raw, radiating, and stifling.

To her right, at the head of the table, was Atlas. His shoulders were rigid, but the power that radiated from him was clear, not only to her but to everyone. Just out of the corner of her gaze, she could see Rowan leaning casually against the wall, but she was certain he was watching everyone, waiting for anyone to step out of line. As Atlas' beta and enforcer, he had a responsibility that he took seriously. While Silas was standing behind her, his hand on her shoulder. A calm presence in the storm.

"So..." Rowan cleared his throat dramatically. "Let's get down to business. We're here because of Calder's actions. These whispers..."

"It's more like actively plotting." She raised her eyebrow, waiting for him to react.

"She gets it." Rowan shot her a smirk.

"Enough!" Calder slammed his fist against the table, making a few gathered jump. "If you can't see what is happening, you're blind. Atlas' judgment is compromised by *her* influence. This liability can't continue. We all feel it every time she uses magic, it's... tainted."

Salis squeezed her shoulder, as if warning her not to rise to Calder's bait.

"Watch your tone, Calder. I've said it before, Lena belongs here, and I won't say it again." Atlas' words sliced through the room like a sharp blade.

"You're growing weak because of her," Calder snapped. "Your father would have never allowed a human, anchor born or not, free range into pack business. At our fire!"

Rowan straightened against the wall, no longer relaxed. Instead, he stepped closer, as if he expected something to happen. Atlas sat there, the rage bubbling off him, but he remained silent.

"Lena's presence changes the pack," Silas acknowledged, keeping his tone firm but steady. "Every member feels the difference, but it's not a weakness, it's balance and strength."

"Or it's what breaks us apart," Calder snaps.

"Everything is changing, Calder. The ley line, the veil, even the forest. When have you seen the forest as dangerous as it is now?" Rowan pressed when Atlas remained silent.

"Calder..." She paused, giving him a moment to look at her. "Why would I want to tear apart this pack when the Otherwood is seeping through the cracks? I..." She shook her head. "No, we need to be at our strongest, not fighting among ourselves."

"Otherwise—" Atlas' words were cut off as the door burst open. A young man stumbled inside. His skin was pale, and he was sucking in air as if he'd run the entire way there.

"It...it's Reggie," His voice cracked. "He's gone!"

"Corbin, start at the beginning," Atlas ordered, coming around the table to the young wolf.

"Patrol..." Corbin dropped onto the floor as if his legs couldn't hold him. "We were on patrol. But he didn't come back. He..."

"See what I'm talking about?" Calder shouted. "Atlas is a liability.

Our wolves are disappearing, and our *alpha* can't protect us. Maybe this is why we need to allow the veil to open."

"Shut up, Calder!" Tuck growled.

"Corbin, where was he patrolling?" Atlas asked.

"I found his jacket near the creek." Corbin stared up at Atlas, fear in his eyes. "It was torn to shreds. Blood..."

"I'm on it." Rowan stepped close to her, ran his finger along the curve of her shoulder until she looked up at him. "Stay with Silas. I'll be back soon."

"Be safe." She reached up and placed her hand over his.

"Meeting adjourned. We need to find Reggie. Calder..." Atlas rose from in front of Corbin and looked at the other wolf. "Check in with the others, make sure everyone is accounted for. Tuck, I need you to go to Reggie's parents. Let them know what's happening. The rest of you, let's go. You can help with the search."

"I'm going with you," Calder argued.

"You handle the patrol rotations. You know those guys better than anyone. I need you to check in with them. Find out if they heard anything. Then join us." Atlas took a step toward him, and the air thickened as his wolf came forward, until it was lurking just below the surface. "You don't have to like how I run the pack, but as long as I'm alpha here, you will follow orders."

"Come on, Calder, I'll help you check in with everyone." Another wolf placed a hand on his shoulder, gently leading him toward the door.

"Wait!" Corbin called out. "You should know...his scent trail stops at the ley line seam."

Her blood seemed to turn to ice. When she touched the forest ground, she witnessed people walking toward the ley line and disappearing. If that is where Reggie's scent disappeared, it was unlikely they'd see him again.

Everyone around the table rose to their feet, heading for the door when Atlas tipped his head toward Rowan, signaling for him to head out with the others. "I'll be right behind."

"Need another moment with the witch," Calder cracked.

"Get out!" Atlas growled.

"I'm not a witch," she mumbled, more to herself.

When they were alone, Atlas came to her, crouching in front of her, and he took her hand into his. "I need you to go back to the house. Don't leave Silas' sight. Understand?"

"I'll be fine. Go." She squeezed his hand as her gaze locked onto his. "Be careful. You and Rowan better come back to me in one piece."

"Always." He leaned in and pressed his lips to hers. The kiss was soft, almost like a whisper, before he stood again and strolled from the room.

The deliberate way he walked, his shoulders squared as if he was ready to take on the world, or the pack, made her realize the simmering rage within him wasn't just anger; it was also concern. It was more than just the pack politics, or the missing members, or even his pride. That alone was enough to terrify her.

"Come on, Lena, let's get back to the house." Silas caressed her back as she rose, clearly understanding what she was feeling even though she hadn't spoken. "Don't let Calder's rebellion rattle you. He's been sniffing around for a while, waiting for something to use to challenge Atlas."

"I just gave him the ammo he needed." She let out a deep sigh as she turned toward him. "Just add it to my list of faults...political disaster."

"Not a chance." Silas wrapped his arm around her, drawing her in close. "Calder and others may not see it yet, but you're what the pack needs. What Atlas needs."

"What about you?" She ran her fingers along his chest, teasing along the contours of his chest.

"You're exactly what I need." Without hesitation, he leaned down, pressing his lips to hers.

Wrapping her arms around his neck, she opened her mouth, allowing his tongue to slip in. A soft moan escaped her lips as she pushed aside the fear and embraced the moment. Her fingers tangled in the edge of his hair. Too soon, the kiss ended, and he pulled back, leaving her breathless and wanting more.

"We need to get you back to the house. There, the boundary and wards will keep you safe." He stared down at her.

"Wait..." She leaned back a little to look at him. "You're not just worried about the Otherwood, you're concerned the pack, no, that Calder may try something."

"Len—"

"Be honest. I deserve that much." She cut him off before he could deny it.

"The pack's not united, and that makes things dangerous. Calder isn't just whispering about you, or challenging Atlas, he's..."

"Talking about breaking open the veil." She finished for him as a shiver went up her spine.

With the unfolding danger, it became clear Hollow Creek was no longer safe. Not just for her, but for the wolves. Two missing wolves were likely just the beginning. She needed to find a way to protect them. Otherwise, everything that Atlas worked for would crumble, and she might lose the ones closest to her.

# Chapter 6

## *Offering*

S tanding on the back porch, Lena stared out at the forest. Something within it was calling to her. Without realizing it, she stepped off the porch and onto the garden path. It was as if she were being pulled forward. "I need to be there. I need to see."

"What?" Silas grabbed hold of her arm, stopping her from moving further toward the stone wall. "What are you talking about?"

"I have to go into the forest." She stared up at him, silently pleading for him to understand. "Something out there is..."

"Which is why you're staying here behind the wards." He stepped in front of her, blocking her path.

"Silas..." She reached out and cupped the side of his face. "You told me that you feel too much. Then you should understand what I'm saying. I have to go. We have to be there. I can't explain why or what we'll find. But I know for certain nothing will happen to us. Not this time."

"Atlas is going to kill me," he mumbled. "Stay close to me. And don't trust anyone besides Rowan, Atlas, and me. Not until we know for certain..."

"Who's on our side." She nodded as she stepped around him toward the stone wall, leading to the woods.

The moment she stepped over the property line, the air changed. The cool air was charged with energy, causing the hairs on the back of her neck to stand up. As Silas stepped closer, she could feel his wolf near the surface.

"This isn't right," Silas whispered.

In the distance, pack members called out for Reggie, yet she knew he wouldn't be shouting back. He'd been gone for at least two hours, and the scent disappeared at the ley line. That told her all she needed to know. Yet they wouldn't give up the search, not yet at least. Echoes of twigs snapping as they moved through the forest drifted toward her as if the forest was leading her closer to the group.

"I think I saw this." Her voice was soft as she moved ahead, not in the direction of the others but closer to the pond.

"What do you mean you *saw* it?"

Just ahead, a howl resonated through the forest. *They found him.* She quickened her pace. As she broke through the tree line, she spotted the pack gathered near the pond, and Atlas crouched down next to something, Rowan at his side, but his gaze on the others. A white wolf stood just beyond him, his head still tipped back as he let out another low howl, a warning. Stepping closer, she realized it wasn't something, but someone. A young boy lay near the edge of the pond. She didn't know his name, but she knew it wasn't Reggie.

She forced her way through the wolves, Silas on her heels, as she did. As she cleared the last of those gathered, she could see the boy's shirt was torn open and blood dried on his chest. She expected to see claw marks, but this was different. There in his flesh was a sigil just like on her shoulder. Only, unlike hers, this one was carved. Jagged and rough, as if he struggled against it. Just like it had been in her dream.

"I thought it was a dre—"

"Not now." Silas' fingers wrapped around her arm, tugging her against him.

Realizing she wasn't completely among friends, she went quiet, just as Rowan came up to her other side.

"Go on, I'll stay with her." His gaze was on Silas as he ran his fingers along the back of her hand before looking down at her. "You shouldn't be here."

"I needed to be." As Silas moved toward Atlas, she inched closer to Rowan. Not out of fear of the others, but because whatever was in these woods had done that to the boy.

"It...it called me." His breathing was steady but shallow as he looked at Atlas before glancing toward her. "It wants *her*."

"Proof!" Calder stepped out of the trees, stalking toward them, with his gaze on her. "It's hunting our wolves because we're allowing Atlas to protect her. This is a message from the Otherwood for her. Maybe if we give her to them—"

"Enough." Atlas rose, blocking Calder's path. "We both know the Otherwood doesn't leave messages. Someone is helping them to tear open the veil."

"Grayson is proof of that." Silas pressed his hand over the wound. His eyes closed, and his lips moved, but whatever he was saying wasn't heard by those gathered. With every second, Grayson's skin stitched back together, and his breathing became steadier as Silas healed him.

She glanced at the pond, and for a moment, she saw movement beneath the water, deep within. Shadows shifted, and the wind carried her name. *Lena.* From the way no one responded, she knew only she had heard it. The Otherwood was reaching through the divide, and it wanted her.

# Chapter 7

## *The Edge*

Samhain had come and gone. The yearly ritual to bind the veil was completed. According to the journals that were supposed to calm things for Lena and the pack. However, things were now more dangerous than they had been before Samhain. People were missing, some presumed dead, and the rest of them were in danger. How was she supposed to protect those she cared about when she felt unprepared for this new magical war she found herself in?

Her gaze dropped to the pond, now producing an eerie glow, and she realized the old rules her Aunt Mira had described in her journals didn't seem to apply. There was no threat just at Samhain. No possible Otherwood breakthrough once a year. This was something she'd always have to keep under control.

*If they let me.* Her gaze shot to Calder, whispering to a couple of others. She mentally took them in, so when they were alone, she could ask Atlas who they were. She needed to be aware of all potential threats, especially those within the group that were supposed to be allies.

"You shouldn't be here," Rowan muttered, his jaw tight, as he watched the pond.

"You say that every time there's danger." Callie stepped up next to them, her bubbly personality out of place. "I heard the howl, what's goin—"

"Callie?" She glanced at her friend when her words trailed off.

"Grayson..." His name came out on a breath as she stared wide-eyed at Silas and the young boy.

"You know him?" She shook her head as she wrapped her arm around Callie. "Of course you do. What was I thinking? He's in good hands with Silas, you know that."

"He..."

"Hurt, but will be fine." Rowan reached around Lena to take Callie's hand. "Silas is healing him."

"I..." She glanced at Lena and then Rowan before shaking her head and leaning in close. "Come with me. There's something you need to see."

"Now?" She glanced at Silas and Atlas, wanting to stay.

"Yes." The conviction in Callie's tone made her turn. "If it wasn't important, I wouldn't ask."

"Okay." She nodded.

Without hesitation, Callie stepped away from them and started to weave her way through the crowd, as if she knew they'd follow her. Rowan placed his hand on the small of her back, guiding her through the path Callie had created, but the stiffness in his muscles made it clear he was concerned for her safety.

"Where are we going?" Rowan asked when they were far enough away from the others that he wouldn't be overheard.

"There's something wrong..." Callie glanced around before turning back to them. "With the ley line."

"What do you mean?" Lena sped up, so she was next to Callie. "How can—"

"I don't know, it just is." Callie cut her off. "You're the expert in this magical stuff, not me. You just need to see it."

The woods grew denser the farther they moved from the pond.

The trees grew closer together, as if warning a person to stay out. The air was dense, almost suffocating, and pulsed with magic waiting to be wielded. She was pushed forward, toward the ley line in question. As she neared, she could see her breath and the figures lurking around. The figures weren't clear enough to make out actual features, just ghostly shapes

"See what I mean?" Callie asked, rubbing her arms as if to keep the sudden chill away.

The ley line pulsed in time with the sigil on her shoulder, warning her the Otherwood was near. The corrupted spirits seemed to notice her as they turned toward her. Or at least she believed they were facing her from what little features she could make out. Even the trees around her appeared different, twisted. She reached out, needing to know if it was reality or her vision.

"Don't touch anything," Rowan warned.

Even as he said it, her fingers brushed along the bark, and darkness swallowed her. One moment she was standing in the woods, the soft light from the ley line casting an eerie glow over the area, and the next she was plunged into utter darkness. The trees around her warped. Their normal straight appearance twisted in unnatural angles. The air was hazy with smoke, just like in her dreams.

Weaving between the trees were people. Some she recognized and others she didn't, but one stood out more than the others. Cliff. He'd been missing, presumed dead, since before Samhain. Yet there he was, walking deeper into the twisted forest, his gaze blank as if in a trance.

Another figure stepped around the trees, and she let out a shallow gasp. Reggie. His jeans were torn and bloody, and his shirt was ripped, but he didn't seem to notice. He followed the others without hesitation.

Although distant and seemingly unreachable, she could see the glow of magic seeping from the ley line seam. Casting an eerie glow over the twisted trees. Underfoot, the ground was parched and cracked, more dead than alive. A shadow shifted, pulling her attention back toward the magical rip, and there, within the blueish glow, were thin, pale fingers reaching out. The cloaked figure pulled itself out, and there before her stood the Hollow-Wight again.

*Anchor born. You can't save him. He's an offering.*

The sound carried across on wind, as there was no mouth to speak from. At least not that she could see. Just hollow eye sockets, so dark they dragged her in like a black hole.

"Lena!" She could hear Rowan's voice, but it was distant, as if across the forest.

A hand dropped onto her shoulder, and fingers squeezed into her flesh, as someone pulled her backwards. The twisted trees vanished, and she landed on the ground as her knees buckled. She took in a deep breath of air as if she'd been underwater.

"I saw him...them." She glanced up at Rowan and Callie. "Reggie...he's there...Cliff too. They were right there. I could have..."

"Where's there? You didn't go anywhere? What do you mean they were right there?" Callie questioned.

"I..." She looked to Rowan as if he could explain what happened. "I was there...the Otherwood."

"Impossible." Callie shook her head.

"I could smell it." Rowan crouched down next to her and took her hand into his.

"Mira wrote about this in her journal. The Otherwood doesn't always kill, sometimes it *collects*." She leaned into him, keeping her voice soft. "They have him. The Otherwood has Reggie. I saw him there. An offering."

"I remember overhearing Mira warning Atlas about this." Callie stepped closer. "The Otherwood doesn't lash out at random, it hunts. First, random people to draw our attention, but they'll come after anchors next. That's what happened..."

"Atlas doesn't like to talk about it, but that's what happened to their mother," Rowan explained, pulling her to her feet.

"Dad went after her and..." Callie's words trailed off.

"We lost them both." He wrapped his arm around Callie's waist, pulling her against his side, while still holding Lena's hand.

"We need to get you out of these woods." She glanced up at Rowan, who nodded.

"You both need to get out of here."

"He's right." Callie nodded. "We're both at risk, you more so than me. Being anchor born draws the Otherwood like a moth to light, but the Otherwood already has your scent. They've marked you. Every time your mark flares, your magic leaks, drawing their attention."

As if on cue, her mark pulsed, burning from the inside out. She reached up and pulled her sweater away, revealing the soft orange light pulsing under her skin. "We need to go."

The wind whipped toward them, sending leaves flying, and Rowan stepped in front of them, his attention focused on the group of trees further ahead.

She could sense movement, but couldn't make out what was coming. "Two anchors in one place, it's bait the Otherwood can't resist."

"Go, I'll be right behind you. Get back to the house, but whatever you do, stay together." He snarled at the trees, as if warning whatever was there, and shifted. One moment, Rowan was there before them, the next, his wolf.

Shadows crept closer, and Callie grabbed her hand. "Let's go!"

She wanted to argue, to stay with Rowan, or call for Atlas and the others, but before she could do anything, the sigil on her shoulder seared with pain as if trying to burn itself off her skin.

Rowan stepped between them. His growl echoed off the trees.

*Please, Atlas, hear his call. He can't stand against the Otherwood alone.*

Not knowing what else to do, she called to the magic within her and pushed back against the shadows. It was as if she was pushing a wall, but with every inch, the air became easier to breathe.

"What are you doing?" Callie's hand tightened on Lena's wrist, trying to pull her toward the house.

"Not this time!" she snapped through clenched teeth. "This is my fight. Go, Callie. There's nothing between us and the house, run now!"

Not needing to be told twice, Callie turned and ran.

As if sensing she wasn't going anywhere, Rowan stepped closer, still cloaked in shadows.

The magic coursing through her was wild and unsteady, but she raised her hand and focused on the darkest part of the tree line. The power answered her call, and sparks lit up the air as it flowed toward the threat.

Unlike she expected, instead of the Otherwood shadows retreating, they lunged faster.

"No!" she shouted at everything and nothing all at once. "This isn't happening. You've taken enough from this town! From this pack! They're mine."

She planted her feet and released the power building inside of her. Sending a violent pulse of white energy through the air. Shrieks echoed through the darkness as the shadows that had been pressing forward peeled back, disappearing until the forest was quiet.

Rowan pressed himself against her side, grounding her.

She dragged her fingers through his fur and leaned back against the tree. Her breath came in shallow gasps. "Row—"

Her words were cut off as a crack of underbrush caught her attention. Footsteps. But this time, from a different direction. She pushed off the tree, exhausted, but not defeated. A whip of Rowan's tail hit against her thigh, alerting her. She focused her attention on the area where she heard the noise just as Atlas, Silas, and numerous pack wolves emerged from the trees.

"We heard Rowan's howl." Atlas' gaze locked on hers as he continued toward her. "What happened here?"

"By the look of things, your lady fought the Otherwood," someone hollered from within the group.

"I'd say that about describes it." Atlas stopped in front of her. "You're still glowing from the magic."

She glanced down at the scorched dirt, embarrassed. Rowan pressed against her thigh and let out a soft bark. "I sent Callie to my house. The Otherwood is hunting anchor borns."

"Then we don't give it what it wants." He wrapped his arm around her, pulling her against him, tight and protective. "Ever."

# Chapter 8

## *The Challenge*

Before Lena could say anything or even calm the power still pulsating within her, others joined them. As they did, whispers rippled through the crowd, but that isn't what held her attention. It was Calder stalking toward them, rage clear in his eyes.

"I warned you this would happen," Calder growled loud enough that it could be heard over the murmurs. "Look at our forest. This is what happens when you let her power loose. Now the ley line is cracked and the Otherwood is clawing its way into our land."

"Calder..." Rowan warned.

She glanced at Rowan, uncertain when he shifted back, but there he stood, naked, and ready to handle whatever happened.

Silas weaved his way around a couple of members coming to stand behind her, and he placed his hand on her waist as he leaned in close. "I need you to be ready to move."

"Wha—" Her words were cut off with a glance back from Rowan, as if he was silently asking her not to make them say it aloud.

"Here." Silas reached passed her and handed Rowan a pair of shorts, which he quickly stepped into.

"We all heard Rowan's howl, and now we stand in the

aftermath." Calder waved his hand around as if everyone hadn't already noticed the scorched earth and the singed trees. "Wild magic unleashed in *our* woods, and now look at the ley line. The crack will let more of those Otherwood creatures break through and attack *us*. Our alpha isn't protecting *us*. This is recklessness, and it's going to get us killed."

A few glanced toward her, suspicion clouding their features, while others she could see fear and concern, clear as the burned marks on the ground.

Atlas stepped away from her, his shoulders squared, ready. "I've seen what a Hollow-Wight does. Rowan and Callie wouldn't have stood a chance against it. Instead, she protected Callie and Rowan. She held the line, protected those we care about. If you call that reckless, you've forgotten what loyalty means."

"Pack protects pack! She's not pack," Calder snapped. "This anchor born is making the Otherwood stronger, and Atlas is too blind to see the danger he's putting us in."

"This isn't on Lena. The Otherwood was clawing at our boundaries before Mira died," Rowan hollered.

"We weren't losing pack members then," Calder snarled. "Atlas, I challenge you."

Silence fell over the crowd, and her stomach tightened. She might have been new to this town, but she knew there was no taking back a challenge. The air crackled as Atlas nodded.

"Let's finish this."

"You're not what your father raised you to be. Protecting her has made you weak, Atlas." Calder's body trembled as he called his wolf forward.

Atlas didn't respond verbally, instead, he called his wolf forward. The crack of bones echoed through the stillness of the night. Almost instantly, fur rippled over muscle, and Atlas fell forward onto four paws. Silver eyes glowed into the darkness as he tipped his let out a growl.

Compared to Atlas, Calder's wolf was darker, more graphite. He was lean, and his eyes burned with fury.

Calder lunged at Atlas as the two wolves fought in a fury of teeth and claws. The pack cried out, shouting, as dirt flew through the air. She must have moved toward the fray because Rowan grabbed hold of her arm, pulling her back.

"Don't, Lena." He wrapped his arm around her shoulder, pressing her against his body, and the warmth of his naked chest made her snuggle against him. "If anyone interferes, it will mean his death. The same goes for Calder. If anyone aids him, he'll be damned."

Magic pulsed within her, demanding she do something, but Silas stepped up on her other side before she could react.

"No magic." Silas wrapped his arm around her waist. "He has to stand on his own."

"How can we just do nothing?" It came out soft, but the determination was clear.

"It's a direct challenge for leadership. If we do anything, it will mean they lose, and it could mean his death. The interfering party as well."

Calder slammed Atlas to the ground, growling, he moved in for the kill.

"Atlas!" she cried out.

Atlas' wolf faltered, pausing for a moment, as his silver eyes locked on hers. The connection between them tugged as her chest tightened.

Calder used that moment of weakness and raked his claws down Atlas' side, blood spilling out onto the burnt ground.

The pack reacted, screaming for Atlas to get up.

Her knees buckled, and the only thing keeping her upright was Silas' grip on her waist.

"Shit!" Rowan cursed. "Get up Atlas!"

Rage made Atlas' eyes burn brighter, and he turned his attention away from her, back to the fight at hand. He growled as he snapped at Calder, pushing him away. Rising off the ground, he quickly pounced on Calder, slamming him to the ground hard enough that the vibration could be felt by everyone around. With Calder on his side, Atlas' mouth went to his throat. A kill bite ready, but he didn't sink his teeth in.

"End this!" someone from within the group shouted, but she didn't turn to look.

Time seemed to stand still as she waited for Atlas to make a move. To finish Calder and this challenge. But nothing happened. Seconds stretched on, but Calder stayed down, eyes open, but the fight was gone. Submission.

Atlas stepped back, releasing Calder. His gaze drifted to her again, but there was no triumph in those silver eyes. In that moment, she realized how much defending her could have cost him.

As he shifted back, Atlas' body shook with effort. His wounds were freely bleeding down his naked body. Yet he focused on the pack. "Challenge is over. If anyone has doubts that Lena belongs here, they can leave. This is my pack, my town, and my choice."

Still in wolf form, Calder slunk into the shadows. Beaten, but something in the way he glared back at her told her he wasn't broken yet. This wasn't over. Today was just a battle in the ongoing war. But at that moment, she didn't care, she wanted to go to Atlas, but something about the way he barely glanced at her warned her it wouldn't be welcomed. Her shout had nearly cost him his life.

Atlas stood tall, even as blood dripped into the dry dirt below, from where claws had ripped into him. The pack began to disperse, and without thinking, she stepped forward. "Atlas—"

"Give him a moment," Silas said as he stepped around her, coming to Atlas' side.

Even though Silas' words were soft and likely true, it felt like a door had been slammed in her face. Before she could say anything, Rowan placed a steadying hand on her back. He didn't lead her away, he was just there, providing the comfort she needed.

"Leave it." Rowan's voice was low enough that the others couldn't hear. "Let him bleed and remember why he fought. Don't chase him. He needs to remember what you mean to him."

Atlas pulled away from Silas, refusing the help he offered, and stalked into the woods, leaving a blood trail in his wake.

"I almost cost him everything." Her voice was raw as she stared in the direction he'd gone.

"That was Calder." Rowan pressed his hand firmer against her back, grounding her. "This isn't on you, Lena, this has been building for some time. Don't let him pulling away convince you that you don't matter because you do. You matter to all of us."

Both the Otherwood and now Calder weren't defeated, they were waiting. Waiting for their next opening. *Or maybe I'm what's going to get everyone killed.*

**U**nable to settle her thoughts or her body, Lena stepped into the kitchen to make a mug of tea. As she did, voices carried on the air toward her, and she inched closer to the back porch door.

"Stop dodging this," Rowan said, his voice sharp.

"Our pack nearly tore itself apart because of *her*." Atlas' words cut through her chest like a knife.

"Because she's not claimed," Rowan growled. "If she were *yours*, officially, Calder wouldn't have been able to challenge you."

"It wouldn't have changed anything."

"Bullshit, Atlas, and you know it." Rowan let out a sigh, as if he'd been through this before. "This is about survival for all of us. If she's anchored to the pack through you...us...then Calder can't use her as leverage. Damn it, Atlas, you felt what happened when she screamed your name. We all did. The bond is already there, pulling you. Claiming her makes it official. It keeps her and you safe."

*Claim. Bond. Safe.* Each word felt like a lead weight in her stomach.

"Safe?" Atlas let out a huff. "You think binding her to us, to this mess, will protect her? No, Rowan, it will paint a giant red target on her back. Mira was right to keep her away. Why did she leave that house to her? She should have just let it—"

"Let it what? Rot away? And what about the pack? We need an anchor born to keep the Otherwood under control. It's always been like that. Mira understood that. The Barkstone family has been our anchor." Rowan's shadow moved, and for a moment, she was worried they'd spot her. "Lena is already a target. You saw it yourself. Those shadows went for her. Not any of us. We can't be fighting ourselves when we have to fight the Otherwood. She's already pack in every way that matters, except the one way it counts the most."

Silence stretched on until she wondered if they were still there. She hadn't heard them move, but it was too quiet. Still, she stayed where she was. Hidden in the shadows, waiting, though for what she wasn't sure.

"She deserves a choice," Atlas muttered.

"Then give her one," Rowan stated as if it were simple. "But we can't wait much longer, or she won't be alive to make it."

With the idea of tea forgotten, she headed back to her bedroom. Her thoughts raced until she wasn't sure where one stopped and another began. She wasn't sure if she was terrified of the idea of this mating and becoming pack or if she already wanted it.

# Chapter 9

## *The Pack*

The meeting continued, only this time without Calder, and Lena wasn't sure if it should have been without her as well. Especially now that the whispers of Calder's defeat hadn't quieted the doubts, it stoked the fires.

Atlas sat at the head of the table again while Rowan leaned against the wall, directly behind her. Unlike last time, Silas was standing near the back of her chair, his hand on her shoulder.

"An alpha keeps order through dominance." Eamon, one of the older wolves, sat forward, his gaze on Atlas. "Calder is alive, and she's still here in the pack business. You're shoring weakness, Atlas."

"She's unclaimed, and the Otherwood marked her. What if they pull her under completely?"

The argument continued until Atlas slammed his hand on the table, quieting everyone. "Like it or not, she's part of this fight. If we tear ourselves apart from within, it will make the Otherwood's job easier. Is that what you want? If so, we might as well walk down to the ley line or the pond and offer ourselves now. Why fight it?"

"What about tradition?" Eamon asked, doubt clear in his voice. "We've always had an anchor born connected to the pack, but never *in* pack business. Not in our meetings, sitting by the alpha like she was claimed. Yet she bears no mark."

"Mateo," Rowan called from his spot near the wall. "This isn't the good old days. The Otherwood has been wreaking havoc on us for the last couple of years. Maybe she's our opportunity to change it."

"Or maybe she's our downfall. A plant. She's marked—"

"You're speaking as if I'm a burden your pack has to carry." No longer shrinking back from the weight of their gaze, doubt, or fear. Instead, she leaned forward, placing her hands on the table, and eyed Mateo. "I protected Callie yesterday. She's one of yours. Your niece, I believe."

"Rowan was there, h—"

"Yeah, I was there," Rowan agreed. "But it was Lena who pushed the Otherwood creatures back. Not me."

"So, as I was saying. What if I'm not a burden but something else? Something more?" She paused, letting that sink in. "Mateo, you said it before that dominance is the way. I've heard others mention that the pack must be bound by blood, mating, and challenges. What if there was another way? A bond forged by choice and trust, not out of fear."

Not waiting for an answer, she glanced over to Atlas before letting her gaze find Rowan, then Silas, before returning to Atlas. "You told me that Mira tried to change things. She failed, but she wasn't wrong."

"Traditio—"

"Sometimes traditions have to be bucked." She spun back to the wolf who was talking. "In the last few weeks, we've lost two already. Now, Callie is in danger. I don't care about tradition. I care about lives. We've spilled enough blood, we've lost enough. Why don't you talk to Reggie's family? See if they'd rather we take a risk now than lose another. They have another son. Think they wouldn't buck tradition to save him?"

"What are you thinking?" Atlas questioned.

"The Otherwood doesn't care about pack rules or blood

dominance. It cares about me, and I think..." She focused her attention on him, ignoring everyone else in the room. "I think it's because I'm not bound. Not completely. If I...no, if *we* were, we could forge something it couldn't touch."

"You heard us." Rowan straightened from the wall, catching her attention, but she couldn't look away from Atlas. "Last night, on the porch, you heard me telling Atlas..."

Her chest tightened as Atlas' gaze shot to hers. Anger burned within as his irises shifted to silver, as his wolf pressed against the bounds.

"Yes, I heard you." She ignored the movement around her and kept her attention on Atlas.

"Do you know why I said it?" Rowan asked, but didn't give her a chance to answer. "Without the mating bond, you'll be prey. It won't matter how much power you have, they'll come after you with everything they have."

"I don't want to be prey or property. Nor am I some prize for you to claim." She let her attention shift to Rowan for a moment. "I will stand with you, not behind you. So, maybe it's time your traditions are rewritten."

Atlas' silver gaze burned. He seemed caught between fury and hope as he watched her. While the others in the room mumbled and adjusted as if uneasy.

This was her moment to prove to the pack that she wasn't an outsider. The Otherwood may have marked her, but she was entirely on their side. Aunt Mira brought her to Hollow Creek for a reason, and part of that was to keep them safe. This was family...her family.

Chaos was the only way to describe the rest of the meeting. As members stormed out, arguing over the correct path to choose, Lena moved to the small coffee bar for a much-needed caffeine fix. It was clear that many of the older members didn't like the idea of bucking tradition, but some of the younger wolves saw it as an opportunity for change. They might be divided now, but she'd find a way to get them to see reason.

With coffee in hand, she turned to find Atlas behind her, his body blocking her way. In that moment, he seemed larger than before. It wasn't his broad shoulders or the way he stared down at her, but the energy his wolf produced that made the hairs on her arm stand up.

"You shouldn't have said that." His voice was sharp with annoyance.

"They deserved the truth." She forced herself to meet his gaze, even as his eyes swirled with silver.

"You undermined me." He stepped closer, crowding her space.

"I gave them what you wouldn't...a choice." She set her coffee mug aside and crossed her arms over her chest. "Atlas, I'm not a fragile doll that needs to be wrapped in bubble wrap for protection. I can take care of myself, and I won't be someone's possession, not even for you."

"Do you really think I don't know that?" He put his hand against the wall, next to her, and leaned in close. "I fight myself every day to not make you mine."

"Why?" She licked her lips as she kept her focus on him. "Why not do it? You know I want it."

His fingers tangled in her hair, tugging slightly, as he leaned in closer. For a heartbeat, she thought he'd kiss her, but then he stepped back and dragged a hand through his hair. "Damn it, Lena, you don't know what you're asking."

"Then enlighten me," she snapped, annoyed.

"Claiming you will put a target on your back bigger than Calder and the Otherwood combine. You'll be hunted. By my enemies and the veil itself. I don't want that for you." Every word comes out more of a growl than the last.

"Atlas..." She stepped toward him, closing the distance he had put between them. "I'm already hunted. Pushing me away isn't going to stop that. Now the choice is rather I'm by your side, or if I'm alone."

As silence stretched, she kept her gaze on him, watching for any sign of emotion. Regret, desire, or anything in between. Nothing. His features gave nothing away. Instead, he stood there completely still.

She nodded, taking his silence for the only answer she'd get, and stepped around him. The room was empty. Even Silas and Rowan had gone, though she wasn't sure if that was because Atlas ordered them out or if they just thought it was needed. In the end, it didn't matter.

Atlas reached out, his fingers wrapping around her wrist, stopping her. "You don't know what you're asking of me."

"Maybe not, but I—" Before she could finish, a howl echoed in the distance. There was a sharp urgency to it that she couldn't deny.

"Stay here!" he ordered, heading for the door.

"Not on your life." She followed close on his heels. Whatever was happening in Hollow Creek involved her, and she wasn't going to sit on the sidelines, waiting. If she wanted to be part of the pack, she had to prove to these wolves she was truly one of them.

# Chapter 10

## *Betrayal*

Outside of The Hollow Tap, Rowan and Silas fell in step with Lena and Atlas, headed for the woods behind the bar. The howl was sharp and desperate. Instantly calling the pack members forward, some in wolf form, others remaining human, but all of them on guard.

The sigil on her shoulder pulsed, warning her that whatever they discovered would be tied to the Otherwood. The energy pulsating from the broken ley line called to her, drawing her toward it. "This isn't right."

"What?" Rowan asked from his spot next to her.

"The ley line. It's..." She took in a deep breath, trying to determine what she was smelling. "Ash...I can smell ash, as if the ley line were burning. It's not like wood ash...metal and blood."

As she curved around the trees, she immediately spotted the rip.

At the shimmering edge of the ley line, a young wolf stood, blood dripping from his sliced palms. He'd been there when she'd met the pack, and she spotted him around town, yet she couldn't recall his name.

"Take her and leave us be!" he cried as they neared.

"Seth..." Rowan snarled. "What have you done?"

She froze. Instantly aware that Seth was offering her up as a sacrifice. What would he do if she got too close? Would he try to throw her into the shimmering crack that the Hollow-Wight had emerged from?

Rowan stepped away from her, stalking toward Seth, but Silas grabbed his shoulder, stopping him. The crack pulsed, growing, as Seth's blood landed within it.

"Seth, you've made a pact you don't understand," Silas hollered over the wind.

"This won't hold." Atlas stepped in front of her as shadows surged from the split.

The sigil on her shoulder flared, searing into her skin, as if it were being burned into her now, but it wasn't. Rather, it was the Otherwood reaching out. It wanted her.

As shadows emerged, Rowan lunged at Seth, slamming him to the ground, while ensuring the bloody hand was no longer dripping into the tear. He held Seth's arm against his body, allowing the blood to drip on Seth's clothes instead.

"Tuck." Atlas turned toward the other wolf. "Help Rowan with Seth. We'll address his actions outside of the woods."

"What's the plan, alpha?" someone asked.

"We need to get out of these woods. Our houses both have wards to give us time." Her voice was low, trying to keep it so that only Atlas could hear her.

"Lena's right." He glanced back at her. "We'll meet back at my place. There, we'll address the situation and put together a plan. The boundary there will keep the Otherwood out and give us time to prepare."

Atlas stepped closer to her and placed his hand on her arm, but she barely noticed, her gaze focused on the ley line. They may have been able to save Seth's life, but the damage was done. The ley line wasn't just seeping magic but now acting as a portal for the Otherwood shadows. How long before others were able to crawl through? Shadows and Hollow-Wights were one thing, but there were more dangerous creatures living in the Otherwood. Beings they didn't want on this side of the divide.

By the time the house Atlas, Rowan, and Silas shared came into view, everyone was on edge. Atlas and Silas stayed by her side, as if they were waiting for someone to step out of line. Unlike other times, when Atlas had kept his distance, he now slung one arm over her shoulders. Gently guiding but also providing comfort.

"Stay close," Atlas whispered as they entered his backyard and he stepped onto the porch, giving himself a little extra height to look out on everyone.

She stayed on the stone sidewalk, Silas by her side, continually scanning the area, and every muscle was tight. He wasn't the fighter, but she didn't doubt he'd throw down to protect her if it came to that.

Rowan pushed Seth to his knees in front of the group, and Atlas cleared his throat. "You offered one of our own to the Otherwood."

"She's not pack!" Seth screamed. "She's part of the curse. If we give her to them, we can b—"

Callie, who had been off to the side, stepped forward and swung, landing her fist against the side of Seth's jaw. Blood seeped from between his lips as Rowan stepped in her way, blocking her from taking another shot.

"Enough, Callie," Rowan ordered.

Shouts erupted, and Silas stepped up next to Atlas.

"The Otherwood won't stop with Lena, they'll come after all of us until we're destroyed." Silas' voice was steady, but it carried enough emotion that everyone stopped and listened. "They won't be satisfied destroying our pack or taking over Hollow Creek. They'll branch out until no one is safe. If we let the Otherwood win, they'll devour everything. Seth's actions today could have doomed all of us."

"I had to try something." Seth spat, sending a tooth and blood to the ground in front of him. "Calder's right, Atlas is too wrapped up in her to see what's happening. This pack has always been the one to suffer the most. No more. I'm tired of bleeding for these anchor borns. As if they're special."

Rage rippled off Atlas as his hand shifted, allowing claws to string free from his human body. "You're pack no longer."

Realizing what was about to happen, she swallowed. From her aunt's journals, she knew executions were rare, but this was something that couldn't be overlooked. There was no turning the other cheek when it came to betrayal. It was one of those crimes an alpha couldn't overlook.

"The Otherwood will come for h—"

His words were cut off by a snarl from Atlas as he shifted mid-stride. His massive silver wolf collided with Seth just as Seth shifted into a much smaller wolf. Atlas' size, power, and rage give him the upper hand, making the fight quick yet brutal. The wolf dug his claws into Seth's side a split second before his mouth clamped down on Seth's neck. Blood spills out onto the dirt, and the silence hangs heavily in the air.

Atlas stands, still in wolf form, and looks over at her, as if expecting to see her disgusted by what she witnessed. Instead, she offers him a weak smile. What he did wasn't just for the pack, but to protect her. That spoke volumes.

Shifting back, Atlas steps away from Seth's now human body and surveys the pack. "This is what happens when you betray your oath and your alpha. Seth turned his back on this pack. He knew what would happen when he tried to make a deal with the Otherwood."

Silas tossed Atlas a pair of shorts that he slipped on before walking toward them. Fresh blood tainted the skin around his mouth and matted in his chest hair.

"You always have shorts at the perfect time," she whispered to Silas while keeping her gaze on Atlas.

"You hang around with wolves enough, you'll start knowing all our hiding spots," Silas teased.

"What now?" Someone from the crowd hollered. "How do we protect ourselves? This pack and her?"

"Fighting among ourselves isn't going to solve anything." Callie stepped out of the pack and moved toward where Silas, Atlas, and Lena were. "This isn't something new, and it's not Lena's fault this is happening. So, stop blaming her and start thinking of ways to keep our pack safe."

"Callie's right." Atlas nodded. "What happened today cannot happen again. I said it before, but it seems I must repeat myself: Lena is part of this pack. If you don't like it, you're free to leave. As long as I'm alpha, my decision is final."

"Years ago, Mira tried to do what Lena is suggesting. She tried to form a multi-tiered bond with this pack, but she was doing it out of obligation, not out of..." Callie glanced back at her and then to her brother. "Love."

Atlas stood straighter, as if he wasn't ready to admit it.

"I was just a kid, but I remember Mira trying to anchor herself to more than one of our wolves. She believed it would strengthen the bond. She failed, and it destroyed something within her. But Mira didn't have Lena's connection with Atlas, Rowan, and Silas." Callie glanced at her brother before turning to Lena.

"I..." She wasn't sure what she was going to say. Whatever was happening between her and the guys was private, and she wasn't ready for everyone to know. She wasn't even sure they were ready to admit what was simmering between them.

"You've already done what she couldn't." Callie spun around to face her. "You're at the center of more than one bond. It's why the Otherwood wants you. Seth thought he could buy freedom from them by offering you, but that's not how it works. The Otherwood will continue to hunt us because we'll be more vulnerable without an anchor born. Lena, the Otherwood doesn't want you gone, it wants you because of all you've accomplished. You're the key, and that's why it won't stop until it converts you."

Murmurs swept through the group, some in support, others with concern. She was a liability, someone who might bring danger to the pack, because they knew, as well as she did, that the Otherwood would never stop hunting her.

# Chapter 11

## *Bonds Unbroken*

Most of the pack scattered. Some of them went to check areas or other members, while some just left to carry on with their day. Nothing had been decided when it came to the Otherwood. No one was sure what their next move needed to be. There were things Atlas had to decide before a battle plan could be drawn up. That meant returning to the ley line to assess the damage Seth had caused.

"You really don't need to be here," Rowan reminded her as they stood by the ley line.

"I know." Her voice was soft as she stared at Atlas. He stood a little ahead of them with Silas, who was crouched next to the fractured ley line. Still in only shorts, the tension in his body was clear. His muscles were rigid, and his jaw flexed. Being back here no doubt reminded him of the betrayal.

"It's done, Lena. He made his choice." Rowan took hold of her hand, gently entwining their fingers and squeezing them lightly.

*Anchor...*

She glanced around, looking for where the voice came from. It wasn't one of the wolves, rather, it was almost as if it was carried on the wind.

"The ley line crack is deeper now." Crouched near the ley line, Silas held out his hand, near the crack, but didn't put his hand over it into the blueish glow seeping from it. "Seth's blood fed the fracture."

"Can we stitch it shut?" Tuck asked. As one of Atlas' most trusted, he was the only one who accompanied them to the woods.

"No." She stepped up closer to Silas. "It's unraveling because of me."

Atlas turned his attention to the ley line, anything but to look at her. Rowan squeezed her hand, reassuring, but it was Silas who spoke.

"You're the tether, not the cause," Silas reminded everyone. "You're the only thing that has kept us from being swallowed by the darkness so far."

"In the clearing..." Rowan stopped glancing at Atlas, as if waiting for something.

"What?" She turned toward him, waiting for him to finish. "What about the clearing?"

"Atlas didn't just hear my howl, he felt the pull." Rowan glanced down at her as he brought his other hand up to her arm, gently rubbing along it as if to chase away the chill. "When the shadows came after you, there was a pull—"

"What do you mean?" she questioned.

"A magical tug," Atlas answered. "It was as if someone was pulling on a rope."

"Why didn't you say anything before?" She glanced over her shoulder at him.

"We only discussed it last night," Rowan answered before Atlas could. "I felt it, but I was there with you. I didn't know that Atlas and the others felt anything until I brought it up. The point is, Atlas and the strength of the pack pulled you back."

"A tether." Atlas stepped toward them, his gaze dark, as he focused on her. There was fury in his eyes, but also something softer, tender. "That's you, Lena, the tether connected to my pack. You're not fragile, you're a warrior. Just perfect for an alpha."

"Not sure your pack would agree." Her voice was soft as he wrapped his arm around her waist, pulling her into his body and away from Rowan.

"You're the only thing keeping them from the brink of despair. Of darkness so black you're essentially blind." With his gaze on hers, he reached up and tucked a strand of hair behind her ear.

"Your pack is fighting over...well, fundamentally me. I'm supposed to bind you, not tear you apart." She kept her voice soft, ensuring that he was the only one who heard her fears. Teasing her fingers along his side, she stared up into his eyes, hoping he'd say something to ease the tension within her.

For a moment, it was just the two of them, everyone else faded to the background. Then Rowan placed his hand on the center of her back, and Silas stepped up beside them. He took her other hand in his, this thumb teasing over her knuckles.

With the three of them touching the connection forming between them sparked within her, burning hotter than the sigil on her arm had ever. What was pulsing between them was stronger than the curse or the Otherwood.

"Look!" Tuck hollers behind them.

She glanced over her shoulder to see the ley line shimmering brighter than before, as if the veil were acknowledging the connection she felt.

"The Otherwood knows what you are and what you mean to *us* and this pack. They'll never stop coming," Atlas growled.

"Let them." She leaned back against Rowan while keeping Atlas tight against the front of her and Silas on her side. She was surrounded and ready. The claim was already forming, even if she didn't carry their mating mark *yet*. "I'm not alone."

As Lena stepped over the wall into the yard at the pack house, she immediately spotted the small group of wolves waiting. Atlas, who had been next to her, took her hand and continued walking when she faltered. Rowan moved to her other side, while Silas stayed close behind. They'd picked up on the tension hanging in the air.

"Alpha..." one of the wolves acknowledged as they neared.

"We know." Calder rose from where he'd been sitting on the porch, but his gaze was low, not quite meeting theirs.

"What do you think you know?" Atlas questioned.

"We know why the Otherwood wants her. We felt it through the pack connection." Eamon stared at Atlas.

Tuck came around there, holding up his hand. "Guys, maybe now's not the time."

"She's bringing danger to our pack. If not now, when? When we lose someone else? Cliff, then Reggie. Who's next?" The same wolf snapped.

"You know your father would have—"

"Enough," Atlas snapped, cutting Eamon off. "If you're here to convince me to feed her to the veil or allow the Otherwood to have her, you're wasting your time. She's not a damn bargaining chip."

"Then bind her." Calder's voice was low, almost bordering on submissive. "Make her yours. Bind her to this pack completely. Now, once and for all. If the Otherwood shadows want to claim her, claim her before they can."

"Calder's right. She needs to carry your mark." Another one nodded.

"Dominance isn't the answer." She looked at Calder and the others. "Being marked by Atlas won't stop the Otherwood. I'm here because I choose to be here. This isn't because of dominance or command, it's choice."

"You show up here, knowing nothing about this place, the magic, or our pack, and in less than a month, you think you know better than centuries of pack law?" An older wolf shook his head.

"I've read about what your laws did to Mira." She nodded.

"It nearly broke Mira." Callie stepped out of the house, determination clear in her stance. "Mira tried to build a bond out of choice with more than one wolf. It nearly destroyed her. But Lena isn't Mira. Lena is stronger, and that is what the Otherwood fears. That's why it wants her."

"When I am marked by Atlas, it will be out of choice." Lena pushed her shoulders back and looked at each of the men gathered. "Right now, we need to focus on keeping the Otherwood out, protecting everyone, and figuring out how to get Reggie back."

"Back?" Tuck questioned.

"He's in the Otherwood." She glanced over at him. "I saw him, alive, but now we have to figure out how to get him back."

"Without offering her as a bargaining chip," Atlas growled, his attention on Calder.

"I've got an idea." Knowing that the others weren't going to like it, her heart skipped a beat. *Saving Reggie will prove to those like Calder that I'm already pack, even without Atlas' official mark.*

# Chapter 12

## *Through the Veil*

L ena's stomach twisted with nerves as she braced for what they were about to do. They'd been planning Reggie's rescue for hours now, and every one of them led them there. Though Atlas and Rowan had been the strongest opposition. Silas had been the one to convince them. Without her, there was no chance of rescuing Reggie.

"You're right." Silas knelt near the fractured ley line. "He's alive. Bound, somewhere past the seam."

"This could be a trap." Rowan stepped closer and glanced at Atlas. "You should stay here."

"No." Atlas turned to her. "I'd like to order you to stay."

"You know that's not how this is going to work." She closed the distance between them and put her hand on his arm. "An anchor is needed, otherwise, you won't make it back. I'm going. We'll face it together, or not at all."

"It's mirrored," Silas announced, pulling her attention back from Atlas. "The Otherwood is a mirror version of Hollow Creek."

"It's too dangerous," Atlas said, ignoring Silas' comment.

"You know it has to be me." Her sigil pulsed, but she wasn't sure if it was in encouragement or warning. "The Otherwood already has its claws in me."

"We're doing it together." Rowan stepped up behind her and placed a hand on her shoulder.

"Then we need to do it now." Silas rose from where he had been crouched. "I don't know how much longer Reggie has without help."

"Your alpha side is showing," she teased as she smirked up at Atlas. "I know you want to protect me, but right now we have to do this."

Without giving him the opportunity to debate, she stepped back from him and walked over to the ley line fissure. In reality, she didn't know what she was doing, but instincts guided her forward. She reached out until her fingers were within the light pulsating from the crack.

A soft growl echoed behind her, just to the right. She didn't bother to turn around as she recognized it as Atlas. His personal dilemma couldn't stop her from doing what she needed to do. Instead, she closed her eyes and focused on the veil. In her mind, she pictured the veil pulling away, creating a doorway.

*Please let this work.*

"It's working, Lena." Silas' voice was low, but the encouragement was clear.

The air around her seemed to drop to below freezing, and as she opened her eyes, the fog flooded through the opening she'd created. Ignoring it all, she stepped forward. Atlas and Rowan come up to flank either side.

Everything about this world was wrong. From the firmness under her feet to the tall, yet twisted, trees. The air even smelled different, coppery as if blood had been spilled recently.

*Come home, Lena. You don't belong with them.* The wind whispered as it rushed forward to meet her.

"This will never be home." She glanced around, looking for any threats, but all she could see was darkness and never-ending fog.

"Where is he, Silas?" The urgency was clear in her tone.

Wind picked up, and the trees groaned around them. In the distance, figures appeared within the fog. More shapeless shadows and glowing eyes than physical beings.

"You were never enough." Rowan snarled, his eyes glowing red.

"What?" She stepped back, uncertain. The spot where Rowan had stood was empty. It was as if he vanished.

"What's wrong, Lena?" Silas asked, his hand coming to rest on her shoulder.

"Rowan?" she screamed, looking around for him.

"What?" He was still right there next to her.

Relief was short-lived as she looked further into the woods. There, nestled in the trees, Atlas was bound in thick black chains. His silver wolf eyes stared back at her, and the claws of his wolf were out, but it was as if he couldn't complete the transformation. His mouth was moving, but she couldn't hear what he said.

Though she saw the ropes around him, she could feel Atlas' hand in hers, steady and sure. "Lies!"

"What's going on?" Rowan asked. "Lena—"

"Not real," she mumbled. "Lies. All lies."

"Reggie..." Silas called out.

She tried to focus on where Silas was pointing, but her vision was filled with more illusions. Even Callie was there, flames licking at her body as she screamed. But Callie wasn't in the Otherwood. She was back on the other side. Safe. This was the Otherwood, a mind trick. "I'm the tether. I know this isn't real."

"Hurry!" Atlas ordered. "Whatever is happening to Lena, we need to go before it breaks her hold on our world."

Rowan and Silas neared Reggie, while Atlas stayed at her side. Little by little, her vision cleared, allowing her to see what was happening.

"Wait!" she hollered as Rowan reached out to Reggie, stopping him just in time. "Something's wrong. Don't touch him."

"Stay with us. No curse, no pain..." Reggie's gaze locked onto her, but it wasn't him. Something else looked out of his eyes at her.

Black eyes, hollow. *We're too late.* Black cords ran across his chest like overgrown vines. Magic ties were holding him against the trees. His skin was pale, almost lifeless. The Otherwood had sunk its claws into him, and unlike her, he didn't have the magic to fight it.

"It's too late." Silas' words were soft.

"No." She reached down and grasped the vein. Burning seared through her, but she pushed back, forcing her magic out through her fingers, breaking the binds that bound him. "You're not taking him! He's ours!"

*Him for you.*

"Neither," she shouted back. She knew the guys hadn't heard the voice, just like they hadn't heard it before, but it didn't matter.

Silver light poured from her fingers, breaking the vines that bound him. As each black cord broke, it burned and disintegrated. One by one, she broke them. *Don't let us be too late.* She waited for a sign, anything to show he was still there. But nothing. With a final spark of her magic, his eyes closed, and he was lifeless. There was a faint heartbeat under her touch, but that was the only sign of life.

"We've got to go." Silas leaned down, his hand on her shoulder as if ready to pull her away.

"Almost." She gritted her teeth, fighting back against the pull. "Be ready to grab him."

"They're closing in fast," Rowan warned.

"When he's free, Silas get Reggie back home. Rowan and I will keep them back." Atlas leaned down next to her ear. "Stay close, but move quickly."

"Come on, Reggie. Come back to us," she urged.

The last vine broke, and Reggie's eyes opened. Hazel eyes stared out at her. Relief and concern blazed in his pupils. "You shouldn't have..." Reggie leaned forward before collapsing against her. "Have come."

"I'm glad to see you, too." She smirked.

"We've got to go," Rowan growled. "Now!"

"Ahh..." Reggie cried as he tried to stand.

Silas hooked his arms under the younger man, lifting him. "It's going to suck for a few minutes, but we've got to move quickly."

She looked down at the burns on her hands, they were healing, but the raw skin was blistered and painful.

"Come on." Atlas wrapped his arm around her, practically dragging her back to the seam between worlds.

She let him pull her back toward their world, but something didn't feel quite right. The shadows seemed to be closing in around her, and the howls of creatures echoed through the air. "This was too easy."

"Easy?" Rowan let out a light chuckle. "Let's get home, and then you can decide that. We're not out of here yet."

As if on cue, the edges of the divide shrank just a little. It was enough that she saw it.

"Hold on, just another minute, veilheart," Atlas whispered before turning to Rowan. "Go. She'll be right behind you."

Without arguing, he grabbed her hand and stepped through, pulling her along with him as he did.

Exhausted, she collapsed onto the hard forest ground and dug her fingers into the dirt. She needed to ensure this was her world. She slammed the portal shut, cutting off the flow of magic that had allowed them to traverse the planes.

Movement from the corner of her gaze pulled her attention away from the dirt. Callie, Tuck, Corbin, and others were there. Even Calder was on the edge of the tree line, and for the first time, there wasn't hostility radiating from him.

"It's been hours." Relief was clear in Tuck's voice as he came closer.

"We're home." Tears filled her eyes as Atlas crouched down next to her.

"Because of you." He pressed his lips to her temple before pulling her upright.

"You shouldn't have come, it was a setup to try to get her. They wanted you, Lena." Reggie's voice was hoarse and full of emotion.

"With her, they don't need to break the veil; if they can corrupt her, they can walk through it with her as the doorway."

"You're pack." Atlas reminded him. "No one takes what's ours. You, Lena, or any member. We'll always come, and we'll always fight."

Her mark hummed, reminding her that despite what Atlas said, she was also marked by the Otherwood. Even now, back in Hollow Creek, she could feel the Otherwood watching.

# Chapter 13

## *The Fire Within*

Standing in the dark forest, Lena pushed aside panic, trying to remember how she'd gotten there. Fog slithered along the ground, creeping closer, but in the distance, a warm amber glow could be seen. *Fire.* As she recognized it, the flames seemed to grow closer, until the smoke clawed at her.

She glanced down only to find herself standing there in her pajamas, and even though she couldn't see her feet through the fog, she knew they were bare. The cold dirt under her feet sends a chill up her spine.

*Break the bond, anchor born. Burn them! Burn them all.*

No matter where she looked, she couldn't see anyone. The words were carried on the wind. Endlessly echoed through the trees.

Fire crept closer with each passing second until her chest ached from the smoke. She spun around, looking for an escape, but flames consumed everything around her.

"This is a dream." She dropped to her knees, pinching herself. "It's got to be a dream."

"Lena!" Someone called her name, but through the smoke and fire, she couldn't see.

179

Her eyes watered as a familiar scent hit her full force. Pine and fresh rain. *Rowan.*

Losing control, she fell back against the dirt, her body convulsing as power flared within her. She felt the rush of magic shoot upwards, toward Rowan, but her body wouldn't respond.

With the release, the burning forest faded, and she opened her eyes to find herself in her bed. Rowan was standing there, his eyes wide, and smoke was rising from the burn mark on his shirt.

"Oh, Rowan!" Her body trembled as she pushed back the covers, rushing toward him. "I...I hurt you."

"It wasn't intentional." He stood completely still, as if he were worried magic would shoot out of her again. "But, you didn't just lash out, Lena. You..."

"What?" she questioned when his words trailed off.

"Tried to burn through the bond itself."

She wanted to reach out and touch him, but she didn't trust herself. Hurting him reminded her how dangerous magic was.

"What d..." Her words trailed off as Atlas and Silas strolled into the room. Their attention immediately turned to Rowan and the scorch mark on the wall behind him. "What does that even mean?"

"That if you don't get control over this, you won't just hurt someone, you'll destroy everything." Atlas stalked further into the room. "You'll destroy the pack bond from the inside out. This time we kept it from the others, but next time we might not be so lucky."

"The pack is already making demands, Lena. We can't give them more reasons to doubt you," Silas added.

With her gaze focused on the burn mark on Rowan's shirt, she dropped down onto the edge of the bed. As if she didn't have enough to worry about, now she was afraid of herself.

"What if I really hurt one of you?" she asked, her voice raw with fear. "If I lose control...burn the bond...I..."

"We bind it together." He stepped closer, coming to the edge of the bed next to her. "We stop running from this."

"This? What is this? What do you mean bind it together?" The questions flowed faster than he could react.

"We make you ours." He reached down and took her hand into his. "There's no breaking that bond. You'll be ours, always."

She glanced at Silas, who nodded in agreement. Then, hesitantly, her gaze drifted to Rowan, who was still standing near the wall.

"Think I'm going to say no?" He cocked an eyebrow in question. "Lena, I've been waiting for this moment since you stepped into my bar."

"But I hurt you."

"Silas," Altas called.

"You're not the first to lose control, Lena." Silas stepped forward, lifting his shirt as he did. "It was after the Samhain ritual, reinforcing the veil boundary for another year, when Mira lost control. She was awake, but had been drinking, and her control was low. She ended up..." He stepped close, allowing her to see the jagged scar running along his back.

"What did she do?" She reached out, running her fingers over the scar.

"You struck out with magic, but she attacked with a knife." Rowan came up next to the bed, joining them. "Silas was in his wolf form at the time, and Mira believed he was from the Otherwood. She tried to kill him. If he hadn't been a shifter and a healer, she would have likely been successful. Silas was able to heal most of the injury, but it still took weeks for his body to recover."

"I knew she hadn't intended to harm me, but it took some time to trust her," Silas admitted. "It wasn't like what happened with Rowan. Mira wasn't asleep when she lashed out. She'd seen me in my wolf form numerous times, but still..."

"Silas is unique." Atlas' lips curled up into a smirk. "Always, but especially in his wolf form. There's a black handprint in his gray coat, near his left hip."

"I was touched by the Otherwood." Silas let his shirt drop back into place and turned toward her. "Their mark will always be there.

Some believe it's why I can heal. I can call upon something beyond my wolf magic."

"Let us make this official." Atlas' words were soft as he took her hand into his.

"All of you...like share?" She glanced at each one of them before adding. "I know there's been something between...I mean between us. Each of us. But isn't that weird for you? Don't you want your own woman?"

"We told you before, the bond formed naturally. It's meant to be, and it works for us. What we have doesn't need to follow anyone's rules." Silas turned back toward her.

"We want you, Lena." Rowan cupped the side of her face, guiding her to look up at him. "We've known it for a while. Some of us just took longer to come around to it." He shot a glance at Atlas.

"Yeah, yeah." Atlas shook his head. "It took me a bit."

"A bit?" She let out a soft chuckle. "I thought you hated me."

"Mira's demand for me to stay away from you was hard to move past." He brought her hand up to his lips, gently kissing it. "Plus, you're Callie's best friend, I don't want to come between you two. But you call to me and my wolf. I want to protect you, Lena, but making you our mate will put you in danger."

"It will also protect her," Silas reminded him.

"The Otherwood will never stop. I know this now—"

"True." Atlas cut her off. "But they'll come after us with everything they have, because you choosing us over them will unleash their fury."

"How can you want that? How can you want *me*, knowing that?" With her heart in her throat, she stared up at him.

"We'd always choose you." Atlas closed the distance between them, pressing her up against the headboard of the bed. "We've all hesitated, but it's time we stop fighting it. This is meant to be, and each of us knows it. We'll be stronger once the pact is cemented. So, stop fighting us, stop fighting me."

"We're not letting go," Silas assured her, still hanging back, watching, waiting for her next move.

She let her gaze drift from Silas to Rowan before coming back to Atlas. "Everything has been leading us to this moment...to this claim."

"To you." Atlas lifted his hand to her jaw, his fingertips teasing along her skin with such tenderness that her knees would have buckled if she hadn't been sitting. "You're ours." His voice was low and dangerous, but instead of making her anxious, it calmed her nerves.

Before she could speak, his mouth crashed against hers, stealing the air from her lungs. As his lips took hers, it was anything but gentle. Within his kiss, his unspent desire lingered. The possessiveness of it broke down her walls, allowing her to surrender to his touch. With her back against the headboard and his arms on either side of her, she was caged in.

"Don't scare her off." Rowan sank down on the bed next to her. His fingers brushed along her wrist, sending goosebumps up her arm as she wrapped her other arm around Atlas' waist.

Silas stayed near the door, watching her every move, as if waiting for her to push them away again.

"Come here." She held out her hand that had been on Atlas' back, needing all three of them.

The moment Silas fingers touched her, the current changed. Each of them pulling at the magic within her in a different way. Yet somehow, instead of it unsettling her, it balanced everything. She wasn't just an anchor, she was the tether connecting their group.

In that moment, even the sigil on her shoulder dimmed. No longer burning bright within her.

Silas, the most vulnerable of the group, stood near the edge of the bed, wearing his heart on his sleeve. "We're not afraid of you, Lena. We're afraid of losing you."

"Then claim me because I'm not going anywhere." *Not voluntarily, at least.* Yet, she didn't express the last part out loud.

Her pulse echoed in her ears as Atlas' mouth found her again. His kiss devoured her, staking his claim before he worked down her neck. Rowan pressed against her side, his hand on her hips, teasing her nightshirt up further. Silas sat on the edge of the bed, his fingers running through her hair, as he stared down at her, as if waiting for her to disappear. Her body vibrated with the touch of each of them.

"You feel that?" Rowan questioned, making her gaze shoot to his.

"You're binding with us," Silas explained.

"Huh?" The question came out breathless.

"Now that you've made your choice. Your magic is creating the multi-tiered bond that you read about in Mira's journals."

Mira's journals hadn't gone into details, but she was able to piece together parts. It hadn't worked for Mira because she hadn't been in love with the men she'd tried to create the bond with. She had been doing it out of obligation, not of choice. Here and now, they were forming a bond woven by will.

"Mine," Atlas growled against her throat as he arched over her, giving Silas more room.

Instinctively, she arched into him as her body burned for him. His teeth clawed against her pulse point, arching her higher. "Atlas..." His name came out on a moan.

"I need this now. I need all of you." The tether between them pulled taut, and magic surged through her, filling the room with light. Her whole body hummed, and the air sizzled with power. Each of them called to a unique part of her, but together, there was unity. Pack.

The bond she didn't realize she was forming snapped into place with warmth, love, and light. It spread over each of them, knitting them together as one. For the first time since *anchor* was mentioned, she truly felt anchored. Not by the veil, or magic, or the Otherwood curse, but to them. For the first time, she wasn't afraid of what the morning light would bring, or what the magic inside of her might do. She'd found her place within the wolves.

# Chapter 14

## *Shadows in the Roots*

Warmth surrounded Lena as she opened her eyes to find herself surrounded by the guys. Atlas behind her, his arm draped over her waist. Rowan half sprawled on the bed, half off, sharing just enough with Silas to ensure neither of them fell. All of them touching her, as if they were afraid that if they let go, she'd disappear.

"Morning," Silas whispered, his words sleep-coated.

Atlas let out a soft growl as he tugged the blanket higher, snuggling into her back. His arm tightened around her, possessively drawing her closer against his chest.

"Always the morning person," Rowan shook his head at Atlas, but also snuggled in closer to her.

"Did it work?" Her voice was soft as she glanced at each of them.

"What do you think?" Silas asked.

"How do you feel?" Atlas whispered into her ear, while Rowan dragged a finger along the sigil on her shoulder, testing her reaction.

The sigil bubbled with power, but instead of glowing or pushing forward, it seemed to retreat into her. Still present, but calmer than before. The magic that had felt like a fire within her seemed to have settled as well. Now low and warm, not all-consuming as it had been hours before.

"I feel...steady." She twisted enough to look at Atlas. "Through our bond, I feel the steadiness from your wolf, Rowan's tranquility, and Silas' empathy. I'm anchored in place by our bond."

"There's no going back." He dragged his hand along her bare arm. "You're ours now, always."

"Always." Silas kissed the back of her hand.

"We wouldn't want it any other way," Rowan smirked.

The world outside was still unraveled, uncertain, but in that room, it felt steady and calm. The Otherwood could wait. For a moment, she savored their new connection. The new beginning.

Suddenly, pounding echoed through the room. Sharp, frantic knocks, shattering their moment with certainty. Besides them, only Callie was in the house, and something told Lena she wasn't bringing muffins and coffee.

"Lena, open up!" Callie hollered, her voice carrying enough urgency to pull all of them from the bed.

She grabbed her discarded nightshirt and slipped it on. Each of the guys grabbed their pants. Bare-chested and jeans barely at his hips, Atlas pulled open the door with a low snarl.

No muffins or coffee, instead a very frazzled Callie. Her hair was tangled and wild, while her eyes were wide. "You need to see this. Now!"

Without waiting to see if they followed, Callie turned and headed toward the front door.

Stepping out into the hallway, the chill hit her. The house was colder than ever before. She briefly wondered about the furnace, but at the moment it was pushed to the back burner. It wasn't the reason Callie was banging on the bedroom door.

As they neared the back door, a strange feeling came over her. "Ahh..." The faint hum grew louder with each step.

"You feel it too?" Callie asked, but didn't stop. She pulled open the door and stepped aside. "It's what got me up, but I wasn't expecting this."

Thick fog made it feel like she was stuck inside a snow globe, looking out. She could barely see the edge of the property, but the wardstones along the edge were no longer glowing. Usually, they simmered with a faint golden glow but were now dark.

Movement just beyond the trees drew her attention from the stones to the woods. Shadows moved, but as if they were human and walked, but as if it pulsed to a beat she couldn't hear. "What was that?"

"The Otherwood." Silas' voice was low as he placed his hand on her shoulder.

"It's not staying on its side anymore." Atlas stepped past her and pushed the screen door open. "It's spreading."

"But how? Why? I thought the seal was stable." She took a step forward only for Rowan to grab her arm, stopping her.

"The seal was stable." Silas shook his head as he stared out at the twisted tress of the Otherwood.

"Something is feeding it again. Stronger." Atlas stood there, unmoving. "We need to find it and stop it."

"It doesn't make sense." Silas stepped out onto the porch next to Atlas. "The veil is stable, it shouldn't be bleeding like this."

"It is." Rowan gestured to the scene before them as if they hadn't already noticed. "It's stronger than before Samhain."

As he said it, her sigil pulsated beneath her nightshirt, hotter than it had been. She stepped out onto the porch, joining Atlas and Silas. The thumping of her mark grew stronger. The forest was aware of her presence, and it was trying to pull her closer.

"Tuck has already swept the area." Callie leaned against the doorframe. "The Otherwood breach hasn't spread far. It's thickest here and fades quickly."

"You called Tuck?" Atlas glanced back at his sister.

Callie's lips curled up into a smile with the mention of Tuck. "He was checking the perimeter, as he usually does in the morning, and noticed it. He came here to alert you."

"Then where is he?"

"I told him I'd alert you. He's calling the guards and checking on people." Callie ran her hand over her arm, as if chasing off a chill.

"Whatever is causing this is close," Silas whispered.

"Then we find it." Lena was surprised by how steady her voice sounded.

Each of them turned toward her.

"Don't look at me like that. We're not waiting for this to spread or for it to come to us. We need to go in."

"It's too risky." Atlas shook his head. "It was too close the first time we crossed over, and this time they'll be waiting."

"I wasn't tethered to the pack then, but I am now."

"She's not wrong, Atlas," Rowan admitted.

"Annoying, but she's never wrong," Callie muttered.

"I don't think we'll have to go into the Otherwood." Silas stepped off the porch and strolled down the path to the stone wall dividing her property from the woods. He stopped short of the fog, holding out his hand. "Our issue is here. I think we'll be able to handle it without crossing at the ley line."

"Callie, you need to stay here." Atlas glanced back at his sister when she stepped forward onto the porch. "Inside and call Tuck. Let him know we're...investigating, I guess, but I want him here with you until we get back."

"I don't need a babysitter," Callie growled.

"We don't know what the blowback might be," Rowan reminded her before Atlas could. "Tuck will know what to do if we don't come back."

"Lena." Atlas' gaze shot to her. "You stay by our side at all times. Don't take a single step without one of us next to you. Understand?"

"Deal." She nodded and stepped off the porch.

The moment they neared the stone wall, Rowan and Atlas flanked her. Their bodies were tight, and their wolves close to the surface. She didn't need weapons, at least not the traditional kind, when she had wolves and magic at her disposal.

Silas was the first across the stone wall, with the rest of them only a step behind. The change was immediate. The morning sun no longer reached them, instead, it was as dark as a moonless night. Birds were silent, and the gentle breeze was gone. The stillness bordered on creepy.

The sigil on her shoulder flared to life, burning with such force that she instinctively reached for it. This place wanted her. Not just her body, but her magic and even her blood. She couldn't explain how she knew it, but if the Otherwood claimed her, it would grow, not only in power, but it would spread into their world, destroying Hollow Creek forever. The magic within her coiled in her stomach, aching to be released.

"It's pulling strength from the ley line, like a parasite." Silas' voice was low as he walked in front of them.

"It's feeding on it," she clarified. "Look."

She pointed to the twisted trees that seemed to glisten and pulse with the same rhythm her sigil did. At the base of the largest tree were shards of bone arranged in a perfect spiral, and the magic pulsing from it, making her stomach tighten. The ritual site was clear. "Someone has been feeding the Otherwood from this side."

"Not just someone..." Silas knelt near the tree. "A pack member."

A growl tore through Atlas, low and dangerous. "Seth wasn't working alone."

The mention of Seth's name stopped her in her tracks. The betrayal still stung, and his execution was raw in her mind. He's betrayed his pack because of her. Now with new evidence etched in the soil, they had someone else to search for. Someone had continued his work, even knowing the consequences.

As she stepped closer to the tree, the shadows reacted. They rose from the ground and seeped out of the trees. One lunged at Rowan on her left, but he was already moving. Another came out from the ground in front of Silas.

"Back." Atlas grabbed her arm, pulling her backward toward the stone divide.

"No." She pulled her arm out of Atlas' grip. "I can stop this."

She called to the magic that had been coiling in her body, ready and waiting, and allowed it to surge forward. Magic exploded, bright and blinding, as the well within her rose to meet the darkness.

The spiral around the tree rippled, no longer just dirt, but like a mirror to the other side. Allowing the Otherwood to come into view. A dark hand reached out from within.

"Not happening." She focused the light spreading around them into the earth at the bottom of the tree.

Whatever was on the other side screamed as the hand pulled back. The shadows that had been attacking were burnt away or retreating, as the Otherwood shrank back into itself. The twisted trees cracked and smoked until only the original trees of Hollow Creek remained untouched. Even the shards of bone on the ground turned to dust.

As her magic returned to her, she swayed on her feet. Lightheaded, her legs gave way.

Atlas wrapped his arm around her waist, catching her before she collapsed. "Easy, I've got you."

"This wasn't a random breach." As her vision steadied, she glanced up to meet his gaze. "Someone *made* a channel."

"Great." Rowan blew out a shaky breath. "They're still out there, feeding the Otherwood. Strengthening it."

Still unsteady, she forced her legs under her to stand again, even though Atlas kept his arm around her waist. "Then we find them and end this before it gets worse."

# Chapter 15

## *The Betrayer's Shadow*

B ack at the house, Atlas stood at the head of the table with Rowan and Silas on either side of him, while Lena sat off to the side. While she was part of the pack now, complete with tether, she didn't want to make this meeting about her connection. It needed to be about what they found.

The group gathered was smaller than at any other pack meeting. Only Tuck, Baxter, and Callie. Atlas' most trusted people.

"None of this is random. The attack, the breaches, Seth's betrayal." Atlas placed his hand on the table. "Someone is feeding the Otherwood, and that person is still here."

"Do we know how they're communicating?" Tuck asked.

"The ley line," Silas answered. "They're using ritual marks to amplify the connection. It's how Seth opened the fracture and why now the Otherwood is pushing the boundaries."

"They'd need access, which means..." Callie's words trailed off as she looked at her brother. "Someone high enough in the pack, not to raise suspicions."

*Someone trusted. Someone trusted by Atlas.* That's what Callie meant, and the very idea slammed into Lena like a lightning bolt.

191

"Silas…" Atlas glanced toward him before continuing. "I need you and Baxter to check the perimeter wards. Reinforce any that need it. Callie, can you help Lena look through Mira's journal for anything that might help?"

"And you?" Callie asked

"Rowan and I are going to meet with the senior wolves. While Tuck here is on guard duty." He glanced at the man in question. "I don't want to believe it, but it's possible someone close to me is betraying this pack. Inviting anyone here is a risk to Lena and Callie's safety."

Tuck tipped his head. "Don't worry about them, I'll keep them safe."

"What if he's the one betraying us?" Callie questioned.

Tuck spun to look at her. His eyes were wide.

"What?" She shrugged. "You're one of Atlas' most senior advisors."

"I trust him as much as Rowan and Silas. If I can rule anyone out, it's Tuck and Baxter. Which is why they're here." Atlas stared at his sister. "You can doubt him if that makes you feel better, but you'll listen to whatever commands he gives as if they came from me. Understood?"

She glanced toward Tuck. "I don't doubt it, but I needed to know why *you* trusted him."

"Come on, Callie." She pushed back from the table. "The journals are in the study. We should get started."

As she stood, Atlas reached out, his fingers brushing along her arm. She glanced over at him, their gazes locked for a moment. So many unsaid words hung in the air, but instead of giving them a voice, she nodded. "We'll be fine. Keep yourself safe. All of you."

"This is ridiculous." Lena tossed another journal to the side. Since she arrived in Hollow Creek and found Aunt Mira's journals, she read every entry at least once. Now, the idea that she'd find something to stop what was happening seemed unlikely. She couldn't remember anything like this happening in any of the journals. Not even the ones from Mira's mother that they'd found stashed away further back in the attic.

"Sitting around complaining isn't going to help. So, what else do you suggest?" Callie leaned back against the armchair, a journal spread out on her lap.

"I—" Her words were cut off when Rowan stepped into the doorway.

"Silas and Baxter are back, and they found something." He tipped his head for them to follow.

"And the other shoe drops." Callie set the journal aside and rose from the chair.

She hesitated a moment before standing up from the sofa. Her chest was tight because whatever was found wouldn't bring relief. Someone had betrayed the pack, and treachery of this depth was met with only one result. Death.

"Lena!" Atlas called when she didn't emerge from the study behind Callie.

"I'm coming." She forced herself forward, and as she stepped out into the hall, the smell of wet leaves and fur hit her, along with the rage bubbling within Atlas. "So, what did you find?"

"Tracks." Silas came closer and wrapped his arm around her shoulder, drawing her against his body.

As he did, the scene of the forest surrounded her, and she embraced him, wanting more of it. More so, she wanted the tranquility the forest had once represented to her. Now it seemed to bring only danger.

"Heavy boot tracks near the ley line fracture," Baxter clarified. "But whoever was there masked their scent, just not perfectly."

"Then we know who it was?" She lifted her head to look up at Silas.

He shook his head. "The boots aren't standard patrol issue. They're older...someone who's been around for a while."

"That's got to limit the possibilities." With her arm around Silas' waist, she glanced back at Atlas.

"By a lot." He didn't quite look at her. Rather, he kept his gaze low. "It's Eamon."

"Eamon?" Silas' body tightened under her touch. "He's been your advisor since..."

"Dad died." Callie's voice was low, as if she couldn't believe what they were saying.

Atlas dropped into the chair. "When I took over this pack, he was the first to swear his loyalty. With Mira and him, I was able to stabilize the territory and keep the Otherwood out. I trust...trusted him."

"Why would he do this?" She stepped away from Silas and moved closer toward Atlas.

"Because..." A man pulled open the screen door and stepped into the house. "When Mira died, the veil should have fallen." His steel gray gaze drifted from Atlas to hers.

"Eamon." As she said his name, Atlas and Rowan stepped closer to her.

"You weren't meant to hold this line, Atlas. It's not what your father wanted. It's why we tried the multi-tier bond with Mira."

"You were *E*." Her voice was soft as the journal entries from Mira fell into place. "You were the biggest supporter, then—"

"I realized no matter what we did, the Otherwood would always be a threat." He glanced at Atlas. "Your father knew it, too. Mira knew the bond needed wasn't strong enough. She wasn't the anchor for the task. What if the right anchor born never appears?"

"What are you saying?" Rowan questioned.

"Atlas, you were never meant to hold the line forever. The Otherwood is power. Our ancestors merged with it, and now we spend all our time and energy trying to keep it out. Generations have choked on this fear."

"Selling out our pack is your solution? Rowan snarled.

"Anchors are keys." Eamon's gaze flicked to her. "You're what the veil responds to. If we stop clinging to our old ways, you could end this curse instead of patching it year after year."

Atlas moved before anyone else could. In the blink of an eye, he was across the room, and Eamon was slammed against the wall. Atlas' hand at his throat, a growl tearing from his throat, like thunder before a storm.

"You risked their lives. You risked her life," Atlas snarled.

"And I'd do it again." Eamon was still under Atlas' grip. "The old ways will kill us just as surely as the Otherwood will."

"People have died and you're not sorry." The surprise was clear in Silas' voice as he stepped closer.

"I'm not," Eamon admitted.

In the deafening silence, she stood there, staring at Eamon, numb. He turned his back on his pack, but what cut the deepest was the betrayal of Atlas, who admired the man. In that moment, Atlas' expression hardened into something she'd only see once between. Primal. The alpha emerged.

"By pack law, betrayal of kin, alliance with the Otherwood, and endangerment of the anchor is punishable by death." Atlas' voice rang through the house.

Her chest tightened as she knew what was about to happen. Before coming to Hollow Creek, she'd have been disgusted, terrified of the actions Atlas was capable of, but since she arrived, she'd changed. Harder, but she also realized there were consequences to their actions.

"Then finish it." Eamon met Atlas' gaze, and there was no fear in his eyes.

One swift, decisive strike, and it was over. There was no hesitation, no chance for regret. When Atlas stepped back, Eamon's body slumped to the floor. His eyes were still open, but his neck was hanging at an awkward angle.

Atlas stood there, staring down at the body for a long moment before he turned toward Tuck. "Burn him and salt the ground."

Through the bond, she reached out to him, but he shook her off. He retreated into himself before stalking off down the hall. This betrayal cut deep and would leave a lasting impression.

Once again, the Otherwood claimed another piece of their world, but this time it was family.

# Chapter 16

## *The Veil Trembles*

The night had been long, preparing for the ritual, but Lena was tired of the Otherwood taking from her, the pack, and Hollow Creek. It was time to strike back. Ash and salt formed a circle around Lena as they stood here at the ley line edge. Runes glowed faintly in her fingertips.

"The ley line bends here." Inside the circle, Silas crouched beside the runes. "Think enough to speak through but strong enough to hold if the Otherwood pushes back."

"*When* they push back." Rowan adjusted the knife on his belt as he stepped into the ring next to her.

In the middle of the circle, she felt alive. Her magic vibrated within her, even as her heart hammered against her chest. Cementing the bond with Atlas, Rowan, and Silas had changed things. Making her more powerful and her magic seemed more alive. As if something had woken within her.

Atlas glanced around the forest before joining them within the circle. His presence was grounding and absolute. His fingers brushed along the curve of her wrist. "If it gets too much—"

"Not this time." She glanced up at him.

With a slight nod, Silas muttered something she couldn't make out. As he did, the ley line answered. The ground shuddered, and the air thickened. She reached inward and pulled her magic forward, letting it rise until it flowed out of her like water out of a faucet. With her eyes closed, she could feel the ley line. What was usually a silver and light, threading through the world like roots, was now fractured, and darkness leaked through.

*Not as long as I'm here.*

She pushed her magic forward, surging into those spots, and the darkness reached back. Shadows crept into her vision, some half-formed, others wolves that didn't appear quite right. Some with too many eyes, others with extra teeth, or one who was larger than any she'd seen before.

*Anchor. You hold the door and the wound.*

Her breath caught in her chest, but the bond surged forward. Atlas' hand on her shoulder, Silas' own magic at her side, while Rowan's voice drowned out the voice of the Otherwood.

"You want to break into our world."

She could feel the Otherwood laugh more than she could hear it. Dried leaves fluttered through the air as if to remind her they were already there in some ways.

*To join, not destroy.*

Images flashed through her mind. Not of the past or what she was protecting, but of what the Otherwood wanted the future to be.

Hollow Creek's main street was dark and foggy. Tree roots curled up from the ground, reaching out across sidewalks. Shadows lingered, and wolves moved as if patrolling. A few humans lingered, their gaze darting from one thing to another, as if scared. Each of them with marks like hers, glowing as if a fire burned within. While the biggest difference was the veil. It wasn't broken, it was gone.

*Merge. One realm, one world, one truth.*

Gasping, she stumbled back, and the vision snapped. Still, she continued to feed her magic into the ley line, slowly knitting back the spaces the Otherwood had broken through. Opening her eyes, she didn't just find the guys around her still, holding the line. She also saw the lightness in the woods. Sun seeped from within the tree branches, birds chirped, and the breeze was gentle. Even the ground under her feet had quieted.

"The fracture is sealed." Relief laced Silas' tone as he rose from where he'd been kneeling.

She could feel it. Her magic had knitted the tears back together, but it wasn't over. Eamon was right, the Otherwood would never quit.

"They're not trying to break through." She glanced at Altas. "They want to merge with us."

"Merge? What does that even mean?" Rowan frowned.

"This curse isn't a curse, it's a transformation. One that my family and your pack have been holding back for centuries."

"Then we hold it harder." Atlas' jaw tightened as he met her gaze. "We don't let it through."

In that instant, everything changed. The Otherwood didn't want destruction, it wanted union, and that meant everything they thought they knew was wrong. The next time the Otherwood tried to break through, it might not be so easy to contain.

# Chapter 17

## *The Pact*

Curled up in a blanket on the sofa, Lena watched the rain fall outside. While the drumming of raindrops hitting the roof was usually relaxing, now, with the pressing issues with the Otherwood, she couldn't relax. Every noise brought apprehension, and the howling wind held warnings she wasn't ready for.

The sigil on her shoulder pulsed faintly, a steady reminder that the Otherwood was near. Even if she left Hollow Creek, she would always be a part of this. Even if she didn't defend the town, the Otherwood wouldn't stop at the edge of town. It would spread outwards, consuming everything in its path.

*One realm, one world, one truth.*

The door creaked open, and Rowan stepped in, his hair and clothes damp from the rain. "Tuck is taking care of the perimeter, and Baxter is with Callie. She's getting stuff from her apartment and will be staying here for now."

Unable to speak, she nodded. Callie wasn't just a wolf and part of the pack. She was also part anchor, which meant the Otherwood would use her if they could. Her power may be dimmed by her wolf, but she was in danger because of her anchor born blood.

Silas stepped out of the kitchen, carrying a tray full of steaming mugs of tea. "Baxter will keep her safe until she's here."

Atlas stepped into the room, slower than usual, as if the weight of the situation was on his shoulders. He barely glanced at her as he dropped down onto the edge of the sofa.

"If the Otherwood doesn't want to invade..." Rowan hesitated, brows knitted together. "Merging means we've been fighting the battle all wrong."

"Merging isn't peace." Atlas leaned back against the sofa and stared up at the ceiling. "It's obliteration. The Hollow Creek we know will cease to exist."

"Maybe it will be something new...stronger," Silas countered softly, handing Lena a mug of tea.

"Stronger?" Atlas shot him a look. "You know the stories. The last time a merge was attempted, we lost over twenty people, and the western territory vanished. How many more would we lose? Are you willing to risk this pack, Lena, for a *maybe*?"

"Mira tried..." she whispered, and they all turned toward her.

"What do you mean?" Rowan sank down onto the edge of the sofa, his gaze on her.

"She tried to form a new bond." She cupped the mug of tea, trying to soak up its warmth. "The bond between magic and wolf. Anchor and pack. It's clear in Mira's journals she believed it could stabilize the boundary and end this cycle."

"She failed," Atlas reminded her.

"Did she?" She glanced over at him. "It was something Eamon said...Mira knew the bond needed wasn't strong enough. She wasn't the anchor for the task."

"What are you saying?" Rowan pushed.

"What if she didn't fail, but stopped. What if the pack wasn't ready?"

"Are you saying you think we could succeed where she didn't?" Silas questioned, sitting on the coffee table in front of her.

"I don't know." She stared down at her tea. "I know that the

Otherwood isn't just clawing at the edges, and it's never going to stop trying to take what is ours. Sealing the fracture or fighting back shadows won't work forever."

"Are you saying you want the merge?" Rowan's voice was deep as he leaned back, as if angry by what she said.

"No, what I'm saying is I don't know if we can stop it." She glanced over at him.

Silence descended over them, thick and uneasy. No one wanted to admit they could fail or that Eamon might have been right. But part of her knew it was true.

"No." Atlas stalked toward the window and stared out. "We hold the line until we have no choice. That's our duty. It's what my father, Mira, and so many others died for."

"What if holding the line destroys everything? Destroys us?" She leaned forward, placing her elbows on her knees. "What about future generations? Do you want our children to be forced into this?"

Atlas froze, his body stiff, but he didn't turn back.

She stood, strolled across the coffee table toward him, and placed her hand on his back. "I'm not saying we give up. What I'm saying is we need to prepare. If we can't avoid the merge, we need to understand it completely. If we can do it on our terms with our rules, then we do it."

"Rules?" Rowan shook his head as if he couldn't believe it.

"Fine, balance." She glanced back at him. "The Otherwood wants our world, then *we* decide what that world looks like."

"You're talking a pact." Silas nodded. "Between the wolves and the anchor. The Otherwood and the wolves. Mira wanted that."

"She tried to create that balance with *E*." She nodded. "I'm tired of reacting. Maybe it's time to take our fate into our hands."

She stood there next to Atlas, her hand on his back, and allowed the silence to wrap around them. Instead of stressing over the quiet, she sank into it.

Atlas turned and slid his arm around her waist. "Then we choose together."

Rowan and Silas appeared at her side. Silas was behind her, while Rowan was taking her other side. The moment their fingers touched her body, the bond between them hummed to life, warm and steady.

"We'll face whatever comes next, together." Rowan pressed his lips to her forehead.

"Always." Silas looped his arms around her waist, pulling her back against his chest.

Together they stood near the window, staring out at the dark forest. Within the treeline, the Otherwood waited. Watched. It didn't retreat.

*Neither will we.*

# Part Three

---

## *Hollow Threshold*

The veil between worlds is thinning, and Hollow Creek is at the center, tearing at the seams. Now that the Otherwood is bleeding through, magic no longer obeys rules. The more Lena uses her newfound powers, the more it costs her.

After sealing the fracture and forging a bond that defies every law of magic and pack, Lena and her mates believe they've bought themselves time. But the truth is, the Otherwood isn't trying to break through, it wants to merge.

When they learn that Lena's bloodline isn't meant to seal the boundary, but to open it, everything changes. Loyalties are tested, and beliefs crumble, leaving the pack splintered. The group has to face the fact that it's no longer a choice of fighting. It's whether to surrender, transform, or be consumed.

# Chapter 1

## *The Fissure*

The heavy quietness pressed against Lena. As if the forest were holding its breath, waiting for her next move. The thick scent of wet earth was overpowering, yet somehow welcoming. The darkness was shattered only by stray rays of moonlight breaking through the tree limbs. She'd once found the woods to be peaceful, even at night, but now the shadows seemed to hold terrors she wasn't sure she was ready to face.

She stood at the edge of the pond, her shoes sinking into the mossy soil. The fissures around the pond and the ley line had returned. A thick jagged crack ran down the area, pulsing light that made her stomach churn. The Otherwood was reaching out again.

The mark on her shoulder flared. She clenched her fingers, resisting the urge to reach for it. A hot pulse of power surged through her. The bond throbbed in response, and somewhere in the shadows, she could sense Atlas, Rowan, and Silas. Each connected to her in a way she couldn't completely understand.

*Lena...* A whisper from within the darkness, silky and sinister.

She froze, muscles tightening. Whatever called her name wasn't human, it was Otherwood. The seduction within it was almost too much to resist. It held a promise of power and freedom. All she had to do was step into the fissure.

"Lena, step back," Rowan called, cutting through her thoughts.

"I...I have to see..." The pull to the other side was warm and welcoming. "I need to know what it's doing."

"No, Lena, you don't." Atlas stepped from the shadows, his boots crunching against the dried leaves on the forest floor. His silver wolf eyes were fierce with concern as he fixed his attention on her. "This isn't meant for you to face alone."

The fissure pulsed again, urging her to take the step into their world, to experience it for herself. Images flashed before her eyes. Twisted trees grown out of barren ground. A fox swallowed whole by the shadows. The Otherwood wasn't simply breaking through, it was adapting.

As her magic spiraled around her, the mark on her arm burned until her skin was on fire. She tried to exhale, anchoring herself in the moment. "I can't just do nothing. The pull—"

"Focus." Silas stepped beside her, so close she could feel his breath on her neck, and took her hand in his. "Focus, Lena. Be the anchor. Don't let it take you."

Her fingers twisted as a thread of power seeped into the fissure. As it did, the light emitted flared brighter. She swallowed hard, trying to prevent the power from escaping her body. The bond throbbed violently, and the tether that connected her to the pack shook. Yet the sensation from the ley line crack was intoxicating.

*You belong here. You're the bridge. Step forward, and you'll understand everything.*

She glanced at the others, looking for any sign that they had heard the voice. But they were still. Their gazes were trained on her, and they weren't looking around to see who had spoken. They hadn't heard it.

"It knows me," she breathed. "More than that, it wants me."

Atlas' hand brushed against her. While Rowan stepped up

behind her, his chest against her back, he placed his hand on her shoulders. With each of them touching her, the bond flared, and the magic swirling within her calmed.

"You're not alone. Not now, not ever. Let it feel us, feel our bond, and know that it can't touch you. You're ours."

Her vision blurred as threads of magic snaked out of the fissure, toward her. Twisted shadows seeped out of the pond, reaching toward her. The Otherwood was brushing against her mind, testing their bond. She didn't have to think. Her body reacted on its own. Heat and energy rippled out of her in waves, rushing toward the crack, leaving her breathless.

"We're in this together," Silas reassured her.

She leaned into the bond, feeling each of their wolves at her back, and allowed the power to flow through her. Her hands trembled, but her vision was clear. The tether that bound them was more than magic, it was life. They were a steady strength that allowed her to push against the seductive pull of the Otherwood.

As she pushed her magic out toward it, the fissure screamed, not verbally, but she could feel the pain and the cries. Pushing back, the Otherwood thrust visions of the merged world into her head. Not one of the joys to come, but the consequences of her actions. Atlas chained to a throne of roots and shadows, his eyes black. Something had changed within him. Same with Rowan, who knelt beside him, thick ropes pinning him in place. Silas was somewhere in the mist, unseen, but she could feel him.

The images were meant to scare her, to make her beg for their salvation. The Otherwood expected her to negotiate. But she wouldn't allow that to happen. Instead, she squeezed Silas' and Atlas' hands while pressing back into Rowan's body. Grounding herself in their touch.

"You can do this," Atlas rasped in her ear.

She focused, letting the power flow outward into the crack. Shadows shrieked, retreating, as if she were burning them.

*Don't. Join us, Lena.*

The silky allure, once seductive, now left her uneasy. The Otherwood was struggling against her, testing her in ways it had never before, trying to pull her into the fissure.

"No!" Her voice was soft, but the determination was evident. The sigil on her shoulder flared. A blinding light could be seen through her sweater. "I am the anchor."

The ley line pulsed violently, fighting as she pushed the Otherwood back again, but finally it gave way, and she staggered back into Rowan. He wrapped his arms around her, supporting her when she wasn't sure she could herself.

"I got you. We got you," he mumbled, nuzzling against her neck.

Atlas squeezed her hand, and the unease settled within her. The heat of his touch centered her, giving her a moment to breathe as the tremors of power eased.

"You did it. You held it back." Silas pressed his lips to hers. "I knew you could."

"I almost lost control," she admitted. "If you hadn't been there..."

"We'll always be there." Atlas ran his hand down her arm.

"Don't forget it. Every surge, every time, we'll always be there," Rowan reminded her.

"Every time your mark burns, it's a warning. The Otherwood is close to or attempting to infiltrate our world. It's like a sensor of their activities." Silas turned to face her. "You're powerful, and the Otherwood knows it. But we need to tune into this hidden advantage."

"Here I thought this sigil was just a fancy tattoo they could use to hurt me." She shook her head. "I can still feel their claws in me. But since we bonded, it's... I don't know less somehow."

As if speaking of her connection to the Otherwood brought their wolves to the surface, she could feel them creep up, giving off more warmth than before. With the Otherwood threat at bay, she allowed herself to sink into that tether, into the safety and heat it offered. Most of all, into the connection she shared with the men she trusted.

In their embrace, she let her fear slip away and allowed hope for the future to take hold.

*Lena, you're the bridge. Step forward.*

# Chapter 2

## *Shattered Truths*

The first time she met the pack, it was in the very same space, even the fire was burning again, but unlike now, that night was full of hope. Atlas and Rowan were in front of the group, while she had hung back with Silas. She was tethered to the pack through the guys, but it was Atlas' pack. He was Alpha, and he needed to embrace that role without her tonight. The future had to be decided by the pack.

"Call this what it is." Calder rose from where he'd been sitting. "The ley line isn't sick, it's evolving. We're clinging to old boundaries that might not exist much longer."

"It's not evolution." Rowan shook his head. "This is corruption. Look at the twisted growth by the pond, and you can see it. This isn't balance, it's an invasion."

"It could be the land trying to heal itself." He glanced around at the others. "What if Eamon was right and we're the infection? What if the merge is the cure?"

A growl ripped from within the wolves, but Atlas raised his hand, cutting it off immediately. In that moment, he was everything an

Alpha was supposed to be. Calm and authoritative. But the pack was divided, and storm clouds were on the horizon.

"This meeting is to inform you, to answer questions, but no decision will be made tonight. We need to think about this logically and not decide out of panic or fear."

"Fear?" Shaking his head, Calder looked at Atlas. "That's what you think this is? It's choosing adaptation over extinction."

"Or inviting annihilation," Rowan snapped. "We lived in peace for centuries, and we can do it again if we get ourselves and the veil under control."

Lena bit her lip, trying to remain silent. She could feel tension crackle through the air. The fissure wasn't just a scar on their land, it was alive and watching. Even now, the Otherwood was listening.

"We can't tear ourselves apart before the fighting even starts," Atlas growled, looking from Calder to the others. "This is our home. Our families. We can't stand by and do nothing as the Otherwood takes what we've built and those we love."

Tuck nodded, his support clear. "We protect our town, pack, and loved ones."

"The Otherwood has always wanted a doorway into our world, and we've kept them out." Atlas paused for a moment. "Now it seems they want more, but we don't know its intent, so until we do, we treat every anomaly as a threat. We must protect the ley line and guard the boundary."

"If the boundary is dissolving?" Calder's voice was low, as if he didn't want to ask the question.

"We adapt," Tuck hollered. "We don't give up. We fight for our way of life."

"We adapt." Atlas nodded in agreement. "On our terms, not the Otherwood's."

The Otherwood was listening, and they didn't like what they were hearing. The sigil on her shoulder burned. She rubbed it gently, hoping it would ease the pain. Instead, her fingers felt electric on her skin, and suddenly the world around her shifted.

"Lena," Silas whispered. "What's wrong?"

She wanted to answer, but the words wouldn't come. Her surroundings grew dark, and the clearing disappeared. It wasn't like the dreams. Instead, the vision slammed into her while her eyes were still wide open.

*Not again...*

Although she knew she was still sitting at the pack meeting, she felt transported to the center of Hollow Creek. But it wasn't the town she saw every day. Now it was dark and nearly deserted. Roots emerged from under the sidewalk, and the world seemed draped in shadows, sending chills down her spine. The sky was dark, obsidian with streaks of deep violet. Abandoned buildings leaned at impossible angles, their windows broken, and their interiors gutted.

Wolves prowled the street, but not Atlas' wolves. These creatures had a hollow glow to them. Their fur shimmered with shadows. Their eyes were deep black, hollow of any light or emotion. They seemed half-shadow, half-animal, but complete predators.

Atlas was in the middle of the town square. Heavy chains bound him, and blood dripped from his body in more places than she could count. Rowan slumped near the fountain, unconscious, as blood pooled under him. Enough to make her wonder if he was still alive. Silas was nowhere to be found. Callie was tied to a post. Flames licked at her legs, inching higher with every second. Her mouth was open mid-scream, but no sound escaped, at least not that Lena could hear.

"No...this isn't real," she whispered to herself with her eyes squeezed shut as if that would stop the vision.

"Lena!" Silas' voice cut through the spiraling nightmare as if she were underwater. "Look at me!"

His arm wrapped around her shoulders, enough to pull her back from the vision, back to reality. The ebony and violet sky popped like a bubble around her, allowing the vision to fade in on itself. Opening her eyes, she found herself back with the pack in the clearing. Silas pressed up against her, his arm around her shoulder.

215

"You're safe." Silas' mouth was next to her ear, trying to be quiet enough that the other shifters didn't notice.

"If the worlds merge, it won't heal anything, it will *destroy* everything." Her breath hitched, and her heart slammed erratically against her ribcage.

At the front of the pack, Atlas stood, his gaze locked on her for a long moment before nodding. "Then we know what we need to do. No merge, no surrender. Whatever it takes, we hold the line. For ourselves and future generations. We protect this pack and this town as we've always done."

*Does that line still exist?*

She wasn't sure, especially when the wind picked up. Gently whispering her name. *Lena.*

Never taking his gaze off her, Atlas made his way through the pack. Every move was careful, as if he were waiting for Calder or someone else to try to stop him. Rowan followed close behind, his gaze monitoring the other pack members, clearly looking for any threat to Atlas or her.

When Atlas reached her, he brushed his finger along her cheekbone before tipping her chin up to look at him. "We'll find a way to stop the merge. My dad died protecting this town. I'm not about to surrender our home to the Otherwood now."

"So what, alpha, you made the decision?" Calder called from behind him. "No vote, nothing."

"My word is law." He spun around to look at Calder and the others. "You know Mira's visions better than some. Lena's are the same. If she says the merge will destroy everything, I believe her."

"Me too!" Rowan nodded. "Calder, you have a young boy. Don't you want him to have a future?"

Calder was silent for a long moment before nodding. "A future where he's safe. The Otherwood doesn't make it safe here anymore. They're poaching our territory, threatening our welfare."

"Joining them won't protect you or your son. You'll be sacrificing everything and gaining nothing." She stepped to Atlas' side and faced

Calder. "You don't have to like me, but what I'm saying is the truth. What I've seen..." Her voice trailed off.

"What?" Callie hollered from within the crowd. "Tell them."

"What I've seen is worse than anything Mira's journals threatened. Your son, along with all the children in this pack, won't have a better life. They won't have a life at all. The Otherwood will take over, and Hollow Creek will cease to exist, including this pack." She stared at Calder.

"Yo..." Calder's voice faltered. "You're lying. You have to be."

Rowan placed his hand on the small of her back, steadying her. Their touch, even Atlas' light caress along the back of her hand, was grounding and insistent. Her anchor woven throughout the bond.

"I wish I were." Lena's words were soft, full of remorse. "I've seen what the future would hold and what would happen to this pack. I promise you, it's not a world any of us would want our children growing up in."

"This meeting is over." Atlas' voice was steady, but she could feel his wolf pressing against the bond. "Rowan will work on the pack's protection, extra patrols, whatever we need. Once I know more, we'll come together again. But if I find out anyone else is supporting the Otherwood, there will be hell to pay. If you have your doubts or concerns, bring them to me. Don't go behind my back and risk this town and our people."

When Atlas fell silent, Rowan cleared his throat. "Tuck and I'll be in touch with new security changes. Everyone needs to be vigilant. If you see anything, report it."

As the members began to clear out, the three men turned to her, this touch still present, grounding her. It was too much, and her knees threatened to buckle. She leaned into Silas and Rowan, who stood behind her. Their bodies firm against hers. The additional contact allowed the bond to pulse stronger, intertwining them.

"Focus on us," Rowan murmured, as his lips brushed the top of her ear. "You're not alone."

The surging rhythm of the Otherwood pulsed under her feet, but she forced herself to focus on their touch and the moment she was living. The threat of the future would wait, even if just a few minutes. She reached out, letting her hand brush along Atlas' chest. His solid frame helped her stay present, even as the visions tugged at the back of her mind.

As her mark flared, she pressed back into Silas. The handprint on his fur from the Otherwood's touch was similar to the sigil on her arm, and their magic spoke to each other, allowing her to ride the wave rushing up on her. As if knowing what she needed, Atlas squeezed her hand, firm and protective. A breath hitched within her as a mixture of fear and exhilaration collided with something darker.

"It wants me," she whispered.

"Well, veilheart, we're not going to let it take you." Atlas pressed his lips to her head. "We've got you."

With his declaration, their connection sang in response, agreeing. The bond they'd formed wrapped around her like a warm blanket, welcoming and protective. Instead of fighting, she allowed herself to collapse into it, allowing their presence and combined magic to fill every cell within her.

The fissure pulsed seductive whispers and brushed along the edge of her consciousness. It was tantalizing, but with their touch, she resisted the call.

She wanted to explain to them the storm raging within her, but the words wouldn't come. Instead, she focused on what she did know. The Otherwood was patient. It would linger and wait, searching for her weakest moment before exerting itself. She also realized that holding the line as Atlas ordered would take more than just magic. It would take everything they had, especially trust, surrender, and the bond between them. Every aspect would be tested, and if one aspect wasn't perfect, they'd lose.

*This is only the beginning.*

# Chapter 3

## *The Hollowed Speak*

Days had passed since the fissure tore through the ley line, and Hollow Creek still crackled with unspent magic. The air hummed, and static electricity was felt even by those with no magical abilities. For Lena, it was like being in a plasma ball from her childhood. The glass sphere, with its colorful lights, stretches from the glowing center. Whenever she touched it, the filament seemed to follow her finger. Now, that same energy seemed to follow her wherever she moved.

Even the pack was restless. They patrolled the woods with urgency, their voices hushed, and every time the leaves rustled or a twig snapped, they turned, ready, expecting the worst. Everyone in Hollow Creek was on edge, waiting for the next move or the next attack.

Unwilling to sit by, she ignored Atlas' orders for her to stay at the house and followed Rowan out to check the perimeter. The forest seemed darker, more dangerous. Even at midday with the sun high overhead, sunrays barely peeked through the canopy of the trees. Another sign of the changes the Otherwood has created.

The pond just past the stone wall rippled without wind,

reminding her that the Otherwood wasn't dormant. It was waiting, patiently, for its opportunity. Waiting for her. She tried to ignore the allure that spot offered. It called to her on a level she wasn't sure she'd be able to deny for long.

As they made their way back to the house, and the pond came into view, she spotted something crouched near the water's edge. It waited still as stone, and from its reflection, it clearly wasn't human. As the figure lifted its head, the eyes were the first thing she noticed. Glowing with a fire she'd only seen in the Otherwood creatures.

"Stop," she hissed. The air around her sparked, waiting for her to call upon the magic within her.

The figure rose. Somewhat human, yet not completely, as if its body was crossed between human and wolf. Yet the creature moved with a predatory grace.

"You're one of them." Her voice was low, but as the creature looked at her, she was certain it had heard.

"We are the Hollowed," the figure said softly, voice melodic and chilling at the same time.

*Hollowed.* Stuck her like a knife to the chest. "Who are you? What do you want?"

"Peace." The figure stepped closer. "No division. Magic and life coexist as one. A place where death does not cage us, but also a place where the rift in your ley line can heal."

"Peace by merging our world with the Otherwood?" Rowan growled, low and warning. "It will destroy everything we know. Everything we built and protected over the years."

"Not destroy, evolve. The merge is inevitable. If you resist, it will only make things sweeter for us and worse for you." The figure tipped its head at Lena. "How many are you willing to sacrifice?"

Her heart hammered against her ribcage, yet there was a pull to its words. It was as if her magic recognized something within the figure's words, even as her mind resisted. Rowan's body next to her kept her grounded, even as her magic throbbed along her skin.

The figure raised a hand, commanding.

"Jacob." Atlas' voice cut through the clearing behind them. "I know it's you."

She turned to see him stepping out of the woods toward them. Rage rippled off him, and his muscles were tight, waiting for a fight. Jacob had been Atlas' father's second-in-command. Just as Rowan was Atlas'. Atlas' father trusted Jacob implicitly, to the point that he was like a second father to Atlas. This betrayal cut deeper than any claw or fang ever could.

"You swore loyalty to this pack!" Atlas hollered, his fists clenched. "How long—"

"Long enough to know that we need to stop following tradition. I'm here to guide evolution. One in which you can't stop." Jacob's lips ticked up into a faint smile.

Her sigil flared hot, and her magic sparked through her veins.

"Focus on me." Rowan pressed against her. "You're here, safe and sound."

Jacob's gaze locked on hers, and there was understanding in his eyes. "You're not the anchor they think you are. You're the key."

There it was again. *You're the key.* She wasn't certain what it meant to be the key, but she was sure it was nothing good.

Atlas rested his hand on her shoulder, pulling her back from her thoughts. "We'll fix this, but for now, it's time to go."

With her gaze locked on Jacob, she allowed Atlas and Rowan to lead her back to the house.

*I'll see you again soon. Soon, Lena, you'll know what the Otherwood can offer you.*

"I already know, and the answer is no," she hollered as Rowan squeezed her hand. *The answer will always be no.*

# Chapter 4

## *Breaking Point*

Night had fallen, but the unease still tightened her shoulders. Usually, sitting in front of the fire, with the guys all at the house, allowed her to breathe easy, but tonight she couldn't let go of the tension that coiled within her. Atlas was in the study with Tuck handling pack business, while Silas sat next to her, and Rowan stood near the fireplace. With every howl of the wind, every bump in the night, he seemed ready to tear the house to shreds.

"Do you think he's right?" Her voice was soft as she stared into the flames, unable to meet either of their gazes. "I mean, about me being the key?"

"It doesn't matter what he thinks." Silas brushed her hair out of her face. "What matters is we're here, and whatever happens, we're facing it together."

She leaned against him, allowing the warmth and the pulse to comfort her. But the doubt still lingered. *What if these visions aren't true? What if stopping the merge is wrong? What if merging with the Otherwood was something this world needed?*

As if realizing she needed it, Rowan stepped away from the fire and joined them on the sofa. The moment he took her hand in his, the relief was undeniable. The more they touched her, especially together, the stronger their bond was, allowing her to find peace from everything outside of it.

The Hollowed were out there, waiting, and stalked their every move, but in their embrace, her mind was clear. This fight wasn't just about boundaries or pack loyalty, the fate of their world hung in the balance. And she was at the center of it all.

"It's time," Atlas announced as he stepped out of the office with Tuck.

"I thought we were waiting until tomorrow night." Rowan stilled next to her as he glanced over at Atlas.

"We've got to stop the Otherwood from accessing our world, which means closing the fissure at the ley line. We can't afford to wait." He tipped his head to Tuck. "The information received from those on patrol means we need to act tonight. He's going to stay with Callie so we can handle this together."

"Let's go." Lena rose from the sofa and started for the door. There was no doubt in her mind that the guys would be right behind her.

The moment she stepped outside, she could smell the difference in the air, the slight ozone scent that reminded her of bleach, and the air sizzled with unspent magic. Even the darkness seemed suffocating. No stars were visible, and the fog seemed thicker, as if it were waiting to swallow the town.

"Lena, wait," Silas called as he stepped out of the house behind her. "We should put together a plan first."

"A plan?" She spun around to face him. "We just go and throw whatever we can at the ley line. There's no planning for it."

"Fine." He grabbed hold of her wrist and turned her back to look at him. "Then at least take a moment to breathe."

"I'm fine," she snapped.

"The ley line will respond to your fear as much as your control. You need to center yourself. Be the anchor that you are." As he spoke, Rowan and Atlas came up to stand on either side of her.

"We won't have another chance at this." Atlas placed his hand on her shoulder. "So, we need you focused."

Her body was alive with power. Raw, unpredictable energy surged through her veins seeking escape, but Atlas was right, she needed to center herself. Her magic and emotions were controlling her, not the other way around. She took a deep breath and then nodded. "Let's do this."

Silas and Atlas flanked her, each of them taking a hand, while Rowan stood close by, ready if anything emerged from the darkness. With the three of them there, the bond hummed between them as if it were a living being.

"Whatever happens, you need to trust that we're here, Lena. We'll pull you out if things get dangerous," Rowan reminded as they cleared the stone wall and stepped into the woods.

With every step toward the ley line, her power became harder to control. She could feel the fissure pulsing, this time stronger and sharper. A growl vibrated through the air from the crack in the ground.

Her fingers tingled with electricity, and she was worried her containment wouldn't hold, causing the energy to shoot from her fingers as it had before. She immediately pulled her hands away from Silas and Atlas, out of fear she'd hurt them. Silas let her hand drop, but Atlas held tight.

"Together," he whispered.

"Atlas—" His voice was firm but reassuring.

"By the blood of those bound in oath and the howl that bridges shadows, I call and claim the ley line." As he continued, Rowan and Silas joined in harmony with Atlas, each voice carrying power. "Bind this wound and seal this rift. Allows the worlds to remain divided until balance wills otherwise."

Thunder rolled in the distance. Atlas glanced toward her, his wolf eyes burned golden in his human face. "Join your power with ours."

She hesitated for a moment before nodding. With her hand in

his, she allowed her power to spring forward. The warmth of it against the cold night air made her want to step forward, chasing off the chill, threats, and danger in the darkness.

Silas and Rowan each touched her arm, strengthening their bond to the maximum. Atlas' fire, Rowan's calm steadiness that balanced him out, and there in the mix was Silas' quiet precision, all merged with her.

"One tether, three wolves. Magic to flesh, blood to bond, seal this wound."

Power shot out from her fingers, wild and hot. Electricity danced through every nerve ending until she felt as though her body was burning from the inside out. The sigil on her shoulder flared to a blinding white. The power coiled around them, tightening until it was hard to breathe.

Rowan's hand found her hip, anchoring her as the energy surged. "Breathe, Lena. Let the power move through you."

The ley line pulsed erratically, and the fissure groaned like stone cracking under pressure. Sparks licked at the edges of the fissure, shadow tendrils twisted upwards, as if reaching for something.

"By the oath of pack and bond we bind the hollowed and the Otherwo—"

Before Atlas could finish, the fissure exploded outward. A wave of raw power slammed into her, and her legs gave out from under her. If it weren't for the three of them, she'd have collapsed onto the dirt. Atlas let go of her hand and wrapped his arm around her waist, securing her against him.

Rowan stepped closer to her other side, his hand still on her arm. While Silas stood behind her, his hand on the nape of her neck. The three of them embraced her as her magic screamed, unrestrained.

"Ahh!"

"Lena," Atlas tipped her chin up to look at him. "Listen to me. You hold the line, not it. You, veilheart!"

"I can't..." her voice broke.

Remnants of the chant twisted through the air, mocking echoes of the words that moments ago held power. Shadows spit out from the ley line in violent bursts of darkness.

*This isn't right. It's too strong.*

"Lena," Silas pressed his fingers into her neck with just enough pressure that it grounded her. "Anchor it through us. Don't fight it. Use us."

"He's right." Atlas leaned down, pressing his forehead against hers as he cupped the back of her head. Their gazes locked, and the heat of their connection was like a weapon. A lifeline. "Use us."

She grabbed hold of the magical lifeline they were offering and, with everything in her, poured herself into it. The bond pulsed between them, supporting her, but she could feel the fissure reaching out and tasting their shared power. Suddenly, it synced with her, echoing her fears. It was responding not to the chants or the command, but to her heartbeat.

*How many times do you need to hear it before you believe it? You're not the anchor they think you are, you're the key.* The ley line shifted violently.

Shadows slithered from the ley line, and hallowed creatures emerged. The pull of the Otherwood was almost too much. The whispers from the fissure clawed at her thoughts, pressing her fears back at her and seducing her with promises of power, safety, and unity. Atlas, Rowan, and Silas fought against the pull, their combined strength barely kept her anchored.

"Lena!" Rowan's growl broke through her panic. "Focus on us! Don't let it drag you in."

Her chest burned, and her muscles were tight as a scream tore from her throat, echoing through the woods. She screamed again, but this time it was out of fury, and she poured every shred of herself into the tether, the bond, and the men holding her steady.

Her magic erupted outward in a blinding golden-white energy. She aimed it at the ley line, focusing everything she had into it. Atlas snarled as power flooded through him, and she felt Rowan stumble back, but never losing his grip on her. While Silas pressed his palms to her, amplifying her energy.

For a fleeting moment, the shadows froze, and the edges of the crack stabilized. Before the ley line reacted violently, sending a shockwave of energy out toward them. The wave sent all four of them to their knees. As the light dimmed, the fissure quieted but didn't heal. Jagged rays of black light shot out of it, as if mocking. It pulsed angrily and alive.

She stared at the burn marks, proof of their attempt and failure.

Atlas was the first to rise, his chest heaving, as he scanned the area before looking down at her. "We stopped nothing. We underestimated it, and it's stronger now."

"It's learning, and it wants her." Rowan's grip on her waist tightened, making it clear what he thought of that.

"It will be expecting our next move now," Atlas growled.

"It knows she's the key." Silas tucked a strand of her hair behind her ear. "I felt it."

"I failed..." she whispered.

"You did everything you could. We all did," Rowan assured her.

"I don't think..." She glanced up at Atlas. "It's about stopping it anymore. It wants me. Maybe..."

"Unacceptable." He reached down, took her hand, and pulled her up onto her feet in one quick move. With her standing in front of him, he wrapped his arms around her, pulling her tight against his chest. "You're ours."

Silas stood up and brushed his fingers along the curve of her cheek. "You're the anchor, but you're not the only one keeping the world together. We're all tethered, and we'll hold it."

"Together." Rowan joined them, wrapping his arm around her waist. "No matter what it throws at us, we'll hold it *together*."

Standing there, nestled between the three men who owned her heart, she wanted to believe everything was going to be okay. But the sinking dread remained. The Otherwood wasn't coming, it was already inside their world. Probing, waiting, and tonight exposing just how unprepared they were.

# Chapter 5

## *The Echo Path*

The mark on Lena's arm flared just as the sun kissed the horizon. It was insistent, pulsing with her heartbeat, and burned every time she closed her eyes.

"What is it?" Rowan stirred beside her, instantly alert.

"I can't explain it, but it's like it's pulling me somewhere." She lifted her shirt, revealing the sigil. "It's tugging me, urging me toward the woods. I need..."

"Then we follow it." Silas hopped out of bed and grabbed a pair of jeans, quickly slipping them on. "Come on, before it fades."

"What if it's a trap?" She eyed him as she sat up.

"Then we'll find out." Rowan squeezed her hand.

"Atlas left an hour ago to check on things. He'll feel us leaving the house, so I'll let him know what's going on." Silas pulled on a long-sleeve shirt and headed toward the door. "Five minutes."

"He's right, we need to follow it." Rowan ran his hand down her back before getting out of bed and dressing.

"Bad idea," she mumbled, but snatched a pair of jeans from the clean clothes basket she hadn't put away yet. "Should we wait for Atlas?"

"As alpha, he can feel us. He'll know where we are, and if he can join us, he will. If we're in danger, he'll be there. No doubts about that." Rowan slipped a sweatshirt over his head and stepped in front of her. "We can't wait for him. We need to go now."

"I know." She stepped into the jeans, quickly pulling them up and buttoning them. Before tugging off the oversized T-shirt she'd slept in and grabbing a sweater from the basket. "Let's do this."

He took her hand in his and led them out of the bedroom.

As they stepped out of the bedroom, Silas was standing in the living room, shoving his phone into his pocket. "Ready?"

"No," she smirked. "But let's do this anyway."

Silas nodded and led the way out of the house and through the garden, toward the stone wall.

Outside the forest was quiet. Not the peaceful quiet she'd hoped for when moving to Hollow Creek. Instead, every step seemed to cause subtle distortions. The light bent wrong, and the air was heavy.

The power within her surged, aligning with something unseen. Instead, she reached out and took Silas' hand, allowing her to touch both of them, centering her in the bond, instead of the Otherwood magic.

When they reached the grove, the world folded in on itself. The hollow ring of trees, impossibly symmetrical. But what unnerved her was the ley line that cut through the center, twisting through the earth like ribbons to form a perfect figure-eight. It pulsed in time with her heart.

As she took a step forward, the air shimmered and the sigil on her arm burned.

"Lena." Rowan's hand tightened on hers.

"I need to see it." Letting go of their hands, she stepped into the center. As she did, the ground rippled beneath her feet. Ancient magic rose to meet her. The ley line didn't resist her touch this time. It opened, inviting. As she reached forward, the light flared.

Two visions unfolded in her mind, overlapping until she was

barely able to contain them. Her body warmed as if overheating from the overload.

In one vision, Hollow Creek was on fire and lay in ruins. The sky was cracked and red, while wolves howled, and the Otherwood bled into town. Only shadows and darkness lingered in the streets.

In the second vision, there was no war, only stillness. Hollow Creek was transformed. Alive but still wrong. Wolves, neither flesh like pack, nor spirit like the Otherwood creatures, roamed the streets. The ley line glowed, not a soft white or golden, it always was, but violet, dark, unnatural. There was peace, but humanity was gone. There were still no boundaries between the worlds.

Tears filled her eyes, but the visions didn't vanish, they sank into her.

"What did you see?" Rowan asked as her knees wobbled.

"Two futures, but both wrong."

"Lena!" Callie jogged into the grove. "I could feel you from the house. You're resonating too strongly. Your magic is running on its own. You must control it."

As if answering, the ley line pulsed beneath her, reacting to her fear and magic. It liked the connection and wanted more.

"Step back," Silas urged. "Now!"

Her mark flared bright and golden. For a moment, it was comforting, but then it lashed out through the air. Realizing what was happening, she tried to sever the pull, but the ley line reached back. It wrapped her in warmth, offering her something she couldn't quite put into words, but it was enticing.

The wind shifted, and Rowan stiffened. He tipped his head back, sniffing the air. "We're not alone."

The scent of decay and smoke drifted toward them before the sound of footsteps on the forest floor, too light for a wolf and too heavy for the shadows. Before she could consider what it might be, four shapes emerged. They appeared to be wolves, with eyes like burning coals, but their bodies were larger, and fur rippled unnaturally. Their movements were jerky and unnatural. Instantly, she knew they were the Hollowed.

"They were waiting for us," she whispered.

One of the dark, shadowed figures lunged at them. Blocking its fangs, Rowan shifted mid-motion, slamming into the Hollowed, and the impact shook the ground. Another circled, focused on Silas. He drew his blade, the one he always carried, inscribed with runes and glowing a pale blue.

Three against four. She reached for her magic, and without hesitation, it was there. Pouring through her veins and burning to be used. Even the ley line beneath her feet thrummed alive and furious.

"We need to go!" Callie snapped.

One of the shadowed wolves caught Rowan's flank, dragging him down to the dirt. She panicked, and the ley line answered.

Light exploded out of the earth. It wasn't a spell, but an order. Her will spoke, and the ley line carried it out. The world shuddered, and shadows recoiled like smoke pulled away in the wind. Only their howls were left in their wake. Peace descended on the grove, and the ribbons of the ley line forming the figure-eight shimmered beneath her, pulsing in rhythm to her heartbeat.

"What did you just do?" Rowan stood, blood streaking his jaw, but he was unharmed.

"I don't know." She swallowed hard. "I didn't cast anything, I just told it what I needed, and it listened."

"You didn't channel the magic, you commanded it." The awe was apparent in Silas' voice.

"Then it's true." Reggie stepped out of the trees before she could respond. His usual calm demeanor was grim. "They're gathered. The Hollowed are preparing a ritual near Blackwater. It's big enough to shift the ley line itself."

"To force the merge?" she questioned.

"Or finish what is already started." Reggie nodded.

"Okay." She looked down at her hands, still glowing with ley line light. "Then they're not the only ones who have started changing."

*The bridge must choose which world to save.* The words carried to her on the wind, and from the way no one else reacted, she was certain no one else heard it.

# Chapter 6

## *Bloodline Secrets*

S tepping into the attic, Lena was hit with the smell of cedar and dust. Forgotten things cluttered the space, except for the right side, where all of Mira's decorations had been stored. Each tote is neatly labeled for its correct season or holiday. Decorating the house for each season had become something Lena looked forward to. But as she set the last box of Halloween decorations in its desired spot, she couldn't even think about the upcoming holidays. Would Hollow Creek still be standing? Would she?

Spinning back to the steps, she watched the light shine through the stained-glass window, reflecting off the rafters. One misaligned board caught her attention. Reaching up, her fingers brushed over a loose board, and as it shifted, something dropped down. Instantly, she reached out to catch it. A small, leather-bound book dropped into her hands. The cover was scorched, and the page edges were charred, but overall, it was still intact.

The handwriting inside was unmistakable. Mira's looping script was faded but recognizable. But the first line formed a ball of lead in her stomach.

*I invited the Otherwood.*

*I thought I could heal the boundary if I offered it a piece of myself. I believed love would bridge the divide, but I was wrong.*

Her fingers tightened on the fragile book before turning the page.

*I'm wondering if my grandmother was right. The guardian line was never meant to repel the Otherwood, but to guide it. With our guidance, we can shape what should never have been divided.*

*Lena, we're not the wall, we're the door.*

"No!" she mumbled to nothing but dust and cobwebs. The visions showed her what would occur if the worlds merged. She'd lose the ones she loves. "Unacceptable!"

Each page was more frantic. Mira's careful research and thoughtful entries of previous journals were now filled with desperation and doubt. She'd drawn diagrams of ley lines intersecting through Hollow Creek and marked runes she didn't recognize. One line echoed through her thoughts: *the veil is not failing, it's awakening.*

As Lena reached the end of the journal, a single folded note slipped out. She carefully unfolded it. The handwriting wasn't as loopy and carefree, but still Mira's. Slanted and rushed, the ink blurred in places where the pen had pressed too hard.

*To my heir, Lena,*

*If you're reading this, you already feel the pull, and the boundary has already begun to move again. I tried to heal it, to control it, to believe I could decide how it ended, but the merge doesn't bargain, Lena. It consumes.*

*I saw what it will demand of you. I've seen what happens when the bridge collapses, when magic consumes its anchor. It ends in your death. I refused to accept that.*

*So, I left this behind, hoping you'd find it in time to do what I couldn't.*

*Find another way. Survive what I couldn't. Don't let the door close with you inside.*

*Mira*

Her vision blurred, not from tears but pain as her sigil sizzled with heat.

A floorboard creaked behind her.

"Lena?"

She didn't turn toward him. Instead, she stared down at the note in her hand. "She knew. Mira knew what the merge would do to *me*."

"What are you talking about?" Rowan hollered as he came into view at the top of the steps.

"She thought she could control it, so she invited it in. I'm not a wall, I'm the door." When he neared, she handed him the journal. "She thought she could control it, and now it's in me."

Rowan opened it, turning to the first page.

Atlas' jaw tightened as he stepped up next to Rowan to read over his shoulder. The muscles in his forearm flexed. "If this is right, then the merge isn't a wound, it's destiny. If Mira says you're the door the Otherwood is trying to open, there's only one way to stop it."

"Don't," Rowan warned.

"If the Otherwood is using her to open the veil, there's only one way to stop it."

Rowan's eyes darkened as he turned toward Atlas. "Say that again."

"If she dies—"

Rowan moved before he could finish. His fist connected with Atlas' jaw in one sharp blow. The echoing crack reverberated through the attic. Atlas staggered back, blood at his lip, but there was no surprise in his gaze.

"Say it again. Say it like you don't hate yourself for even thinking it," Rowan growled.

"You think I want that? You think I haven't spent every night wondering how to stop this without losing her?"

"Enough!" Silas snapped as he climbed the steps.

"You think I haven't wondered the same?" She stared at Atlas. "I wake up every night feeling it trying to pull me apart. But if I'm the door, then I'll decide who walks through it. No one else."

"I don't want to lose you, Lena." Atlas stepped toward her, but Rowan blocked his path. "I'm alpha, I have to..."

"Sacrifice one for the greater good," she supplied without looking at him.

"If the cost of saving the pack is—"

"Stop it." Callie hollered as she climbed up the steps. "Mira's mistake wasn't in trying to stop it. No, she did that for us, for the pack. Her mistake was trying alone."

"What are you saying?" Silas asked from the bottom of the steps.

"You think this bond—the tether between you four and the sigil on her shoulder—exists to give the Otherwood something to target?" She shook her head. "It exists because it's stronger together. We're stronger together than she ever was. And I'm not going to let you die, Lena."

Silence descended over them. At least three of them were on her side. Atlas remained torn between his duty to the pack and her. In some ways, that terrified her, but in others, she could understand his position.

Lena bent down to pick up the journal that had fallen when

Rowan punched Atlas. Her fingers brushed along Mira's ink-stained truth one final time before slamming it shut. "We need to find out where the Hollowed are building their ritual and stop them."

"Blackwater clearing." Atlas met her gaze. "It's old ground. Unprotected. Basically, the perfect place to punch through."

"We end it." Rowan wiped blood from his knuckles.

"Or we learn how to turn it against them." Atlas nodded.

She glanced out the window at the moon hanging low over the forest. Somewhere beyond those trees, the Hollowed were waiting.

"Maybe I can be the key, but I won't be the door," she whispered to both herself and to Mira.

# Chapter 7

## *Hollowed Rising*

The forest surrounding Blackwater was unnaturally still. Even the wind was calm. Making Lena's heart beat faster as she crouched behind a thicket of frost-slick ferns. The cloak she'd found in the attic while they were cobbling together a disguise to blend in among the Hollowed smelled of mothballs and ash.

"You don't have to go in." Rowan adjusted the hood over her head, hiding her identity from anyone who got too close.

"I do." She nodded. "They're using my bloodline, and I need to know why."

"Just remember, we're ghosts," Silas whispered at her side, as his gaze scanned the area. "We get in, listen, and get out before anyone figures it out. We've got to be quick, otherwise they'll sense our bond."

*Or the ley line will sense me.* She could already feel the pull. The energy was already humming along her skin. The fissure they'd tried to stabilize had stretched all the way here, longer than they'd expected, and now hummed through the roots of the trees. The air was charged and reeked of a sweet rot.

"Let's move." She straightened and stepped out from behind the ferns.

They slipped from where they'd been hiding and merged into the slow procession winding through the trees. Dozens of figures stood near the half-buried stone altar, while candles burned, casting an eerie glow over the area. In the center of the altar, a figure raised its arms into the air.

Instantly, she recognized the person—Jacob. He'd once been pack. Family. Now he betrayed them all. Turning his back on kin and pack.

"The forest remembers every death, and every broken bond. We are the chosen, the forest's Hollowed. We're not destroyed, but remade." Jacob's voice carried through the crowd, eliciting cheers. "The merge is not the end, it's the return. Hollow Creek will be remade. A world without decay or division of flesh and spirit. The threshold walks among us. The door is flesh and blood."

"Lena! Lena! Lena!" The crowd changed, voices rising with every syllable.

The sigil beneath her shirt ignited, pulsing in answer to the chant. Within her mind, she could hear the seductive whisper. *Join us.*

"Stay with me," Rowan murmured, his hand squeezing hers.

The chant grew louder, as if the forest itself was echoing it.

On the altar at the center of the crowd, Jacob gestured toward two Hollowed shadows, and they dragged a wolf forward. The wolf struggled against the ropes, and the scent of blood filled the air.

"No," she whispered.

Jacob placed his palm on the wolf's side. Light flared, molten gold and black veins lacing through it. The wolf screamed, a mix between human, wolf, and something else. Bones cracked, reforming, as it twisted on the stone in agony.

She couldn't move, and even her chest felt tight as she tried to breathe. This wasn't faith, it was desecration.

Her mark burned white-hot, and the light seeped through the cloak she was wearing.

Jacob turned in her direction, and through the crowd, his gaze found her. A smile curled at the corner of his lips. "Ah, there you are, threshold."

"Run!" Rowan's grip tightened on her hand as he pulled her toward the forest and hopefully safety.

The clearing erupted in chaos. Shadows surged toward them. Half-formed wolves and twisted black shapes of bark and smoke lunged for her.

Silas tore off his cloak and shifted. His body rippled with fur and power. Rowan followed, but the ley line sparked, sending a bolt toward him.

Instinctively, she threw up her hand, and the ley line responded. The pulse of raw energy shot outward, knocking the Hollowed back like leaves in a storm. The force was so strong that even the trees bowed.

A familiar roar cut through the clearing. The pack of wolves burst into the clearing, coming to their rescue with Atlas leading the charge.

"This way!" Atlas shouted as he took down a Hollowed attacker before it could reach them.

"Stop them!" Jacob hollered. "The door cannot run from the house. Lena, this is your destiny. We're the house, you're the door."

Grateful to see him, Lena stumbled toward Atlas. His hand closed around hers. Solid, even amid chaos. Together, they ran until the chanting behind them faded. Rowan and Silas, still in wolf form, were right beside them. While the rest of the pack brought up the rear.

When they reached the ridge above Hollow Creek, Lena collapsed to her knees, gasping. The others fanned out around them, looking back at the forest as if waiting to see if they'd been followed. But only silence and darkness waited.

"They're more than a cult, they're an army." Tuck stood next to Atlas, his arm bleeding.

"Jacob knew me, Atlas." She rose from the ground and looked at him. "He called me the threshold."

"They might be right." He looked at her, but his expression was shadowed and unreadable.

"Don't start this again." Rowan turned toward Atlas.

"You saw what he did to that wolf, what they're willing to become." He didn't look away. "I love you, Lena. But I also have to do whatever I can to stop that. If that's the future they want, then I'll burn every ley line to stop it, even if that means—"

"Even if that means killing me?" Her voice was barely above a whisper.

The silence that settled over them was worse than any scream ever could be.

"I..." He closed his eyes and took a deep breath. "I don't want to, but if it's you or the pack—"

"Don't you dare!" Rowan growled, low and dangerous.

With magic coiled tight like a storm ready to unleash, she stepped toward him. "I can't be your enemy and your mate, Atlas. You have to choose."

"I'm alpha." He glanced at her as if that should explain it all. His gaze held a pain that she could feel. "I don't get to choose."

Her chest was tight as she stepped back from him. It was just a fraction, but in that moment, it felt like miles. The bond between them cracked with doubt.

Jacob's earlier words echoed through her mind. *The door cannot run from the house.*

As she stood there, overlooking Hollow Creek, she wasn't sure if she was running from the Hollowed or from what she was becoming. *Maybe I'm the problem and the solution. Maybe being both will allow me to end this.*

# Chapter 8

## *The Burden of Choice*

**B**ack at the house, there was a chill, not from the approaching winter but of something splintered and unseen. The bond was changing. Where the walls had once thrummed with shared energy, they now felt hollow, empty. Every silence stretched too long, and every glance carried blame or uncertainty.

Atlas had barely shared a dozen words with her. When he dared to speak to her, it was the alpha of the pack who spoke. Not the man who had claimed her heart. Any feelings they once shared were buried beneath the mantle of command.

Even Rowan's calm, steady presence had transformed. His temper flared at everything, even little things like the tea kettle whistling or the howl of the wind.

Silas was always nearby, as if shielding her from Atlas, but he'd gone quiet. His nose was always buried in a book, looking for an impossible answer.

She hadn't attended the last pack meeting, but Callie had stopped by to fill her in. The pack was split. Half of them were whispering that the merge might be destiny and that resisting it could make things worse. Others wanted to fight as they always had against the Otherwood. Yet others spoke of leaving Hollow Creek before the Otherwood swallowed it whole.

Every thought, word, and argument weighed heavily on her chest until she could hardly breathe. There was no easy answer, no right thing to do to save everyone.

Needing air, she stepped out onto the back porch. Her gaze lingered past the stone wall, to where she didn't doubt a creature from the Otherwood was staring back.

"You look like you haven't slept." Callie strolled toward her.

"I haven't," she admitted, as she dropped down onto the step. "I keep hearing the Hollowed in my dreams. Chanting. *Threshold, bridge, door.*"

"You think it's about you." Callie sank down next to her.

She let out a soft chuckle. "Isn't it? Mira invited the Otherwood, and now I carry the mark. I can feel it growing stronger. Am I not the reason this is happening?"

"Stop." Callie turned toward her. "You didn't start this, but you're trying to end it. That makes a difference."

"What if the only way to end it is for me to—"

"Don't." Callie snapped, cutting her off. "Don't finish that sentence. You think dying fixes everything? That's what Mira believed, and look where it got us. You're not her, and you're not alone. We're going to figure this out."

Tears sprang forth from Lena's eyes. She tried to blink them back, but they fell anyway.

Callie wrapped her arm around her, pulling her into a rough embrace. "You don't have to be strong every second, Lena. We're all here for you. Even my jerk of a brother."

"He has a funny way of showing it," she mumbled through tears.

"He's trying to shut you out because he's afraid of losing you." Callie let out a sigh. "We all are, but he's just not sure how to handle it. He's trying to find a way to protect the pack and the woman he loves."

Callie might believe that, but Lena didn't. Atlas had shut her out.

Even the bond could feel that, and it was impacting all of them. *It's what's allowing the sigil on me to grow powerful. It feels the weakness.*

The storm that had threatened the town throughout the day finally rolled in after midnight. The wind howled, and the pulse from the ley line hummed through her body. She lay in bed alone, and every time she closed her eyes, she could see Jacob.

*The door must open before it can close.* Words from Mira's journal circled within her mind.

She forced herself to close her eyes and take a calming breath.

Suddenly, she was standing in the woods. Her bare feet could feel the cold, damp earth under her, but she knew she was still in bed.

"Lena?" The voice came from within the fog.

Mira stepped out of the mist, just as Lena remembered her. The same wild, curly hair and a flowing dress that embraced the flower-child personality.

"Why didn't you tell me?" she questioned.

"Because you wouldn't have listened. You'd have thought I was mad. Just as I had with my mother, your grandmother." Mira gave her a soft smile. "You needed to find the truth on your own."

"Your journals say the boundary was to protect us, to protect the pack."

"Protection is only one side of the coin." Mira ran her hand down her dress. "The boundary was never a wall, Lena, it was a bridge."

"To where? Or to what?" She wasn't sure which was more important.

"My sweet Lena, bridges go both ways." Mira's smile turned sorrowful. "The question isn't can you cross, it's can you keep what crosses with you?"

She reached out for Mira, needing more answers, but her hand passed through the mist. "Mira!"

Bolting upright, she gasped. She was in her bedroom, the sheets tangled around her as if she'd been tossing and turning, and the sigil glowed faintly.

"Another dream?" Rowan asked, pushing the door open more to step into the bedroom.

"I'm fine," she snapped, then softened. "Mira was there. She said, the boundary is a bridge, and bridges work both ways."

"It's time." Silas stepped up behind Rowan. "We need to stop waiting for the Hollowed to make the next move. We can't keep walking around this house on eggshells. It's time we act."

"You're right." She leaned back against the pillows. "We can't keep reacting. We need to see what they're building. We need to understand their plan. Then we need to end it before it ends us...me."

"Then we go to them." Rowan crossed the room to stand near the bed. Silas followed in his wake.

"It's time we ended this on our terms."

# Chapter 9

## *Splintered Loyalties*

Traditionally, the full moon for the pack meant strength and unity. But as they gathered, it felt like it was the eye of the storm. Unlike previous meetings, every pack member was gathered around the bonfire. Some were sitting or standing, while others were in their wolf form. The air pulsed with magic and rage. Every eye seemed trained on her, glaring, making Lena regret attending. Unlike before, it didn't feel as if she was welcomed. She was an outsider looking in, regardless of her connection.

"The Hollowed are building something at Blackwater." Atlas stood near the bonfire. His voice was calm and steady, but the circles under his eyes revealed his exhaustion. "Intel says they mean to finish the merge before the winter solstice. If they succeed, none of this will survive as it is."

Even with the tension between them, Rowan stood to Atlas' right, his arms folded in what she considered the enforcer's stand. His gaze scanned the crowd as he picked up the same thing she did. The pack wasn't unified. Not tonight, and maybe never again.

Murmurs ripped through the crowd, and she could feel sides forming. The pack was splintering like glass.

"They said the merge will free us," Tomas, a younger wolf, called out. "If we accept this, we'll be free from death and this curse. Maybe we shouldn't fight it."

"You want to become one of them?" another snapped. "You think those shadow things are freedom?"

"They're not all monsters," a woman hollered. "My cousin joined them, and she said she can feel the forest breathing in her now. She has peace now. Something we don't have."

"Enough!" Atlas growled, cutting through the chatter like steel. "This pack stands on one truth, and that's we survive together. The Hollowed broke the second they turned on their own. We don't negotiate with those who want Hollow Creek consumed."

The silence was thick with hesitation. As she looked around the pack, she saw it in their eyes. Doubt and fear. They weren't in this together.

*Did I divide them?*

The bonfire flared, stealing her attention, and for a moment, she thought it was the ley line reacting. Then, a shape formed within the flames. Unmistakably human.

Jacob's projection flickered before them.

"Still pretending you can win, Atlas?" he asked. "I know you. I know everything your father taught you. You won't win."

"You don't belong here." Atlas' body was rigid as he stared at the figure within the flames.

"I do." The projection turned from the crowd. "The Hollowed offered freedom that the old ways couldn't. No more death, fighting, or fading magic. The forest wants to live through us."

"How?" someone asked, but she didn't turn to look.

Jacob's gaze landed on her. "The bridge is already built, we just have to cross it."

The sigil flared with heat, making her cringe. Still, she didn't react. She wouldn't let Jacob see it.

"Join willingly, and the merge will be gentle. Resist, and the forest takes this world." With that, Jacob vanished, and the flames returned to normal.

"He's lying!" Atlas hollered over the crowd. "Anyone who believes otherwise—"

"Enough, alpha," Calder interrupted as he stepped forward. "Threats won't hold this pack together."

"You'd rather we bend a knee to Jacob?" Atlas turned his attention to Calder. "He was one of us, and he's betrayed the oath we all took."

"I'd rather take time to think before we start calling our own traitors."

"This is bad," Silas whispered, stepping up next to her. "We're losing them. If the pack splits, we're finished. The ley line responds to unity, it breaks..."

He didn't have to finish. They both knew what would happen. If the pack broke, the Otherwood would devour Hollow Creek from the inside out.

The back and forth continued until she had to step away to clear her head. When she returned, the fire was nothing but ash, and Atlas stood near the edge of the clearing, head bowed. The alpha mask was cracked, revealing the man underneath, drowning beneath impossible choices.

"You think I went too far," he said quietly as she approached.

While it wasn't a question, there also wasn't a clear-cut response. "You called them traitors."

"They are." His gaze met hers, and the hardness was back. "You witnessed Jacob's spell and how it swayed them. If we don't draw a line, they'll tear the pack apart."

"Fear isn't loyalty."

"No," he admitted. "But it's all I have right now."

Before she could respond, Rowan hollered. "Atlas! Lena!" The urgency in his voice was sharp.

They turned and found Silas standing next to an open supply

crate. His expression was grim. "They're gone. The warding stones we prepared for the perimeter. Every single one of them is gone."

"Who had access?" Atlas demanded.

"Half the pack." Rowan ran a hand over his face. "Whoever did it knew what they were taking. They left this."

Silas hands Atlas the paper. *The boundary was a cage. You're too afraid to open the door.*

This theft felt like another stab in the stomach. It was getting difficult to deny that someone inside their home, their family, was already turning hollow.

The pack wasn't splintering, it was rotting from within.

# Chapter 10

## *Shadows in the Veins*

E very move the forest made mirrored her own. It was as if the branches kept time with her heartbeat. Whenever her heart raced, the wind picked up. When she was calm, so was the wind. Now with her chest heaving, her palms outstretched, the wind howled, and the ley line hummed through her live electricity.

"Focus," Silas reminded her. "You're letting it pull you again. Remember, you're in control, not it."

"I'm not," she snapped as the power flared.

With the rush of power, trees bent lower, bark creaking under invisible strain.

"Lena!" Silas' eyes widened.

She realized his panic too late. The tree groaned and toppled, directly above him.

"No!" The word tore from her throat, and she pulled all her will into a single wave of raw energy. The tree froze midfall, suspended only by her will, before she pushed it upright again. The last few remaining leaves fell to the ground in protest.

Silas stumbled clear, his eyes wide as he stared at her as if maybe he considered her now a threat.

"I didn't mean to." Her hands trembled as she stared down at the grass, now silver, drained of its natural color.

"I know." He let out a deep breath. "That's the problem. You should be able to control it by now."

"I..." She let her words fade off, uncertain what to say.

"I think you need to hear what Callie found." He tipped his head back to the house. "Come on."

"What do you mean, she found something? What is something?" she questioned, even as they headed back to the house.

"About anchors and magic. She'll be able to explain it better." He glanced back at her before stepping over the stone wall, leading to her garden. "Maybe it will explain things."

"Could it make things worse?" She let out a soft breath. "I shouldn't have said that."

"Probably not." Silas took her hand in his. "We'll get through it."

She wasn't so certain, but she followed him across the stone wall and into the house. Only to find Callie at the kitchen table, notes spread out over the wooden surface.

"How did it go?" she asked without looking up.

"As expected."

"Did you find something that will explain what's happening to me?" she questioned, without acknowledging Silas' comment.

"I found too much." She slid a yellowed page across the table toward her. "Mira called it anchor corruption."

She glanced down at the faded ink to find Mira's elegant handwriting.

*If an anchor draws too deeply from the Otherwood, she ceases to balance the threshold. The bridge decays. The anchor becomes the conduit, and through her, the forest will feed.*

"So, what if I lose control, I allow the Otherwood to come

through? To merge?" She looked up from the paper to focus her attention on Callie.

"You have to stop channeling the ley line."

"I can't." She shook her head. "If I stop, we lose any chance of fighting them."

"If you don't, you might not come back." Callie reached across the table and placed her hand on Lena's. "I can't lose you."

Like Atlas, Lena found herself in a position of impossible choices. If she didn't pull from the ley line, she couldn't fight the Hollowed. If she did, the pack may win the war, but she'd still lose herself.

Dusk had painted the garden a pale pink, casting shadows, when Calder came running from the southern ridge. His fur half-shifted, and his eyes were wild.

"They found Malric."

"Found him?" She raised an eyebrow in question.

"What's left of him."

"Let's go!" Atlas grabbed his coat from the hook and pulled open the door.

Atlas, Rowan, Silas, and Lena follow Calder out to the ridge to a spot where the forest opens into a small clearing.

Malric's body lay twisted among the roots, his chest torn open. Veins threaded through his wounds, pulsing with dark sap. Around his neck hung one of the missing warding stones, cracked and drained of light.

"He was carrying the stones." Rowan crouched next to Malric.

"Why?" Atlas' voice was rough.

"Here." Calder handed Silas a piece of paper. "I found it in his fist."

"I'm sorry, alpha. The merge will heal everything. No more pain and no dying. I did this for the pack. Not against you," Silas read.

"He betrayed us, and they killed him anyway." Atlas shook his head.

"Or they killed him because he was one of us." Rowan tipped his head, considering his words. "It's a possibility we haven't considered."

The ley line prickled inside of her, full of sorrow and fury, begging her to reach into it and claim some of the power for herself. Rather than giving in to the temptation, she focused on the issue at hand. "Either way, he still deserves a proper burial."

"I'll handle it." Calder glanced at Atlas, as if waiting for him to veto the idea.

"She's right. Thank you, Calder." Atlas nodded. "Silas, can you inform his family?"

"On it." Silas squeezed her hand before stepping away from the group.

"Everyone else, take this into account when considering your next move. No matter what you think about how I'm leading the pack, I don't want to see anyone else end up like Malric." Atlas glanced around at those who were there. "You're family. Be safe."

"Let's head back." Rowan wrapped his arm around her shoulders.

"Go on, I'll be along soon." Atlas didn't bother glancing at them. "I need to be here."

Even with the tension between them, she reached out, gently squeezing his forearm before stepping back. It was all the comfort she had to offer.

As she headed back to the house, Rowan's arm was still around her shoulder, offering comfort and protection. "He betrayed the pack, and still the Otherwood killed him. That's got to show the pack what it means to help them."

"It will make some hesitate, but others will see past it with the hopes of a safer future. We always think the grass is greener on the other side." He ran his finger along the curve of her shoulder. "We can't focus on that right now. Our attention needs to be on the war at hand."

"The one inside or outside the pack?" she questioned as they stepped over the stone wall leading to the house.

"Both, but right now the one outside is a bigger threat." His steps faltered.

"What?" she questioned as she glanced at the stoop.

A bundle wrapped in black vines sat on the steps. The scent of blood clung to it, taking her breath away.

"Stay back," he ordered as he stepped up to the bundle.

With a quick flick of his wrist, he snapped the vines holding it closed, and the fabric dropped away, revealing a severed wolf head. Eyes still open, unblinking, and vines threading through the fur like veins.

Then, she noticed the word stitched into the fabric. *The merge beings at the next blood moon.*

"Then we strike first," she mumbled.

"Before the moon turns red," Rowan agreed.

No more waiting. No more hiding. If the Otherwood wants war, then we will give them one.

# Chapter 11

## *The Blood Moon Offensive*

The blood moon hung high in the sky, the red light bleeding down onto Hollow Creek like an unfortunate omen. The air trembled as the Hollowed chant echoed low, causing the ground to pulse beneath her feet. Lena could feel the ley line current being pulled toward whatever Jacob had set into motion with his spell.

"Ready?" Silas asked, brushing his fingers along the back of her hand.

"Yes." She tried to put as much confidence in that word as possible, even as uncertainty fluttered within her. This was the moment she'd been preparing for since she arrived in town, and she was determined to win. If she lost, she was going down fighting.

"Everything must be perfect. The counter-ritual needs to invert the Hollowed's pattern, not block it. We must unbind, not seal." Callie came to stand next to Lena.

"Unbind." She knelt in the center of the circle they'd prepared earlier and brushed her fingers over the runes. The ley line stirred beneath her touch. "Like cutting the threads that tie both worlds."

"The ley line will pull through you. Every line they've corrupted will try to anchor to you," Callie said.

"You have to let it and then, when the time is right, release it," Silas reminded.

"If I can't?" She glanced up at him.

"Then the ley line keeps pulling until it burns you out," he admitted.

The words hung in the air like smoke, choking her.

"You've got this, Lena." Rowan placed his hand on her shoulder and squeezed gently.

"They're coming." Callie's voice was low as she stared off into the distance.

Lena couldn't see them yet, but she knew the Hollowed were coming, she could feel them.

"Hold the perimeter. Keep them off, Lena!" Atlas' order cut through the hum of the ley line as he headed toward the other wolves.

"It's time." Silas stepped to the edge of the circle.

Wolves surged into motion. Shadows clashed with fur, and the clearing exploded into violence.

Still kneeling, she closed her eyes and allowed her heartbeat to sync with the pulse of the ley line. She could feel Rowan and Silas flanking her, forming a triangle around the sigil she'd carved into the dirt before dusk. Callie crouched near the edge, chanting the counter-script under her breath.

Instantly, the mark on her skin flared, and fire ran through her veins. Her vision narrowed to the red light of the moon and the thump of her heartbeat.

"By reflection and root, by breath and blood, I unmake what binds." With the first words of the unbinding, the ground shuddered.

Magic tore through her like lightning, making her gasp. Her fingers dug into the soil as the ley line screamed through her palms. The visions from before flashed before her eyes again.

"Lena!" Silas' voice cut through the storm within her. "Stay with me. You're pulling too much."

"I can handle it!" she shouted.

The ground split open beneath the sigil, allowing light to pour out.

"It's working, but she's the conduit. She's the bridge!" Callie hollered over the wind that had picked up.

The ley line surged, desperate and full of wild, untamed energy. With it, the bond to her mates flared, and she could feel them. Atlas fighting alongside the pack, smeared in blood: his own and his enemies. Rowan's protection and Silas' own magic on either side of her. That tether kept her steady. It kept her human.

"You're not alone in this." Without touching her, Rowan leaned in close, his breath brushing along her ear. "Take what you need. Use Silas and me."

She understood why he left out Atlas. The last of her mates was leading the pack, fighting to keep the Hollowed back. Siphoning off of him would weaken him when he needed it the most.

She let the bond between them flow, and energy rushed through her like heat from an oven. Instead of fighting it, she allowed it to take her breath away. This wasn't just magic, it was them. Every beat of love, fear, and need anchored her to the world she was fighting for.

"Unbind the living root." She screamed the final word of the counter-ritual, and the clearing exploded with light.

The Hollowed chants faltered as the ground fractured beneath their feet. The mirror-world shimmered. Hollow Creek and the Otherwood flickered like twin flames in the same body.

The woods glowed, not with fire, but with magic. The air rippled with the hum of power, stretching as if the earth were splitting in two.

The counter ritual she'd unleashed was unraveling the ley line's surface, waking the forest in ways she never expected. It shouldn't be happening like this, but whatever the Otherwood was doing was changing the outcome.

"Protect Lena, whatever's coming—" Atlas's words were cut off.

A scream tore through the clearing. Whether it was human or

wolf, it was unlike anything she'd ever heard before. Even the shadow shuddered and drifted away, fearful.

From within the trees, a creature that never should have existed crawled forward. Limbs too long, and the skin shimmered under the moonlight. Its eyes burned a bright violet. A Hollow-Wight, but this one was different from the previous one she encountered.

"Do you see now?" Jacob's voice drifted toward her, but she couldn't see him. "The merge offers us no boundaries, no death, just perfect unity."

The Hollow-Wight turned toward her, and the gravitational pull was undeniable. The sigil on her shoulder seared as if she were being branded. The Hollow-Wight knew her, and it wanted her.

*It's made of us, an anchor soul twisted into eternal servitude.*

She wasn't sure how she knew it, but it was undeniable.

Her magic surged, and the ley line beneath her feet responded. "It's drawn to me."

The creature lunged.

One moment, Rowan was at her side, the next, he was between her and the Hollow-Wight. His body glowed faintly as his wolf emerged, blurring fur with shadow, as he bit down on the creature.

The Hollow-Wight howled, light spilling from the wound like smoke. Striking back, its claws raked Rowan's chest, and Lena felt it too. The tether between them flared hot before dimming as if the creature was sucking it dry. Rowan's strength wavered.

"Go," Rowan rasped.

She couldn't. A scream erupted from within her that didn't feel human. It cracked through the clearing, shattering the Hollowed chants. Power erupted from her palms as the ley line answered her call.

Trees bowed and roots wrenched from the soil as light the color of sunrise shot from her hands. The Hollow-Wight turned toward her a second before it was gone. Obliterated in a surge of unfiltered magic.

With the creature gone, Rowan's body dropped to the ground.

He lay motionless, but she could see his chest rising and falling. He was alive.

"Go to him!" she ordered Silas.

Trembling, she sank to her knees as magic still crackled in the air. The magic was wild and bent to the light around her. The ley line thrummed through her veins, still feeding her the power.

"What did you do?" Atlas stared at her with wide eyes.

"What I had to. I saved him."

"Look at you." His voice was softer.

She glanced down at her arms. The light hadn't faded as it had in the past. This time, it spread and grew brighter than before. Threads of energy pulsed out from her, shooting up toward the horizon, like veins from within her. The boundary that separated their worlds was no longer holding.

"She didn't stop it." Silas glanced over at them from where he was still kneeling next to Rowan.

"No, she made it worse." Atlas stared down at her. His eyes were dark and unreadable.

The ley line pulsed, but instead of it being under her, it felt like it was within her, and she realized the truth.

*We're not stopping the merge, we're accelerating it.*

# Chapter 12

## *The Hollowed War*

The world around them was breaking. It began as a tremor beneath the ground, but as the light shifted, she saw it. The ley line wasn't flowing through the forest, but upward.

*The current is reversed.*

Magic surged in impossible ways, sending dust and leaves spiraling in ribbons. The forest around them groaned, as if pulled in a direction it didn't want. In the sky above hung a second moon. It was a perfect white reflection of the first, but haunting and wrong. The heart of the Otherwood was bleeding through the veil.

"It's begun," Atlas mumbled as he stared upward.

In the distance, the Hollowed chants echoed, voices rising with determination. The earth pulsed with every word, and the moon grew brighter.

The sigil burned brightly from underneath Lena's shirt. She could feel the ley line pulling at her, beckoning her toward the heart.

"I can stop it," she whispered. "The flow's unstable. If I fuse with it—"

"What does that mean?" Atlas asked.

"If I become the seal, it will close before it fully breaches."

"No." Rowan staggered toward her. "Absolutely not."

She wanted to reach out to him, to cup his cheek, to make certain he was unscathed, but he wasn't close enough. She needed to stay where she was if she was going to perform the ritual. The circle would be the only protection she had against what the Otherwood would throw at her.

"It's the only way." She focused her attention on him. "The ley line needs a living anchor. It always has. Mira tried and failed because she didn't belong to both worlds. I do."

"Lena." Atlas grabbed her shoulder, drawing her attention. "You're not offering yourself to that thing. It will burn you out. You'll die."

"Maybe." With unshed tears in her eyes, she stared up at him, their gazes locking. "But if I don't, everything dies."

Silas stepped forward. "Then I'll go with you."

"No." She turned toward him.

"I can anchor it, too. I belong to both worlds." He reached down and took her hand in his. "We can bind it together and share the weight."

"You could die. All of you could." Her voice broke. "I can't lose you, any of you. That's not what this is."

"You think we're going to stand here and watch you sacrifice yourself?" Atlas shook his head, his fingers tightening on her shoulders.

"Not happening." Rowan stepped into the circle next to her and placed his hand on her other shoulder. "We've said it before, we're in this together."

Before she could respond, the ground split again, and a fissure raced through the clearing like a bolt of lightning. The Hollowed chants that had been going on since the start grew louder, and the second moon turned blood-red.

It was now or never because the merge was seconds away. If she didn't become the living anchor, sending the Otherwood back to where it came from, she'd lose everything anyway.

Her power surged out of control as the ley line reached for her. She coughed, choking on the pull, but they reached for her, each of them finding bare skin, grounding her. As they did, their bond flung open. The rush of their power warmed the cold magic of the ley line.

"You're not alone. You'll never be alone," Rowan whispered through the bond.

"Take what you need," Silas added.

"But don't you dare leave us," Atlas commanded. The authority was clear in his voice.

Without directing, their power surged into her. Not merging, but lending. Her energy burned brighter, coursing through her veins without consuming her. With them, she wasn't fighting the ley line. She was guiding it.

She rose to her feet, her hands raised out in front of her, and the clearing exploded with light.

The Hollowed's chant stopped, and Jacob screamed. The second moon cracked like glass, sending shards raining down on the Hollowed.

Ley line energy tore a cry from her lips as the seal formed.

The Otherwood creatures and shadows were thrown back, and the vines disintegrated into ash.

"You can't undo what's already begun!" Jacob shrieked.

"You're wrong," she whispered.

Light collapsed inward as howls echoed through the darkness. Her body arched, caught in the magical current. Somewhere in the distance, she could hear Rowan's voice shouting something, but she couldn't make it out. All she could hear was the forest and the Otherwood.

*You were meant to open the way!*

"I choose the way it opens." She pushed the magic outward.

As if to answer her, the ley line recoiled. The air imploded, sucking the light inward. She was unmaking the merge the Otherwood had tried to create, but it also tore through the ley line, unraveling every anchor they'd bound. So, she could become the living anchor. She could feel it trying to pull her down, into the core.

"Lena! Hold on!" Atlas' voice cut through the static of the collapsing magic.

The power was so warm and welcoming. It recognized her, making it difficult to break.

She reached back out for the bond with Atlas, Rowan, and Silas, and it flared, raw and alive. Three bright cords of magic reached out to her, refusing to let go.

"Come back to us." Rowan wrapped his arms around her. "You're ours."

The ley line screamed within her mind, and everything went white.

*Don't let this be the end.*

# Chapter 13

## *Threads of the New World*

Sitting on the porch steps, Lena pressed her palms against the cold stone. The ley line hummed, no longer violent, steady, and alive. While the rest of the world seemed too quiet.

They'd won the fight, but the war wasn't over. Even this small win didn't feel like much of a victory. They'd pushed back the Otherwood, but at the cost of many pack members, people she'd come to care about. Perhaps the one that hurt the most was the loss of Calder. He'd once been an adversary, but when it counted the most, he'd stood with Atlas and the pack and fought. Now he was one of the ones presumed dead.

Then there was Rowan. He was alive but changed. Out of the corner of her gaze, she could see him slumped in the porch chair. His skin was pale, and one arm was in a sling. When he had stepped between her and the Hollow-Wight, the ley line had nearly burned through him. He was now touched by something beyond the pack. Not quite Otherwood, but a deeper, darker magic.

Atlas and Silas stood nearby. Both stood tense and ready as if they still couldn't let their guards down.

"It's over," Silas said quietly, his voice raw.

Closing her eyes, she took in what she was feeling. The ley line was not just quiet, it was balanced. "Not over, but held."

"We'll hold it with you." Atlas kissed the top of her head. "I knew you could do it, veilheart."

"Always," Rowan mumbled.

"We should go inside." Atlas took her hand in his.

"Go—" She shook her head, stopping herself. She wasn't ready to go inside, but she knew they wouldn't go without her. Instead, she nodded and allowed him to gently pull her up onto her feet.

"I'm fine." Standing, Rowan snapped at Silas, who was standing there as if he expected to be needed.

"Such a great patient," she teased as she let go of Atlas' hand and went to him. She needed to feel him to be certain he wasn't a figment of her imagination.

"Now you can help anytime." He draped his good arm around her shoulders, drawing her close. "I'm fine, darling."

"Darling..." she whispered, more to herself than anyone else. "I like the way you say it. A little southern twang in there."

"Let's go, you two," Silas ordered. "You both need some rest."

Atlas held open the screen door for them, a smirk curling up the corner of his lips. "I'll make it an order if I have to."

"That will only work for one of us." She raised an eyebrow at him, daring him to try, as they walked inside.

The moment she glanced around the living area, she remembered why she'd stayed outside. The living room was crowded with those waiting for any word on the missing.

In the corner, Reggie was stretched out on the recliner, his breathing slow but even. His tether to this world was thin yet unbroken. Faint veins of light pulsed along his skin, proof that the Otherwood and the ley line had claimed part of him, too.

"Lena..." Callie's eyes were wide as she stared at her.

She glanced down, following where Callie's gaze seemed to be locked.

The sigil on her shoulder had changed. It branched outward as if roots and limbs entwined in a living pattern that pulsed with rhythm. Gold shimmered through the lines, treading with veins of green and silver.

"It's a tree." Silas stepped around to get a better view. "Roots below with branches above. The symbol of the threshold."

"The merge didn't die, did it?" It was a question she didn't want to ask, but one that carried an answer she needed to hear from someone else.

"No." Callie rose from the sofa and came to stand near them. "It's adapted. The boundary is different now. It's not sealed, it's...I don't know how to describe it."

"It's breathing," Rowan supplied. "I can feel it. Magic is still bleeding through."

"So..." She let her words trail off before swallowing. "We didn't stop it, we only changed it."

"Change always carries a cost." Atlas let out a sigh.

The words echoed in her mind as she reached out for the back of the sofa, her legs suddenly weak. For a heartbeat, the air shimmered, and then she saw Mira standing at the edge of the room.

*You did what I couldn't. You made the veil live again. But it will ask something new of you now. The veil has changed, Lena. You must change, too.*

In the blink of an eye, Mira was gone.

"Lena?" Atlas' voice held an urgency she hadn't heard before.

"I'm fine." She leaned into his body, letting the comfort flow from their bond.

"What did you see?" Rowan slid his hand down her arm.

"Mira..." She reached out and took his hand into hers and looked back at Silas, who seemed to understand she wanted him there, too. He came up behind her and placed his hand on her shoulder, his thumb gently brushing against the side of her neck. "She said the veil will ask something new of me now that I've changed it, and because of that, I must be ready to change too."

"We'll be ready," Atlas assured her. "Everything is changing. The town, the pack, and even us. We'll be stronger for it."

It wasn't until night fell over Hollow Creek that Lena realized how true Atlas' earlier words were. Everything was changing. It especially seemed true about the town.

It wasn't long after dusk that the calls and reports from patrol teams rolled in. Ghost lights weaving through the pines. Shadows in mirrors. Reflections in windows when there was no one else around. Echoes in the halls and whispers just behind a person.

Hollow Creek was no longer a border town. It was a place where the two worlds touched. Now they had to learn to coexist.

With a few key members still gathered around the house, Atlas stood near the fireplace with her at his side, while Rowan sat nearby on the couch. Silas tossed another log onto the fire.

"For generations, the guardians protected a line...a wall that kept one word from devouring the other." He paused, and she could see the weight of leadership hung heavy on his shoulders. "The wall is gone now, and what's left is new. The veil moves and breathes. It shifts through us, this land, and Lena. We can't hold it back anymore, but we can guide it."

"So, what does that make us?" Rowan adjusted in the chair, his gaze on them.

"Guardians of a threshold that now moves and breathes." He glanced at each of them before turning back to Rowan. "The old world ended with the merge. Ours begins now."

# Chapter 14

## *The Last Howl*

With others in the house, the only place besides her bedroom that had held any privacy was the attic. But as Lena stood there with Atlas, Rowan, and Silas, she wished she could be anywhere else. This was the place she found Mira's journals, the ones that held all the secrets her aunt never told her. Her heritage and duty. It was where Mira had left her warnings.

*Where I truly learned what my bloodline carried.*

Atlas leaned against the pillar as he stared out the window. "We should discuss what comes next."

It was the reason they were gathered in the attic, away from the others, but the topic still hit harder than she expected.

"You mean if we can keep the pack together?" Rowan dropped into the rocker.

"If the pack can survive at all," Atlas admitted, his jaw tight. "The world's shifting under our feet. We've already got wolves leaving Hollow Creek. Some for cities, others to follow what's left of the Hollowed. We're not sure what happened to Calder or a few others. The ley line..." His gaze found her. "Answers to you now, not to us."

"What's that supposed to mean?" She crossed her arms over her chest as annoyance flared within her.

"I see what it's doing. The way the ley line spikes when you walk by it and how the wind moves around you. The pack feels it. They're loyal, but they're also afraid."

"They should be." Rowan nodded.

"Fear doesn't mean faith is gone. It means they still understand how much it costs to stand near the fire." Silas reminded them before glancing toward her. "I'd follow you into it anyway. Even if it burns everything down."

She wanted to tell him no, that she wasn't worth following into another inferno, but the truth was she believed they were already inside the fire.

"I can feel it inside me now." Her words came out lower than she had expected. "The Otherwood. It's not separate anymore. It's in me, in my blood and in my dreams. I can even hear it. Sometimes it sounds like Mira, but other times it's someone else, and occasionally it's my voice."

"What does it say?" Rowan leaned forward on the rocker.

"That this isn't ending." She let out a soft breath. "Something new is happening in the cracks we left behind, and it's changing me. I...I don't know how long I'll still be—"

"Don't," Atlas growled. "Don't finish that sentence."

"He's right, words give it power." Rowan nodded.

"We've already watched the world break once. You rebuilt it with your hands, so if it's changing again, we'll change with it." Silas put his hand on her shoulder, gently squeezing.

"You sound damn certain." Atlas glanced at him.

"I am." Silas nodded. "She's the ley line's heart. Veilheart, as you call her. We're its echo."

"Then we make it official." Rowan stood, glancing at each of them before letting his gaze settle on hers. "A pack. Not of blood or magic, but of choice."

She looked at them, her bonded mates, her anchors. They were both her undoing and her salvation. Atlas was protective and a pain in her butt. He had trouble balancing his duty to his pack and his commitment to her, but there was never any doubt in her mind that when it mattered, he'd be at her side. Rowan had always been the protector. It was clear to see why he was Atlas' right-hand man. Not only was he an excellent enforcer, but he also had a way with words that could bring any situation down two levels. Lastly, there was Silas. Sweet, steadfast, and a healer in numerous ways. He was the calming nature to their bond.

"He's right." Atlas nodded before she could speak. "No more walls, no more running."

"We aren't just a pack, or a bond, or whatever the ley line made us. We're woven together through love. Whatever comes, we face it as one."

"Together," they said together.

As they did, the air trembled, and the sigil on her shoulder flared, joining them.

Outside, the wind howled. It was the kind of wind that carried whispers not meant for this world.

"Do you hear that?" Atlas stepped toward the wind as she nodded.

It wasn't just the wind that she heard, but voices. The sounds of the Otherwood breathing through the cracks of reality, through the town, and through her.

The boundary wasn't a wall anymore, it wasn't even a line. It was a living, fluid thing. Eternal. And it was waiting. Not for fear or surrender, but for guidance.

A new world.

In the distance, the faint sound of a wolf's call rose from the woods. Fierce and full of promise. Seconds later, another joined. Then another. Until it sounded like the whole town was howling.

"Our wolves," Atlas glanced back at her.

As she stood there listening to the wolves howl, she wasn't just Lena, she was the last of the guardian line and the first of the threshold keepers. The start of something new in a new world.

# Preview: Christmas with a Bear
## Timber Ridge #1

One rental cabin and an angry shifter create a Christmas that changes everything.

Maddie Garrett's life fell apart right before the holidays. Now, without a job, boyfriend, or even a plan. A cabin in Timber Ridge seems like the perfect escape, until a furious owner shows up at her door, demanding she leave.

Nico Matthews doesn't want a tenant. Especially not a beautiful human woman that his bear insists is their mate. He's got enough to handle as a widowed single father and alpha of his clan. But his six-year-old daughter has other ideas.

When Maddie discovers the truth about shifters, she has a choice to make: run back to her safe, ordinary life, or stay for something extraordinary.

A heartwarming paranormal romance about second chances, found family, and choosing the impossible over the safe.

# Chapter One

## Silent Pines

At the end of a long winding driveway, surrounded by towering pines heavy with snow, sat a small, rustic cabin. It was isolated and precisely what Maddie Garrett needed. When a friend of a friend presented the opportunity to rent the cabin for a few weeks, she didn't waste a moment, just threw clothes into a suitcase, grabbed her laptop, and left with her last shred of dignity. A six-hour drive north into the mountains seemed like the perfect way to spend the holidays. No more pitying looks, no more passing the office building that had been her life for the last six years, and best yet, she didn't have to return to the apartment she'd shared with Derek.

*Merry Christmas to me.*

Visible through the trees about a hundred yards up the hill was a large house, more of a lodge than a private home. Lucia had mentioned something about the main house, but explained that the property owner was hardly ever around. It didn't matter to Maddie as long as she got out of the city. She wasn't there to make friends. She needed to figure out what she was supposed to do with her life now.

Maddie climbed onto the porch, carrying the few groceries she had purchased from the last big town and her suitcase. She grabbed the key under the mat and quickly unlocked the door before toeing off her soaked, snow-covered sneakers. The chill of the cabin hit her as her phone vibrated in her pocket. She set the groceries on the counter and pulled out her cell phone. Derek's name flashed on the screen.

> You can't just disappear like this, Maddie.
>
> We need to talk.
>
> Maddie, come on. This is ridiculous.
>
> I know you're upset, but ignoring me won't fix anything.

Message after message flooded her phone. "Why couldn't there be no service?" she muttered. She silenced the phone and tossed it onto the table. The whole point of this trip was to ignore her problems, not have them texting every five minutes.

The kitchen opened into the cozy living room, where a sectional sofa dominated the space in front of the fireplace, and the large glass windows offered a magnificent view of the Christmas tree farm that bordered the property. Yet what she noticed was the quietness. The silence was startling. No traffic or sirens that seemed to echo through the city round the clock. No neighbors arguing through the thin walls.

"This is what I need."

She glanced around the kitchen. The kitchen was updated and modern, though the cabin was rustic. Spotting the kettle on the gas range, she filled it up with water. Unpacking and exploring the rest of the cabin could wait until she had tea. With the kettle on the stove, she turned to the market bags and quickly put them away. The market was surprisingly well stocked, and she was able to pick up everything she needed. Allowing her to relax and enjoy her time away from civilization.

Pulling out the bakery box of fresh gingerbread cookies, she noticed the top one was cracked. Right in the middle of his chest, it was broken in two. "Just like me," she mumbled as she reached into the box. "How had I not seen this coming? At Christmas..."

The kettle whistled, startling her, and the gingerbread man fell to the counter, crumbling further. "Great." She pulled the kettle off and poured the water into the waiting mug before dropping a tea bag in.

"The cookie is just like my life, shattered." With her tea steeping, she gathered up the cookie crumbs and dropped them into the trash can.

A heavy knock rattled the cabin door.

Maddie jumped. She wasn't expecting anyone. She didn't even know anyone within a hundred miles, at least. A knock came again, hard this time, and impatient.

Brushing off her hands, she crossed over to the door. Rising onto her toes, she peered through the small window. A man stood on the porch. Tall, broad-shouldered, with dark hair that was dusted with snow. Dressed in a heavy work coat and boots, he had an expression that caught her attention. She could only describe it as thunderous and certainly unwelcoming.

She cracked open the door. "Can I help you?"

"What are you doing here?" His voice was rough, deep, and unfriendly.

"Excuse me?" She raised an eyebrow at him.

"What are you doing in this cabin?"

"I..." she bristled. "I rented it. Not that it's your business."

"From whom?" His jaw tightened.

"Lucia." She met his gaze. "I don't know what your problem is, but—"

"Lucia. Of course she did." He shook his head as he pulled his phone out of the pocket of his coat, jabbed at the screen, and pressed it to his ear.

She could hear the ringing, and ringing, but no answer.

The man stood there on her porch and lowered the phone from his ear, scowling. His gaze fixed on her. His eyes burned an unusual amber, almost gold, as tension carved sharp lines along his jaw.

"I'm Nico Matthews. I own this property. The main house on the hill, this cabin, and all the land you can see. My sister had no right... no right to rent this place out."

"I paid..." Maddie's stomach sank. "I paid her for the month upfront in cash."

"Figured." He dragged his hand through his hair, snow falling from the dark strands. "This is unbelievable. She knew..." Trailing off, he looked at her. "Look, Miss...?"

"Maddie Garrett."

"Miss Garrett, I don't know what my sister told you, but you can't stay here."

"Excuse me?" After a long, exhausting day of driving, her patience was thin. "I have a rental agreement, and I've already paid for a month stay. I'm not going anywhere."

"It's not safe."

She glanced around the porch, looking for anything that would make the place unsafe, because she had found nothing concerning inside yet. "Cabin looks fine to me."

"That's not what I meant." He stopped, brows furrowed. "There are things happening on this property. Especially in the winter. Potential dangers. I can't have a stranger—"

"Then your sister should have considered that. Take it up with her." She stepped back and started to close the door. "I'll be out of your hair in a few weeks. Until then, I'm staying."

He held up a hand, stopping the door before she could close it. "Miss Garrett—"

"Goodnight, Mr. Matthews."

For a long moment, they stared at each other. His eyes seemed to glow in the darkness, and her chest had a strange flutter, though she wasn't sure if it was from fear or something else.

"Lock your doors and don't go wandering around the property after dark," he warned, stepping back. "If you see or hear anything unusual, you come straight to the main house. Understood?"

"What do you mean by unusual?"

Without answering, he turned and walked away, his broad form disappearing into the snowy darkness. With her heart pounding against her ribcage, she closed the door and locked it.

"What have I gotten myself into?"

She stepped away from the door and grabbed her phone from the counter with the intent to call Lucia and demand an explanation. Before she could dial, she noticed three new messages from Derek.

> Your mom is worried about you.
>
> Tell me where you are!
>
> Maddie, please.

"Forget it." She powered off the phone and put it down on the table again.

Instead, she grabbed her tea and headed to the living room to start a fire. Tomorrow she'd call Lucia. For tonight, she was going to pretend the angry, golden-eyed man and cryptic warnings didn't exist. She was going to enjoy her mug of tea, a fire, and try to remember what peace felt like. Even if it only lasted until morning.

# Preview: Carved in Timber Ridge

## Timber Ridge #2

**She came home searching for answers. She found her destiny instead.**

Aleece Reeves never quite belonged anywhere, not in the shifter town that raised her, and not in the human world where she went to college. As the adopted human daughter of Timber Ridge's mayor, she's spent her whole life caught between two worlds. Now, graduated from college, she's back home for good, and more lost than ever.

When bear shifter Charles Monroe shows up to fix her father's burst pipes on a freezing January morning, the instant connection between them takes her breath away. Charles is everything she didn't know she needed: patient, kind, and building his dream home with his own two hands. Working alongside him on his renovation project, she finally feels like she's found where she belongs.

Just as Aleece begins to imagine a future in Timber Ridge and with Charles, her biological father appears, bringing devastating truths about her past. Now she must choose between life in the city and the terrifying possibility of loving a bear shifter who could break her heart.

Sometimes the bravest choice isn't running away, it's standing still and building something that lasts.

# Chapter One

## Coming Home

The town limit sign appeared through the light snow flurries like an old friend waving hello. Aleece eased off the gas pedal, slowing as she took in the familiar sight. *Home.*

The word should have brought comfort, but instead, her stomach twisted with an uncomfortable mix of relief and dread. She'd been making this drive every weekend for four years and knew every curve of the mountain road, but this time was different. This time, she was finally moving back home. It had been four long years, but this time, as she drove into town, she was a returning resident, not a visitor.

The thought made her grip the steering wheel tighter as she navigated down Main Street. Timber Ridge looked picture-perfect in the winter afternoon light. It was the kind of small mountain town that belonged on a postcard. Storefronts lined both sides of the street, their awnings dusted with fresh snow. Warm lights glowed from the shop windows already decorated for Valentine's Day, though it was only mid-January. Mrs. Appleton was hanging a new sign at the diner. Ricky was shoveling the sidewalk in front of his dad's hardware store, his breath forming clouds in the cold air.

He looked up as she passed, raising his shovel in greeting. She waved back automatically, her chest tightening. Everyone knew her here. They'd watched her grow up, asked about college every time she came home for the weekend. They'd all be asking about her plans now, about what came next. The problem was, she didn't have an answer.

Aleece turned into the residential area where she'd grown up. The houses were older, well-maintained, with large yards and that established feel that came from generations of families putting down roots. She'd always loved the neighborhood. The way the neighbors actually talked to each other, kids still played outside even in the winter, and the way everyone looked out for each other. But lately, she'd started to wonder if that closeness was comforting or suffocating.

Her father's house came into view. A two-story craftsman with a wide front porch and a porch swing where she'd spent countless summer evenings. The sight of it made her throat tight. Her father, Mayor Thomas Reeves, had already shoveled the driveway and scattered salt on the walkway. The light by the door was on even though the sun wasn't down, a beacon welcoming her home.

She pulled into the driveway and shut off the engine, sitting for a moment in the sudden silence. Through the front window, she could see movement. Dad was likely watching for her and probably had been for the past hour, knowing him.

The front door opened before she could even grab her purse. Dad stepped onto the porch, and the smile on his face made her eyes sting with unexpected tears. He was a big man with broad shoulders and kind eyes that crinkled at the corners. His dark hair was graying at the temples. She wasn't certain when that had happened.

"There's my girl," he called out, already heading down the steps despite the cold. He wasn't wearing a coat, just his usual sweater and jeans. Shifters ran hot. The January chill didn't bother him the way it did her.

She climbed out of the car, and before she could say anything, he had pulled her into one of his tight hugs. The kind that lifted her off her feet and squeezed the air from her lungs in the best way possible, while also making her feel safe and that everything would be okay.

"Hi, Dad," she mumbled against his shoulder, breathing in the familiar scent of him that reminded her of home.

"Welcome back, sweetheart." He set her down but kept his hand on her shoulders, studying her face. His smile faltered slightly. "You look tired."

"Six-hour drive," she deflected, but she knew that wasn't what he meant. The exhaustion went deeper than a long drive. It had been building for months. Through finals, the stress of graduation, and the slow realization that finishing college didn't magically provide her with answers about her future.

"Well, let's get you inside and warmed up. I made your favorite, beef stew. It has been simmering all day." Thomas grabbed two suitcases from her back seat like they weighed nothing. "We can unload the rest later."

"Dad, I can carry—"

"I know you can, but humor your old man."

She grabbed her backpack and followed him up the walk, her boots crunching on the salt crystals. The porch swing swayed slightly in the breeze, and she remembered sitting there a few months ago, telling her father about her classes and how she couldn't wait to be home for good.

Graduation had come and gone, but her lease hadn't been up until the fifteenth of January. She'd spent the holidays in Timber Ridge in a weird limbo. She was done with school but not quite home. All of the limbo gave her time to overthink her future.

Inside the house was exactly as she remembered, though the Christmas decorations that had been up when she went to pack her apartment were now down. Warm and cluttered in a comfortable way, with her father's collection of books on the shelves and photos covering every available surface. Photos of her first day of school, soccer games, prom, high school graduation, and most recently, college graduation. A whole life documented.

She set her backpack down by the stairs and stood in the entryway, suddenly overwhelmed by the weight of everything. This house, the town, and the life waiting for her. She'd wanted to come home so badly during college. She had counted down the days to each weekend visit. So why did she feel like she couldn't breathe now that she was here?

"Aleece?"

She blinked, realizing her father was watching her with concern. "Sorry, just...processing, I guess."

"It's a big change." He set her suitcase down at the base of the stairs. "But you've got time to adjust. No rush on anything."

Except she felt like there was a rush. She was twenty-two years old with a degree in business administration and no clear direction. She couldn't just live in her childhood bedroom indefinitely, working part-time at the diner as she had in high school.

"Go ahead and get settled," he said, his voice gentle. "Dinner will be ready soon. Your room is all made up."

She nodded, grabbed her backpack, and one of the suitcases. The stairs creaked in the familiar way as she climbed to the second floor. Her room was at the end of the hall. The same room she'd had since her father had brought her home as a baby.

She pushed open the door and had to smile despite the swirling thoughts. Her father had clearly been busy. The room was spotless, her bed made with fresh sheets, and there were fresh flowers, winter jasmine, her favorite, in the vase on the dresser.

Her bookshelf still held her childhood favorites alongside college textbooks. Her desk sat under the window that looked out over the backyard, the same desk where she'd done her homework, filled out college applications, and written countless papers during weekend visits home. Everything was the same, yet it was all so different at the same time.

She set her suitcase on the bed and moved to the window. The backyard was blanketed in snow, the old oak tree bare-branched against the gray sky. Beyond the fence, she could see the mountains that cradled Timber Ridge, their peaks disappearing into low clouds.

She'd missed this view. During college, she kept it in mind during every stressful moment, especially when she was homesick or felt like she didn't quite fit in with her classmates, who didn't understand why she went home every single weekend. But now that she was here, looking at it in person instead of in her memory, she felt uncertain. Trapped almost, but that wasn't quite right. Like the view was asking her a question, she didn't know how to answer.

A soft knock on the door made her turn, and her father stood there, hands in his pockets, with that concerned dad expression on his face.

"You okay, sweetheart?"

She forced a smile. "Yeah, just tired. Long day."

She could tell from the way his eyebrows pulled together that he didn't buy it, but he didn't push. That was one of the things she loved about him. He gave her space to figure things out on her own, but he was always there when she needed him.

"I've been meaning to ask," he said, leaning against the doorframe. "How's the job search going? You mentioned some applications the last time we talked."

There it was, the question she'd been dreading.

"I've um...I've applied to a few places." She turned back to her suitcase, unzipping it so she wouldn't have to look at him. "I sent my resume to the county office. They have an opening in the administrative office. I also sent it to the A-Z accounting here in town. I saw that Mr. Ross is looking for a business manager. I know I don't have the experience, but—"

"Both solid opportunities." His voice was warm with pride. "County jobs have good benefits, and Mr. Ross, you did your internship with him."

"Yeah." She pulled out a stack of sweaters, buying time. "I also applied to a couple of places in the city. Just...you know, keeping my options open."

The silence that followed was heavy. She risked a glance back at her father and saw that his expression had shifted. Still supportive, but with an underlying sadness that made her chest ache.

"The city," he repeated carefully. "That's a good idea. Cast a wide net."

"Dad—"

"No, really. You should explore all of your options. You worked hard for that degree and graduated with honors. You shouldn't limit yourself." He was trying so hard to sound encouraging, but she could hear the disappointment underneath.

She set the sweaters down and turned to face him fully. "I don't know what I want yet. I need to figure things out."

"Of course you do. You just graduated. Nobody expects you to have it all figured out right away." He crossed his arms over his broad chest. His version of keeping himself from reaching out to fix things. "But I need to ask, are you happy to be home? Or do you feel like you have to be here?"

The question hit harder than she expected. "I don't know," she admitted quietly. "I missed this place so much while I was at school. Every weekend I was here, I dreaded going back. But now that I'm here for good..." Her words trailed off, not sure how to finish.

"Now that you're here, it feels different," he finished for her.

"Yeah." Relief flooded through her that he understood. "Is that terrible? You took me in when nobody else wanted me, and you gave me everything. Yet, I'm standing here wondering if I can actually build a life in Timber Ridge."

He crossed the room and pulled her into a hug, gentler this time. "That's not terrible, it's honest. Aleece, you don't owe me anything. Not your whole life, not your future. I took you in because I wanted to. You needed a home, and I had one to give. That doesn't mean you're obligated to stay here forever."

She pressed her face against his shoulder, fighting back tears. "But what if I leave and I'm miserable? What if I stay and I'm miserable? How do I know which choice is right?"

"You don't. Not yet." He pulled back, cupping her face in his big hands. "But you've got time to figure it out. Send out those applications and see what happens. Maybe you'll get the perfect job here in town. Maybe you'll get an offer in the city that's too good to pass up. Or maybe something completely different will happen. Either way, you don't have to decide today."

She nodded, blinking back tears. "I'm scared I'll make the wrong choice."

"Then you'll make a different choice. That's the thing about life, sweetheart. Very few decisions are permanent." His smile was soft. "Except for adopting kids. That one's pretty permanent, but even that turned out pretty well."

Despite everything, she laughed. "Pretty well?"

"Okay, amazingly well. You turned out perfect." He kissed her forehead. "Now, come on. Let's eat. You can unpack later. Or tomorrow. Or next week. The suitcases aren't going anywhere."

Dinner was comfortable in a way that only came from years of shared meals. Dad ladled out generous portions of beef stew. All it took was one bite to remind her how delicious his cooking was. Throughout dinner, the conversation was easy. He filled her in on the town gossip. The clan alpha, Nico, found his mate at Christmas, and Maddie was making herself an essential part of the clan.

"Can you believe Maddie convinced me to have the town sponsor a Valentine's Day decorating contest? All the storefronts can enter by decorating their shopfronts, and residents will vote for their favorites."

"What's the prize?"

"Gift certificates to a bunch of stores in town, a beautiful handmade quilt donated by Kate from the general store. Then, each month this year, we're doing a different theme window display competition, with the town picking a winner each time. Then at the Christmas festival, we'll draw one final winner. We haven't announced the grand prize yet since some of it is still in the works." He shook his head. "Maddie and her event planning business have really taken off, but she's always got these great ideas for the community as well. I've asked her to help with the Christmas festival."

"Seems like she is the perfect mate for Nico." She brought a spoonful of beef stew to her lips before smirking.

"What's the smirk for?" he asked.

"Maddie isn't just good for Nico. Seems like she's got you wrapped around her little finger, too."

"How's that?"

"Really, Dad?" She took a piece of the fresh Italian bread he'd placed in the center of the table and buttered it. "Maddie's been here a month, and she's already got the town and the mayor doing more community engagement."

"Maddie and Nico also convinced the county to finally repave Main Street." He took a bite of the stew before glancing up at her. "I don't know how she does it, but she's very convincing. You can't say no to her."

"I see." She dunked her bread into the bowl, allowing it to soak up some of the delicious broth.

"So..." Dad's tone turned careful. "Any idea what you're looking for in a job? Besides a paycheck, I mean."

There it was. Just like that, the conversation turned serious. "I don't know. Something that matters. I didn't spend four years studying business just to push papers around."

"The county position would involve some community outreach," he offered. "Working with local programs and all sorts of things."

"Yeah, that could be good." She stared into her soup. "But the city jobs...they're with bigger companies. More room for advancement and better pay."

"Also, more hours, a longer commute, and a higher cost of living."

"I know." She sighed. "See? This is what I mean. Every option has pros and cons. How do people make these decisions?"

Thomas was quiet for a moment, then said, "Can I tell you something? You don't have to agree with me, but...hear me out."

"Of course." She looked up at him.

"When I was younger, I had opportunities to leave Timber Ridge. Good opportunities. There was a construction company in Denver that wanted to hire me, back before I went into politics. Big money, important projects." He leaned back in his chair, his gaze distant. "I turned them down because I knew, in my gut, that I belonged here. This town, these people, these mountains, they were my place, and I've never regretted that choice, not for a single day."

"But?" she prompted, sensing there was more.

"But that was *my* choice, based on what *I* needed. You're not me, sweetheart. You might need something different or somewhere different." His gaze found hers, serious but loving all at once. "Don't stay here because you think it's what I want. Don't stay here out of obligation or guilt. Stay because you can't imagine being anywhere else. Anything less than that, and you'll always wonder what if."

She felt her throat tighten. "What if I don't know? What if I can imagine being happy in both places?"

"Then you pick one and see what happens. If it doesn't work out, you'll figure something else out." He smiled. "You're twenty-two, Aleece. You've got time to make mistakes and change your mind."

She nodded, but the knot in her stomach didn't loosen. Time felt both infinite and terrifyingly short. She could spend years making the wrong choice before realizing it.

It was late, but Aleece couldn't sleep. Usually, when she had trouble sleeping, a nice hot cup of tea helped, but tonight she found herself with a mug of hot chocolate standing by the window looking out at the snow-covered neighborhood.

A few houses down, she could see the lights still on in the Patterson house. The teenage daughter was probably up late studying, just like Aleece used to do. Across the street, old Mr. Mason was out on his porch in his bathrobe, smoking his evening pipe despite the cold. He'd been doing that for as long as she could remember. Some things in Timber Ridge never changed.

She pressed her forehead against the cool glass. Four years ago, leaving for college had felt like an adventure. She'd been so ready to experience the world beyond Timber Ridge, to prove she could make it in the human world even though shifters raised her.

She'd made it. She'd gotten good grades, made friends, and learned to navigate a city where nobody knew her name. But she'd also been homesick in a way that felt like a physical ache. Every Friday afternoon, she would pack a bag and make the six-hour drive home, arriving just in time for dinner with her father. Every Sunday evening, she'd make the drive back, already counting down the days until she could return.

Her human friends had thought she was crazy. "Don't you want to stay for the parties?" they'd ask. "Don't you want to have a college experience?"

But they didn't understand. They had families they could call, siblings they could text, and parents who visited. Aleece only had her father, and he was in Timber Ridge. He'd come to Denver when she had something happening, but preferred to remain in Timber Ridge.

Except now she was there too, and the homesickness hadn't gone away. It had transformed into something else. A restless feeling that maybe she was supposed to be somewhere else, doing something else. Or maybe she was just tired and overthinking everything.

She pushed away from the window, set her mug of half-finished hot chocolate on the counter, and headed upstairs. Her suitcase still sat on her bed, half-unpacked. She should probably finish, put her clothes in drawers, and make the room feel like hers again.

Instead, she pulled out her laptop and opened her email. Three new messages: two automated responses from job applications and one from her friend Kathy from college, asking how the move went and demanding photos of the adorable small town. She ignored the messages and opened the search engine, but her cursor hovered over the search bar.

*What am I looking for?*

The question echoed in her mind, louder than it should have been at nearly one o'clock in the morning. She closed the laptop without searching for anything.

Tomorrow, she'd figure it out.

She finished unpacking mechanically, hanging clothes in her closet, lining up shoes, and setting her few framed photos on the dresser. Her college diploma, still in its cardboard tube, went on the desk. She'd frame it when she figured out what it was supposed to mean.

Finally, she climbed into bed, the same bed she'd slept in since she was five, when her father decided she should have a big girl bed. Instead of a twin-size mattress, they went shopping for one. She ended up with a huge full bed, because she was a princess and should have a big bed. It still had the same quilt Kate had made her for her sixteenth birthday, each square a different pattern coming together to be beautiful.

As she lay in bed, she could look out the window toward the mountain. They appeared just as dark shapes against the slightly light sky. Somewhere out there was the rest of the world. Cities and opportunities and futures she couldn't quite imagine. But here, in her room in her father's house, everything was familiar and safe.

She closed her eyes and tried not to feel like she was suffocating. She was home, and she should be happy. So why did happiness feel so far away?

# About the Author

Kelsey Karson is a lifelong romantic who believes love always finds a way, no matter the odds. Married and living with her two dogs, she writes emotionally driven romances that explore forbidden attraction, societal boundaries, and the courage it takes to choose love when the world says you shouldn't. Whether her characters are defying expectations or fighting impossible circumstances, Kelsey's stories celebrate passion, resilience, and the belief that no rule is stronger than the heart. Through her work, she invites readers to believe in love without limits and to let no one else define how or whom you love.

www.KelseyKarson.com

# Also by Kelsey Karson

**Hollow Series**

Hollow Inheritance

Hollow Anchor

Hollow Threshold

Hollow Pact

**Timber Ridge**

Christmas with a Bear Shifter

Carved in Timber Ridge

Return to Timber Ridge (October 2026)

Her Mountain Christmas (November 2026)

**Stand Alone**

Temptation